Man's Last Song

To the post-modern savages,
the future is not science fiction,
but a lonely journey of self-discovery
for themselves and mankind.

James Tam

JAMES TAM was born in Hong Kong. He lived and studied in Canada in the 70s and returned to Hong Kong in the mid-80s to work as an environmental engineer. He started his own environmental engineering practice and additionally a software company. The latter won the premier IT Excellence Award and the HK Industry Award in 1996. In 2008, Tam realised his long-term plan to leave business before too late, and sat down to write. He now writes fiction and non-fiction, sometimes in English, sometimes in Chinese. His short stories and occasional poems have received honorary mentions in competitions and appeared in anthologies. **Man's Last Song**, Tam's first full-length novel, was a finalist for the International Proverse Prize 2011, and won a supplementary award. As a scientific realist often mistaken for a morbid cynic, he sees abundant evidence that *21st Century Homo Sapiens* is a delusional and self-endangered species. Nevertheless, he remains irrationally optimistic, happily married, with two lovely daughters.

In **MAN'S LAST SONG** the human race faces imminent extinction. The year is 2090. The global population has shrunk to less than half a million; median age about sixty. After forty years of near-universal sterility, humanity is vanishing while the rest of the planet makes a healthy comeback. A few survivors in Hong Kong face the challenge of adjusting to life as *post-modern savages*, rediscovering instincts that have long been suppressed by civilisation. To these post-modern cavemen and cavewomen dwelling in the concrete remains of an empty metropolis, life has become a lonely journey of self-discovery in which they reassess also mankind. Their relationships with nature, each other, and themselves have fundamentally changed. The dilemma, pain and pleasure of love, friendship, compassion, ageing, and loneliness have been heightened by pragmatic dictates. The unknowable – God, *Dao*, death, even reality – has assumed new and shifting dimensions in man's dying world. How did *Homo sapiens* reach this dire situation? Looking back with hindsight borrowed from the future, readers may join characters in this book in finding today's world absurd, even suicidal. Others may hang on tenaciously to one thing that has not changed: hope.

Man's Last Song

To the post-modern savages,
the future is not science fiction,
but a lonely journey of self-discovery
for themselves and mankind.

James Tam

Proverse Hong Kong

Man's Last Song.
By James Tam.
2nd pbk edition published in Hong Kong by Proverse Hong Kong,
November 2015.
ISBN 978-988-8228-16-4
Copyright © Proverse Hong Kong, November 2015.
Printed by CreateSpace.

1st E-book Edition published in Hong Kong By Proverse Hong Kong,
January 2014.
ISBN 978-988-8227-42-6
Copyright © Proverse Hong Kong, January 2014.

1st published in Pbk in Hong Kong by Proverse Hong Kong, 11 April 2013.
ISBN 978-988-8167-34-0
Copyright © Proverse Hong Kong, 11 April 2013.

1st pbk edition(s) distribution
Hong Kong & worldwide: The Chinese University Press of Hong Kong,
The Chinese University of Hong Kong, Shatin, New Territories,
Hong Kong SAR.
E-mail: cup-bus@cuhk.edu.hk Web site: www.chineseupress.com
Tel: [INT+852] 3943 9800; Fax: [INT+852] 2603-7355
United Kingdom: Christine Penney, Stratford-upon-Avon, Warwickshire,
United Kingdom CV37 6DN.
Email: <chrisp@proversepublishing.com>
Distribution and other Enquiries: Proverse Hong Kong, P. O. Box 259,
Tung Chung Post Office, Lantau Island, NT, Hong Kong SAR, China.
E-mail: proverse@netvigator.com Web site: www.proversepublishing.com

British Library Cataloguing in Publication Data.
A catalogue record for this book is available
from the British Library.

Man's Last Song

ONE

James Tam

FOG

Dogs can be heard barking in the distance. Song Sung finds that relatively reassuring; some have started to howl, especially on a full-moon night, to declare their return to nature, reversing centuries of fussy breeding. It gives him the creeps nonetheless. Now that there are no more dog biscuits with nutrient labels, they'd eat anything, including people. Preferably people?

Yes, they must find humans tasty, even rotten ones. The feasting faces of the German shepherds remain vivid in his mind after all these years. He can still hear their ravenous sounds; every slurp, snap, yank, squirt, and grunt. The stench had made the air viscous, keeping everything in suspension, trapping the flies in its space. Blood dripped in slow motion from slimy jaws, like molten plastic.

He shudders.

Man's best friend. Sure, when we manufactured dog food. Wolves. That's right. Wolves.

I'll end up wolf breakfast.

He wonders how thoroughly wolves kill before muzzling in. They're supposedly smart hunters, like humans; perhaps just as cruel. He sees himself pinioned by four big dogs. Canine teeth penetrate his flesh like ceramic nails, clamping the bones, pushing deeper into his guts. He writhes weakly, keeping his eyes closed, trying to relax, submitting. Entrails are being ripped out, but there's no pain, just a feeling of becoming lighter, being reduced... to dog food.

Stop it! He curses his silly imagination.

Why not turn back for a warm drink and more sleep then? No. Keep going. No backtracking. Call it pride, stupidity, whatever.

He clutches the walking staff tighter, and treads on.

6

Dense fog covers everything like a divine correction fluid, attempting to smother the creator's faulty designs. Why bother anymore? There's hardly anyone left. He takes a deep breath; gummy air sinks inside damp lungs. The atmosphere seems anoxic. Can asphyxiation happen gradually, imperceptibly, like boiling frogs? Probably. The misty world started out enchanting this morning. He even thought it romantic, and gaily pronounced it so. Then it turned insufferable without changing appearance, suddenly. Or is it me again? But at least it looked calm from the house. Suffocating, but calm. Out here, in the middle of the grey viscous air, he's flustered by the roiling turbulence. He opens his eyes wider, as if that would help him see further; but depth has been lost, compressed right against his face.

It's silent, eerily silent. How come? Where are the birds and their clamorous twittering? There should be hundreds of them about the big banyan. This time of the day? He's not sure...

Am I still alive? Do lost souls know they are dead?

Rhea's right; it's dumb to go downhill in this weather. Even dumber to take the footpath rather than the main road. "Dumb it is then," he mutters grumpily. Pushing the whiteness in front, he walks trancelike towards the overgrown Old Peak Path.

* * *

What's another day? It's just a few hours to wait out the fog, Rhea had urged gently. What's the hurry? Is everything OK?

Yes, of course. Everything's OK, he assured her. Just can't stand this fog; got to go where there's air.

Where there's air... ? Right now?

Yeah, right now, sorry. I can't breathe. Fogs up here last forever, you know.

Sure. Whatever you say. She returned to the dishes.

She normally leaves the evening dishes for the next morning; cleaning up in candlelight is a pain. Scratching absentmindedly at a speck of food on the porcelain dish, she considered different approaches. A soft purring? Matter-of-fact announcement? A light-hearted "guess-what" surprise? One way or the other, it must come out, soon. He must be told, soon. Why not now? The secret that shouldn't be has been growing inside, like indigestion: burning, gurgling, refusing to go through, too chicken to come out.

Just turn around and say it. Speak! That's all it takes.

That's right; that simple. But she said nothing, and stared at her hands instead. How pampered they once were. How silky and diaphanous their skin used to be. And how impermeable and slack they now looked. The tiny furrows and creases seemed a touch more prominent, a bit more assertive then... the last time she checked? Just a bit, hardly noticeable, but she checked often. Ageing doesn't just happen does it? It creeps, steadily, stealthily, relentlessly, all over you, and stays.

The knuckles... look at them. One molecule at a time, they swell. One of these nights, while sleeping, unsuspecting, the last breaking molecule would be deposited; the final straw. She'll wake up to the arthritic pain of red, swollen knuckles – a trademark of old ladies. Time was undoing her. All quite subtle, but nothing escaped her unforgiving self-scrutiny. These hands, under a thin lace of suds, bluntly reminded her that she was forty-eight. So what, she thought, with a burst of positive energy. I'm still the youngest woman around.

Fine, but old enough to know not to confuse men at the wrong moment. When is the right moment though?

Not today. Not today anyway.

She could hardly believe the hesitation. Why do I need courage, as if guilty of some unforgivable wrongdoing? Oh well, be patient, time's ticking, slowly for once, on my side for once. Before long, I'll be able to sit back and let events take over. In the meantime, I can afford to dither. Can I?

Too late now anyway. Song was antsy, eager to get out, pausing at the door for a recognisable farewell – any sign to demonstrate her wholehearted acceptance of his sudden swing of mood and anxious departure. Rhea swallowed her brooding thoughts, but refused to lessen his unease. Such a petulant man sometimes. She scratched at the dish again. It squeaked; the speck of food had long gone.

Fog had sneaked through every crack and joint of the lavish mansion, creating big wet patches everywhere. Water droplets slithered down the walls as if they were melting. Everything smelled of mildew. A dull silence throbbed in Song's head, pouncing on him from within. Silence is supposed to be relaxing, but... He had to go. Now.

"Sure you don't want to come?"

"No. I've got lots to do here. You go."

"Should I get a few buckets first?" He saw the pails sitting in the living room, ready for their daily trip to the stream.

"It's OK. I'll do that a bit later, when the fog has cleared."

Just a bit later, it would clear. Not forever my love. Do you hear?

GUJI

Living on the Peak used to mean many things. Whereabouts do you live? "The Peak," ostentatiously understated, nonchalant, would have commanded immediate respect, highlighted your position, and established instant credibility in Hong Kong.

Not anymore.

Now that it's free, only Rhea and a reclusive woman live there, and they don't talk to each other. Song nicknames her Guji – Lonesome. Who isn't though? Tiny Hong Kong has become huge, spreading thinly the few thousand elderly residents left. Stripped of its vanity value, and without transportation and dehumidifiers, nobody wants to live amidst the clouds with rheumatism.

When Rhea moved here two years ago, Guji was just down the road. In the first week, Rhea didn't know she had a neighbour. One morning, sitting by the bay window, daydreaming, watching tree shadows dancing and wrestling on the pavement, she saw Guji appearing around the corner, walking briskly in her direction. Tall and slim, in a flowing purple dress, she looked tenuous. But her strides were springy, loaded with intensity, ready to leap. Wavering in the breeze, she shimmered against the morning sun like a precariously tuned video. Her arms hung purposefully from the sides, as if holding two invisible buckets, careful not to spill their contents.

Is she talking to herself?

What a handsome old lady. So unearthly, so... the word ghostly sprang to mind. At that instance, as if prompted by sixth sense, Guji looked up to meet her straight in the eyes. The hair on Rhea's neck stood up. She sucked in a deep breath; it felt cold. She recovered quickly, waved and smiled.

Guji smiled back.

No... she did not. The smile was already there, cast in her icy and delicate countenance. She just let it be seen, then walked on, pace slowed down somewhat. Cascading grey hair bounced against the small of her back. A few steps past the house, she paused, held out her hands as if to take stock of the fingers, then disappeared into the shifting light.

She returned late in the afternoon, staring straight ahead this time, arms swinging freely. She had dropped the invisible buckets. The smile was still there, crystalline and brittle. Her steps were lighter, determined. Rhea wanted to go and introduce herself right away. How exciting to have a neighbour. But... she was evidently avoiding looking Rhea's way.

It took a few days for her feet to warm up for a trip down the street. Aren't we all in a strange mood all the time these days, she told herself. Don't take it personally. She brought along half a dozen goodwill eggs.

What should I say? Why has it taken so long?

She didn't need to say anything. The house was empty. Guji had moved, leaving it in good shape: garbage taken out, floor swept, curtains tied into neat bundles, as if expecting a full refund of security deposit.

A week later, Rhea and Song went for a walk after breakfast. They strolled over the ravine to the west end, and there she was, engaged in an animated soliloquy. They gawked silently from a distance. All of a sudden, she froze. She must have sensed them without turning. She stood still with her back against them, waiting.

It was a quiet morning. They could hear sunbeams striking the leaves, making some curl, others uncurl.

They looked at each other. Let's leave, Song signalled with eyes. Shhhh, Rhea rounded her lips, exhaled silently. They turned in slow motion. The ground crackled underfoot.

From then on, partly out of pique and partly out of respect for the uncanny lady's privacy, they stayed clear of her territory marked with a poignant air of loneliness.

PATH

Song looks down as if to give his feet a final inspection before negotiating the banyan roots undulating across the footpath. How quickly the trees have taken over.

The flora and fauna used to know their place: stay out, or perish. Now they spread out with total disregard, chewing up the artificial pavement at an astonishing speed. Like a well-commissioned demolition team, they seem committed to the task. When a pioneer seed or wandering root has subdued a small crack, others take position to expand, propagate, and penetrate, fast.

When Song was a boy, gaggles of tourists crowded this same junction for a better view of one of the most photographed skylines in the world: in fact just huge blocks of concrete and glass stacked near the waterfront, against dusty hills. On a nice day, the city still looks almost the same, but somehow not quite. After staring at it for a few minutes, you can sense the absence of life even from this distance. It's creepy.

Tourism had been booming. There's a market in adventure, the analysts said. To most, it meant taking a plane ride, shopping and dining under foreign shop signs. Nonetheless, there was an urge to spend, and travelling was a convenient means. People used to save for old age, and to secure future generations' right to consume. When old age approached faster than expected as usual, childless couples panicked. They didn't want to die with a positive bank balance. "Your days are numbered," the TV goaded with subliminal messages, many times a day. "Book now; call this toll free number and get a plastic suitcase for free. Book now." So they did. The senescent world was poised for an economic boom grand finale.

Not everyone agreed.

Those less adventurous and more conscientious were wary of the apocalyptic atmosphere. Look, they said, all the classical symptoms are here: denial, irresponsible spending, depression, improvidence, moral collapse, hysteria, paranoia, and so on. Has it not always been like that? Yeah, but it was now backed by statistics, tracked by indices, revealed by opinion polls, discussed on TV. The future was ending more blatantly than ever.

Others were rapturous. It turned out they had been requesting big time punishments from God, for and on behalf of humanity, for some time now. Finally, thank you Sir.

"Repent now! Drop everything. Join us in repentance. Immerse in pain while you still can feel."

To their indignation, hardly anyone listened. Imminent extinction didn't change people. After a brief stir, the same old pattern resumed. They worked, shopped, ate and played just as before, committing familiar sins. The options were to adapt or deny, or both. Either way, they had to live on. Very few knew how to live on differently. The ruck couldn't get out of the ruts.

* * *

Song's familiar footpath has become wild and assertive over the years, like a freed slave, having discarded its historical function. It is no longer there to serve. Now it is just there, to be, like everything else.

Song and his father used to walk the path nearly every morning. His mother would join half the time. It was his father's favourite strip of land on Earth. He even kept a dossier labelled "The Path", as if there were no others. In it were old photos he had collected, printouts of newspaper clippings, more recent news (such as Government proposing to build a high fence along the whole path to keep pedestrians from rolling off, something that had not happened for nearly two centuries), photos that he occasionally took, with related anecdote and his own comments. "Unlike most places in Hong Kong, it has escaped change for nearly two centuries," he wrote at the back of the front cover. Of course it'd changed in detail, but basically it had been the same since 1860.

It had been first cut by Governor Robinson in 1860, to allow the passage of sedan chairs. He did not seem to have any particular reason to access the peak, other than to spend a gorgeous day outdoors, being carried. His successor MacDonnell built the Mountain Lodge, an atypically overstated name for the first Governor's Summer Residence at hilltop, in 1867. Other dignitaries swarmed in, to be near him. It became a prime location for those permitted.

To prevent moneyed Chinese doing the same later on, just in case, a Peak Reservation Ordinance was passed to make it unlawful to let such land or building or any part thereof for the purpose of residence by any but non-Chinese... above the 788 feet contour. Song's father kept a copy on file, passed by the Legislative Council and assented to by His Excellency the Officer Administrating the Government, the 29th day of April, 1904.

"Did people talk like that?" Song was at a questioning age.

"No. Nobody ever talked like that. They only wrote like this to let people know it's serious stuff. They still do."

"How high is 788 feet?"

"About 240 metres."

"Why 788 and not 790 or 800?"

"Good question. Don't know. Maybe it was a lucky number."

Above the 788-feet contour was the Hill District, exclusively for the felicitous domicile of the privileged from 1904 until 1930: opium drug lords with titles, bankers, policemen, missionaries, compradors, magistrates. All respectable neighbours; fellow expatriates privileged by law.

"What are expatriates?"

"People who live outside the country where they were born."

"Did they go home later?"

"Many did not. But they remained expatriates anyway. Any more questions?"

"Why didn't all of them go home?"

"How do I know. Too cold and wet back home? Lost their accent? Now, do you want me to show you the rest or not?"

Thanks to Robinson's rudimentary design, the footpath remained off-limit to cars throughout its life. In the nineteenth century, after the Peak District became residential, and until the Peak Tram was built, colonial gentlemen and their behatted ladies were carried up and down in sedan chairs. The dark skinned coolies, two per chair, looked impossibly skinny for such a heavy task.

"They don't look very strong."

"But yes they were. They had no choice."

The summer heat and the creaking of rattan came through the yellowish pictures – eeek-aaek eeek-aaek. Song imagined fleshy buttocks, slippery from sweat, wallowing to the squeaky cadence.

Eeek – one step less.

Aaek – another step overcome.

Just one thousand more.... With each conquered step, their passenger must have felt heavier.

HUE! – one of them would bellow, punctuating the hypnotic drudgery, or hawked and spat piercingly, disgusting his starchy client. He would then return to a muted focus on the next step.

"It's hard work. Experienced coolies knew not to think beyond a single step, so as to keep going. Too much expectation could crumble the spirit, bad for survival. You know what I mean? One day, you'll need to be tough like them, to focus on your next step, one at a time." His father used every opportunity to offer him a bit of survival training.

"How do you know what they were thinking?"

"I read novels."

Be like them? Song took another look at the gaunt men in the printout. Big straw hats in hand, they stared back lifelessly. Their indifferent expressions conveyed neither expectation nor curiosity. There might be a trace of contempt for the photographer, who was probably making a lot of fussy demands, muttering incomprehensible complaints about the little Chinamen not knowing how to stay still for his camera. I don't want to be like them, thought young Song, but grunted in agreement, as always, with his father anyway.

At the top, the passenger would alight, temporarily relieving the burden on their shoulders. "But there's no muscle on them." Song's still staring at the gaunt figures. "Oh, you'll be surprised. These guys were strong, made of rice, lots of it, and a few pickles or fermented tofu."

The ladies and gentlemen were dressed as if they were in the Highlands: corset, waistcoat, jacket, tie, the whole lot. They must have sweated profusely in the sweltering heat. The coolies, being at the wrong side of the sedan chair, must have sweated more. Trailing behind them was a complex miasma of multicultural body odour that you could almost see, mixed with eau de cologne.

All that's history. The only thing young Song was supposed to learn from this piece of history was this: focus; keep going.

* * *

Song could jog up and down the short steep path in half an hour. The Friends of the Path – that's what the morning hikers called themselves – were impressed. They were impressed by everything he did. He was the only youngster, a celebrity and great kid, dotingly adored.

The Friends of the Path were familiar strangers. They met each morning, knew each other's names and a few peculiarities, very little else. Protected by anonymity but emboldened by familiarity, they felt free to be themselves, often different from their daytime personas, with much wider latitude in weirdness.

For example, Wan Lao – Old Mister Wan – an otherwise conventional gentleman in his late seventies, walked backward. He claimed it helped to release stress accumulated over a lifetime, and improve balance. He actually attracted a dozen or so emulators. Walking in reverse became a common sight.

A lady in her fifties, invariably dressed in pink, sang O Sole Mio continuously, repeatedly, like a broken gramophone. "Good morning!" She would smile and wave back, performance uninterrupted. Song eventually learnt the lyrics by heart, and sang along sometimes to tease her. It made her sing louder. One day, she handed him a sheet with the Neapolitan lyrics on it, English translation on the side, all neatly hand written. Song thanked her, surprised. She smiled, singing. That was her only known contact with her morning buddies. Otherwise, she remained anonymous, friendly, and, no doubt, non compos mentis.

Even in this non-judgemental circle, there was gossip about her. The mistress of a government minister, someone said. Nearly seventy, five feet three and a bit in his shoes, a mouthful of crooked yellow teeth as if he was born in an earthquake, with artificially greasy hair. Yuck. But she loved him, deeply too! How do you explain it? She was from a rich home, and once pretty. Really! Must be those pink glasses don't you think? It ended badly anyway, like so and so, you know. Aiya, so cold-hearted, makes me sad just listening. Why? Politicians you know, they're all like that. Oh dear, no wonder she's short-circuited. Shhh. Poor girl. Things like that.

That was as much curiosity as was permitted on the Path.

They were each other's morning sun in an ageing city where everyone was negligibly one in ten million, competing for jobs, money, resources, time, recognition, water, air, space, space for their cars... everything.

O sole mio...

VICTORIA

Since Rhea moved to the Peak, Song's been taking the path regularly again, but he hardly knows it anymore. Everyday it looks different, more alien. His childhood playground has become strange and spookily mutable. He can no longer walk through it with eyes closed like he once could.

It's as if the guardian spirit, banished long ago by humans, has returned from the land of timeless myths. She talks to the trees, roves among the bushes on the back of butterflies. She wakes petrified fairies and little elves from their hideouts, coos them into taking possession of their woods again.

Hey, wake, liberation.
It's been so long, centuries...
Look, the humans are gone.
Yes. All gone.

All but a few, a very few.

Song now feels a trespasser, stared at suspiciously by the trees, bugs, birds, trolls, fairies, ghosts, dogs – damn dogs. Wherever he turns, there's a hush. Everything hushes and stares, making faces at his back.

He stops at the small clearing where the sky usually hangs. This morning, it has fallen, splashing greyness all over. A warm moist breeze rushes past him. He turns to see its faint eddies twirling up the peak. Reinforcement. The air is cool for mid-June, but humidity is high as usual. What about global warming? Didn't they say it'd take centuries to return to normal? This is only 2090. But... what's normal?

Central remains shrouded. Through the dense mist, a ghostly hum rises on the thermal of extinguished prosperity; Victoria drones at him unseen.

* * *

Nobody spoke of it as Victoria. It was much better known by a less regal name: Central. Perhaps there were enough "Victoria"s in the vicinity. Tai Ping Shan itself, Peaceful Mountain, 552 metres high, was renamed Victoria Peak by the British. So was the adjacent gap, the harbour it drains into, the road that skirts west, the great park on the east side, the prison, barracks, school, pier... Her Majesty's popularity had evidently overwhelmed imagination.

Starting from the Peak, the footpath zigzags through a precious patch of subtropical forest, then straightens out precipitously after the clearing. It then plunges through the Botanical Garden at Mid-Levels – an upper-middle-class residential area in the past – where Song lives. Further downhill are streaks of narrow streets once packed with cars, wet markets, antique shops, and eateries. Lively, Bohemian, chaotic, noisy. The air changed hue below the 788-feet contour. The small streets cascade steeply towards the sea, following gravity, intersecting at obscure angles. City planners drank liberally in the good old days, and were prone to spontaneity.

The gradient falls abruptly before an unnatural expanse of flat land. Welcome to the City of Victoria, aka Central.

For decades in the 1900s, millions of tonnes of construction debris were dumped into the receding Victoria Harbour every year: a "one-stone-two-fish" solution. Garbage disappeared, new land sprung up, making room for new growth. With growth came new garbage, and the promise of more prime land. The coastline rolled on out. The majestic harbour shrank, becoming modest. One Victoria flourished; the other dwindled.

Song had lived just ten minutes above Central all his life, but had never quite known the area. He was too young to be part of its story. Some said it was there that East met West. "I'd say it's just another district," his father said. "Banks, bars, restaurants, shops; like everywhere else in Hong Kong. Air's bad."

His friend John Johnson worked there for years, and still misses it. "Central was unique, dynamic, different even from itself everyday. It was the last refuge of Capitalism," he had told Song. "The enterprising spirit failed elsewhere because of political contamination, but survived here. That's why Hong Kong had oomph, and most of it in Central. OK, the air was not as good as the Rockies, but electric, and moved with a sense of purpose, let me tell you."

Just walking through Central used to invigorate me, John Johnson had said. The tide of humanity made me feel part of a grand scheme. I know some – he raised his eyebrow; Song understood he meant Ma – would say, *Money money money; all about money, because of money. It stank.* He couldn't be more wrong, I tell you, full of shit. Wealth was just a thermometer testifying to a system's health. Central was healthy. Liberty had been upheld, gently guarded by reasonable discipline; not castrating intervention; not self-righteous and mindless constraints which choked the life out of my old country. Just sensible discipline that promoted orderly liberty and human ingenuity. Song thought John was going to stand up in reverence.

Song expected his Tai-chi guru to give a drastically different picture, and he did.

Garbage, Ma said. Pure garbage. Through and through, left, right and centre, on top and underneath. Underneath? Yes. Do you know what passed under that artificial landmass of junk? he asked. Shit, raw shit. He answered his own question. Excessive shit from people who over-ate but didn't want to wipe themselves even though they had the money, lots of it. To them, money was to be made, not spent on toilet water. They built giant pipes instead: took it out to sea for marine treatment. Fancy that term, *Marine treatment!* So assuring, almost organic. The smart ass must have giggled when he came up with the term. Nature swallowed anyway, gagged. A sanitary headache was resolved through this fish-eat-pooh-man-eat-fish symbiosis. I suppose this is the kind of much-ado-about-nothing that John admires?

Yet what was happening above ground stank more, Ma said gravely, as if confiding a terrifying secret to Song. On top of consolidated waste, bankers crafted and traded investment instruments and derivatives, and derivatives of derivatives, making simple transactions impossibly complex for the general fool. All it took was simple arithmetic; easy. And greed; plenty of it. And lawyers; also plenty of them.

"Now," Ma asked his young friend. "Would you question the judgement of someone who wears a tie and jacket in this heat?"

"You probably would," Ma answered himself again. But people back then didn't. Ties were a sign of trustworthiness, steady like anchor lines; don't ask me why. People trusted bankers, but bankers didn't trust them. Just in case, lawyers would make sure the derivatives and derivatives thereof could stand forthright and unassailable in front of the law. Firewalls were erected between bankers and losses. The two didn't mix. Investors took risks; bankers took returns, all legal of course. Hong Kong had inherited an unquestioning faith in the rule of law, administered by people who wore wigs, dressed like Mozart, spoke like Shakespeare.

And look who made the laws? Ma gestured expansively to Song who had no idea who made the laws. A bunch of boisterous opportunists in their air-conditioned Legislative Council, also founded on garbage. Have you noticed the titaness Themis anchored to the roof, bolted through her feet? A rather ridiculous thing isn't she? blindfolded while her job was to see things clearly. Most pedestrians at street level used a handkerchief to cover the nose instead, not eyes, to filter out traffic fumes. And don't you think coercing with a sword unseeingly is a bit ironic, if not outright dangerous? And the empty balance... that vacant gesture of justice. *Huh.*

In Ma's opinion, John loves his role in Capitalism à la Hong Kong because he was a lackey of the princes of economic freedom, on lavish expatriate terms. "I fail to see how being a capitalistic minion could have been fulfilling," he explained. "I knew the account clerks who crouched over transaction receipts all day, polyester neckties dangling forlorn over balance-sheets, searching for the missing penny. I had worked with sweaty techies who slaved overtime to maintain air-cons, so trustworthy folks could keep their jackets on."

Lunch hours in Central were particularly distasteful, Ma continued. I couldn't help but see the entire process. I was a professional you see. *Dong!* Lunch hour. Hungry people poured from office buildings, instantly sweating upon exposure to ambient temperature, spectacles fogged up, anxiously looking for something fast and cheap to eat. *Dong!* The hour's up, boys and girls. They'd carry poorly digested food back to the office in peristaltic intestines, and flush it down the harbour for marine treatment later.

Energetic for sure, like a nervous breakdown.

Do you know the vibrant economy was supposed to grow perpetually? Yes, rather exceptional compared with the rest of the universe isn't it? But hey, all these people needed to be occupied, or they would have caused trouble for themselves and others. How do you grow an economy? Easy. Print some money, then make a few versatile data points, project strong growth. Done. The developers will take it from there, and turn it into a vision for the Government. Before you know, engineers would be pulling down old buildings for new ones, dumping them into the sea, taking another bite at the harbour. Giant sewer pipes would be made even larger and longer to catch up.

The engine had started, belching a sense of urgency into the air. Electric!

Couriers ran between offices, plastic envelopes bouncing inside satchels. *Urgent!* Ma stood up, moving his hands to the left, then right, then quickly left again to demonstrate frantic urgency. Garbage-men ran between buildings to collect the shredded remains of documents labelled "IMPORTANT AND CONFIDENTIAL – *URGENT*", and took them to the landfills. Buses and underground trains and garbage trucks and construction vehicles rushed in and out as fast as they could, nervous of the competition. Slowing down was detrimental. Stop, and you got swept away.

"Vibrant? Right, I'm still shaking."

The economy grew as projected, as ever, expanding, heating up, full of miracles. Let there be light! And there was light. Let there be cool air! And there was cold air. Somewhere, workers in boiler-suits generated electricity round the clock to keep the miracles going 99.999% of the time – a service pledge. Somewhere far away, someone dirty as hell was mining coal to feed the power plants. Somewhere else further away, soldiers tortured and blew up humans, whole families, entire nations, so SUVs back home could idle in a traffic jam.

But all that digging, pumping and burning could not last forever, right? That much, everyone knew, and in great detail. Log in for a transparent look. Everything was disclosed; more than enough information to make you gasp, boo, scream, panic, applaud, then go away for a drink. Remember the airlines? Ma asked Song. Of course you do, they sponsored your "lifetime" free tickets didn't they? But no you don't. You were much too young to know sustainability. It had become irrelevant by the time you could read; totally out of fashion. Yes, airlines competed to disclose mammoth carbon footprints on fancy websites. Then? Everyone flew away to attend conferences on sustainable development, collecting mileage. Disclosure made problems transparent; transparency made problems invisible, and disappear. Everyone disclosed.

So, Central − Victoria − started with nothing, thrived on garbage, ended in nothing. Ironic don't you think? Did John really call it the last refuge of capitalism?

*   *   *

Song wonders what exactly Capitalism was. It sounds familiar; something to do with money and expectations; one of those simple words covering big vague ideas. These words can still arouse passionate debates among his ageing friends, John and Ma, but mean nothing to him. These ideas belong to a thriving community rather than a dying one. What does it take to survive in a competitive economy? He can't even imagine, but would love to know.

He has heard Ma grumbling about the modern world often enough. It does seem dumb. Yet, if he has a choice, he would like to venture into such a world, and be stupidly busy for no reason, just for the experience. He is being stupidly *not* busy for no reason now, anyway. He would like to know what it's like to have a job, mortgage, family, kids, insurance, career, competition, ambition. He had seen all that from the distance of a kid. But as he grew into them, they disappeared like a mirage. Ma tells him he's lucky. John says it's a pity, but "Hey, don't give up, kiddo." His father smiled and sighed. "That's the way it was. We don't look back."

He doesn't.

Unlike the elders, he has nothing to look back to. He can't join them in reminiscences or debates. The past had always been ahead of him.

Right now, the ghost of Victoria, hiding behind the fog, has seized him. He stares at it like a stunned prey. The leaden sky shifts about like an extraterrestrial amoeba, engulfing him.

* * *

Song Sung's torn within himself again. He feels melancholy and restless, desperate for a sense of purpose that he sees no point having. Part of him is full of verve, confident, ruthless and free. Part of him is uncertain, sentimental and wretched. He loves Rhea dearly, yet doesn't know what love is. Lately, their lovely time together has been ticking away tentatively.

Last night was great. He enjoyed his quiet birthday party; just the two of them. The chicken was perfect, the wine unbeatable. Rhea seemed faraway at times but she insisted nothing was the matter, just tired. Was she? She came sensuously alive when they made love later.

Their love making was... yeah, wonderful.

But something feels uncertain these days. His head? Perhaps. It does seem more easily distracted. His heart? No. Hers? Hope not. His body? More precisely, his penis? That self-serving thing does seem more complacent. Age? Boredom? Itch? It's been seven years so...

This morning, they woke up nicely from a good sleep. He was refreshed, cheerful. He looked out of the windows and commented how beautiful it looked. "Kind of romantic isn't it?" he said. Rhea gave a big happy smile. Barely an hour later, out of the blue, he found it suffocating. He needed air, real air, right that minute, petulant like a kid.

What's wrong with me?

Don't know. Just don't know. Andropause?

"Come on," he reminds himself. "I just turned forty-two, probably the youngest man alive."

In fact, Song is the youngest person alive.

SWEEP

Song Sung turns away from the hypnotic mist. He takes a deep breath to regain focus. "Here. Here. Move on." Repeating the simple mantra helps to rescue him from these recurrent doldrums.

Gingerly, he descends the steep slope, leaning on his staff. The pavement is a mosaic of dead leaves on slimy mulch. A Burmese python greeted him here last year. It must have been three? five? metres long, growing steadily in recollection. Startled, he slipped and fell. Luckily, it glided away in gracious fright rather than trying to swallow and digest him over the next few days.

It reminds him of Chung. He swept the path for decades, and was Song's favourite man because he never called him Baby Song.

"Chung Bak seems so steadily content and happy without trying don't you think?" So his mother once remarked to his father. Everyone called him Chung Bak, Uncle Chung. "He has such a positive vibe. Why can't everyone be like him?"

"Because he's not from this planet," said his father.

"Now, be nice. He's lovely."

Chung was lovely, of course, but also out of proportion for an earthling. His ears were far too big for his tiny head. On a windy day, you couldn't help expecting them to flap. His eyes were two mere dots above a brass knob nose so taut in shiny skin you could see yourself reflected upside down, talking to him. His mouth stretched like a hammock, supported from ear to ear, more cartoony than a yellow smiley face. His short legs terminated in very long feet. Gumboots stuck out under the furrows of his grossly oversized pants like kayaks chased by a tsunami.

Garbage-men, like diplomats, were regularly rotated; but Chung had never moved from the Peak Path. It was a hardship post, full of gravity, heat and bugs, especially on sultry summer days. Rich folks in the neighbourhood also had high standards, quick to complain as a matter of principle. His streetwise supervisor understood all that. Since Chung liked the path, and had never requested a transfer, he stayed.

After his department dissolved, he continued to get paid through automatic transfer, and to sweep. Then the banks stopped. Not a big deal; money didn't mean much by then anyway. A rudimentary barter system had emerged. There was an abundance of leftovers, but what everyone wanted most was fresh food. People would offer their Nintendo, even a Ferrari, for a bag of carrots. The economy had moved in reverse; supply and demand had been rearranged. Many private farms sprung up; most produced nothing. "These people can hardly sprout beans," his father noted. "Imagine, descendants of the largest agrarian civilisation, farming with a manual in one hand."

With or without pay, Chung continued to sweep. It was his life, meant to be. He was fascinated with leaves in an oddly romantic manner, often admiring how beautiful they looked. Song's father once tried to explain photosynthesis to him, thought he might find it interesting. Chung laughed incredulously. "You make it sound so complicated Mr Song."

"Listen to this." He worked his giant bamboo broom like a musical instrument especially for Song, scratching the pavement. "It once had leaves of it's own," he murmured, referring to his broom. "Doesn't it sound great?"

"It does, kind of meditative." Song agreed diplomatically, borrowing his Mum's favourite description of anything repetitious. He thought it sounded just like someone sweeping. "Why are you still working, Chung Bak?"

"Because it makes me happy." His face shifted happily. He then resumed sweeping, watching every leaf as he did. "Leaves must return to their roots you know. We say that about people in Chinese. Has your father never told you?"

"No. But he has a book called Returning to the Roots."

"See." He herded a pile of leaves over the side slope, spreading them over tree roots. "I can listen to this all day."

But not forever.

Years ago, he stopped. Song can't recall when.

He can't pinpoint when the government shut down either. It was a gradual process, kind of sneaky, in traditional low profile. Department after department would declare itself indispensable, committed to service, then vanish the next day. It was to avoid panic, someone explained. No one cared.

The power stations were an exception.

As a privately owned utility, they switched off in style. The Songs were invited to the closing ceremony. Song Huan, with his son's future safety in mind, had lobbied for the methodical decommissioning of hazardous facilities. "Power plants, petrol stations, and a few surviving factories must be properly shut down before too late," he explained, pleaded. They finally agreed.

Song went along. Cocktails were served. A stage was set up outdoors. It was a blustery day. Soon, light and air-conditioning would be off. The indoors would become a trap. Speeches were made. "There's hope," the VIP said. A steady wind picked up a carefully arranged wisp of hair across his crown, twirling it distractingly. It looked as if the whole strand might uproot itself and fly off any moment. "This is only temporary and precautionary, I assure you." That was the giveaway. On his assurance, everyone knew that was it.

Three, two, one. Off.

Many, including Song Huan, had tears in their eyes.

Song might have been the only one who felt a twinge of excitement, anticipating something that he was not supposed to. A new life, one that he had been prepared for since birth, had commenced. A new era had begun at 14.00h, 2nd July 2075, a Tuesday. The PA system went dead. The audience remained silent and motionless, almost incredulous, until someone on stage waved. Some turned around and shook hands with their neighbours, like Catholics exchanging blessings during mass, wishing each other luck.

A few dumb ones applauded.

The Songs could have kept the fridge and light at home going with a generator, but decided against it. No point hanging on noisily for a few more months. Better get on with the new world now rather than later.

Song's father also proposed culling potentially dangerous zoo animals but failed to gain enough support. Even Song thought it unnecessarily cruel. After the python – evidently a retiree from the Botanical Garden Zoo – he now agrees with his father's foresight. Come to think of it, they should have culled all the dogs as well. Well, too late.

Nothing pleased the Songs more than the "temporary" closure of the Education Department in 2062. "About time," they cheered, after having resisted the government's offer to provide private tuition to their son. Song's parents preferred him to learn wilderness survival rather than urban renewal. But infertility was officially temporary so it had to be business as usual as far as the government was concerned, and that included their archaic syllabus. "The crisis will soon pass. Everything will return to normal, with a new baby boom." Good governments were universally delirious back then, so nobody took any notice.

The median age in Hong Kong reached an all-time high of seventy-something in the early 2070s, nearly half a century after the fertility plunge had started. The average age then dropped paradoxically, as the population became older. The apex of the demographic curve had sloughed off. Life expectancy plummeted the minute the power supply was turned off, pulling the plug on medical services. No more deaths postponed by electricity at the expense of the patient. No more questionable lives kept dangling with silicon tubes, pulsating to electromagnetic signals.

This is 2090. Song wonders what the current population profile is. Everyone he knows, except Rhea and himself, is in their sixties. What does it matter though? The dots that make up the demographic curve – the data points that give statistics authority and manipulative power – have all but vanished.

A SAMARITAN DILEMMA

Half way down, the fog has thinned into a light mist. Song's head seems to have cleared with it.

Birds trill and jump in bushes; Song smiles to himself. No canine skirmishes. No hungry embrace from the big snake, just like all the other times. He feels a strange anti-climax, but relieved.

Coming out of the forest, to his right lies a desolate estate. Air-conditioners and sprawling fig-vines hang side by side on fractured walls – one ready to let go, the other to spread. Wild plants overflow from opulent lobbies, as if seeking fresh air. Awnings dangle above collapsed Porsches and Mercedes half-buried in yellow sand. From caved-in sewers, saplings emerge as if to survey a promising new world.

So full of life. So dead.

At the acute bend ahead, a huge boulder had settled after a big storm last year. Soil and branches have since piled up behind. He climbs up, following his own step marks from previous trips. Just as he comes down and around the corner, he notices a dark object at the bottom of the slope.

Dog?

Too big. A lone dog would have turned and fled. They don't usually hunt alone.

Visibility is better now, but anxiety is undermining his vision. He squints, and sees it leaning closer against the soil bank. But was it real? He feels beastly eyes watching behind dense fur. It just moved again! This time he is sure.

The thing is now perfectly still, blended into the bank. Ready to attack? Song assesses his situation. Climbing back up the boulder and running uphill away from a four-legged animal is not a good idea. No short-cut through the overgrown bank either.

Shit. His heartbeat gathers pace.

Without taking his eyes off the thing, he checks his grip on the staff, squeezing and relaxing it subconsciously. His palms feel moist against the wood.

* * *

Wild boar? Bear? This climate must surely be too warm for the furry beast; but then there were quite a few bears and pandas in the zoo weren't there? He feels damp air warming up against his face, as if someone has just splashed the rocks in a sauna. All kinds of animals were freed by ageing zoo keepers. God knows what creatures are out there trying to establish their rightful position on a brave new food-chain right now. He wonders where humans fit in. Bub was right; they should have closed the zoos down properly, with a slaughter.

It's moving again, swaying slightly.

What the...

No eyes. No visible features at all. Just fur.

It's stopped.

Song senses the penetrating gaze of unseen eyes, the warm stench of measured breath. Better get on with it. Even tigers and wolves are wary of humans who aren't afraid; especially if the animals have spent time in a zoo... He inches forward, sidling along the far edge, training his stick on the thing. The pole feels heavier than usual, loaded with anxiety and aggression, or fear. He gingerly approaches the... Oh no...

A man... It's a man.

* * *

An old man kneels with his shoulder against the side slope, curled up like a giant rodent. His hands are under the chest. His face is pressing against the ground. Every now and then, he shudders as if jolted by a deep spasm, and rocks sideways, releasing a barely audible moan; an eery sough; a ghostly whine.

Clumps of long grey hair have fused with his grimy fur coat – forming a pointillist crust of human sludge across his back. He and the mink had merged. Fur coats had been popular in Hong Kong. Rich women used to wear them with antiperspirants. On the old man, it looks bizarrely suitable even in June.

Hair, hair, everywhere.

* * *

Song studies the stranger from the far side, unaware that he's still training the pole on him.

"You OK?"

No response.

"Hello?"

He takes a step back uphill to give himself distance, to think. He stands the pole up, towering like Moses over a repentant soul. The profile of the man's sunken face lies just downhill from Song's shoes. Poor guy. He needs help. But how to help him? The question feels half-hearted. He's aware of a shameful reluctance bubbling inside. I can't help. I don't need this. I can't help.

A foul stench rises to greet him, leaving an aftertaste in the throat. He feels nauseous.

Hot air rises.

He comes down a little along the far edge. A shaft of diffused light finally makes it through the canopy, falling on the man's back. A plume of stink can be seen leaving, like a skunk's tail in cartoons.

He's disgusting.

He needs help.

He's half dead – half man half ghost already.

Is this the odour of putrescent flesh, or just bad hygiene?

Can people decompose alive?

Song's nose tells him the man has been peeing and pooing inside his fur coat. His father used to remind himself it's a blessing not to die in a hospital, without a big sloppy diaper between the legs, tubes coming out or going in every orifice. The stranger, however, seems to highlight the need to wear diapers during one's final moment.

Song is experienced in corpses, but has never witnessed death-in-progress. It's disconcerting, repulsive and disgusting. He feels ashamed of these heartless reactions. Must one feel bad for reactions that are honest and beyond control? He leans forward a few inches to compensate for the callous thoughts anyway.

"Do you need help?" He sounds hollow to himself. What a stupid question.

Unexpectedly, the old man moves a little in response. Then, in suspended motion, he turns his head askew, as if adjusting for maximum discomfort. He's now facing Song's feet from the side, his visible eye barely open. His lips are parted heavily, spread sideways on the ground, exposing a mouthful of dried mucous. No teeth. The nose is bruised, badly swollen. Song can hear a laboured and irregular wheeze through his mouth. He bends over to check – What a whiff! – and nearly vomits over the man.

* * *

With his breakfast quivering at the top of his throat, Song struggles to find his emotional bearing. He can't just walk away.

But why?

Indeed. Why?

He can't think of a reason. He doesn't know this man who is at most days – more likely hours – from death. He can't possibly take care of him. Whatever he does would be futile under the circumstances. He wants to have nothing to do with this. He curses the encounter under his breath; he curses this whole damned morning. Why couldn't you be properly dead by the time I got here? I could have given you a decent disposal.

He regrets not staying another day at Rhea's.

It's difficult to tell the stranger's age given his condition. What difference does it make though? His life is pointless now, whenever it commenced.

Just walk on!

Yet... he can't. Now that he has bumped into this hapless situation, he feels compelled to do something, whatever, in the name of... what? Human fellowship? Come on!

The old man stares vacantly at Song's shoes. He let out another muffled moan – all that he's got left. All that he's been, all that he's done, everything converged into a half-moan at this pathetic moment. He presses his face into the ground, and sways his shoulders weakly, as if trying to burrow.

It suddenly occurs to Song that he might have crawled out here to die alone, in solitude, with dignity, or like elephants, at least according to his father.

Did Bub end up this way?

His eyes redden at the thought. He smacks his lips, and swallows hard. Well, in that case, he might have interrupted a solemn occasion, a grave and private moment.

Go away quickly then...

He starts a few steps downhill, then stops and turns to face the raised rear end of the man. *Now that I've interrupted, why not speed things up to reduce his suffering?* One good whack over the neck. All would be over in a second, in the name of humanity. No, not with his favourite staff. He'd find another one. Ah, a rock would be better wouldn't it? It leaves the hand before the, uh, execution. No physical contact at the moment of death. It somehow seems less distressing.

He leans his staff against a tree, and gathers three boulders. Just in case. Can't do it halfway. Three would do. He places them about a meter above their target.

One. Two. Three.

They look nearly identical, about ten kilos each. Cold; mercenary; they suddenly seem loaded with a sense of purpose. A strange thought strays into his mind. When was the last time a human was stoned to death? The old man has maintained a lifeless gaze at the spot where Song's feet were.

He'll drop them from uphill, for obvious reasons.

Uneasily, he takes position. Should he signal something? All departing souls deserve some form of ritualistic farewell. He and his friends have been affording funeral rites even to liquefied corpses. Should he explain that this is an act of quietus for the old man's sake, to lessen his pain?

Cut that crap. Just do it. Or walk on.

Be on your way brother.
If you have a god, go to him.
May you reunite with loved ones lost to death.
Don't reincarnate though; nobody's around.
We'll soon follow.

Or just, *Bye now, good luck.* Good luck?

He finally decides on, "Be on your way, rest in peace."

Hang on, his head should be covered – for respect? Or to spare himself the mess and gore? Whatever. There's a fountain palm nearby.

When he returns with a few leafy fans, the old man has managed to tilt his head a bit further uphill by bending his neck further.

He's looking. Staring, actually, blankly.

For the first time, Song sees his full face, and the netherworld gleaming darkly behind opaque eyes.

GOODBYE HOUSE

"Where're we moving to Mama?"

"The other side of the ravine, Sweetie."

"Why?"

"Some strangers have moved to the house down the street. I don't want them to see you. They may hurt or take you from me. Lots of bad people out there."

"Is it the lady who waved?"

"I told you not to mention her again. Have you forgotten?"

"Sorry, Mama."

"Promise you'll never, ever, ever, ever, do that again OK!"

"I'll never, ever, ever, ever, do that again."

"That's my good girl. I didn't mean to yell. Don't cry. I worry about you because I love you so much Sweetie. You two are everything I have."

"I know Mama."

"Where's Tommy?"

"Right behind you Mama."

"Tommy you scared me! Never, ever, ever, ever, do that again OK?"

"Tommy never says anything Mama."

"I know. But he's a good boy. Have you got your teddy bear?"

"Yes, and my purse with all the cards, so I can introduce myself to people."

"But not to strangers remember?"

"Only to you and Tommy. When I see strangers, I disappear!"

"That's my girl! Now, was it you who tied up the curtains? Such neat and tidy bundles!"

"You like that Mama?"

"Excellent! Good job, Sweetie! I'll take the garbage out now. You take Tommy's hand. Say good-bye to the house, say good-bye to the piano."

"Good-bye, house. Good-bye, piano."

TWO

SMILE

"Yksi. Kaksi. Kolme." One. Two. Three, Sari Salonen whispers in Finnish.

Blank your mind.... Just count.

She pauses to examine the toque-in-progress. So tiny. How can anyone be that tiny? Should I make it a few stitches bigger? "Neljä, viisi, kuusi..." – Four, five, six....

She speaks four languages, mostly English now, but still counts in Finnish. Numbers are like that, stubbornly native. Her man Song Huan uses English at work and home, but mumbles numbers in Cantonese. Ah, that's easy, *yat, yi, saam*. Anyone can manage that. In Swedish, her other official language, it's ett, två, tre, cut and dried. German exactness starts quite simply with eins, zwei, drei. Even the French manage to curb their passion for complexity, and settle for the prosaic un, deux, trois. Why are numbers so uncharacteristically lengthy and complex in Finnish? Why do the taciturn Finns make so much sound to say one, two, three? God knows. It gets worse. Seitsemän, kahdeksan, yhdeksän, and kymmenen for 7, 8, 9 and 10? Imagine. One needs big lungs to go beyond single digits. In Finland, it takes twenty seconds to countdown to a new year; and Seven Eleven – Seitsemän Yksitoista – doesn't exist for obvious reasons. Maybe that's why Finns don't talk much?

Amused by the mental detour, a gentle smile surfaces like a bubble rising from the bottom of a still lake, spreading soft ripples, ruffling the agreeable expression that Sari wears like a mask these days.

For months, she's been focusing on positive thoughts only. To the outside world – the irritating outside world – she has erected an impregnable shield around her, barring traffic from either direction. Her thin lips, tucked determinedly at the corners, give the ambiguous expression of both content and annoyance: annoyance at the core, content at the surface.

Everything, including her capricious hormones, particularly her capricious hormones, is testing her resolve, trying to nudge her over the limit of sanity.

They won't succeed. No, they won't.

Maintaining a constant smile helps to internalise focus. It reminds her of Mona Lisa. When she first saw the famous painting in Paris, she was shuffling behind Mr and Mrs Tourist Bob in an endless line of visitors.

"Look Bawb, that's the famous Mawna Leesa."

"Yup, here she is! Cool! Beautiful right?"

"The color's kinda dull and blurry though. Like, so brown?"

She looked at Lisa. The Florentine lady was politely giving her celebrated smile, dutifully displaying mystic femininity. Wait, behind that smile was something else. A plea?

Sir, Signore Bawbo, move on now. Per favore.

She imagined what it must be like to face an interminable onslaught of visitors. Fatuous comments, affected admiration, nine to six everyday except Tuesdays when the Museum closed. How many understood what immortalised her enigmatic expression? How many cared?

"She ain't that pretty though. Who painted her, again?"

I beg your pardon Signora Bawbo?

"Da Vincent. It's worth millions I tell ya."

Alas...

"Good art's never cheap Bawb."

If you don't mind...

"Hey, don't know 'bout you but think I've earned a good burger and Frenchie beer with all that artsie farting. What'd you say?"

A marvellous idea, Sir. Now move on. Arrivederci Signore Bawbo; and don't forget your wife.

Sari gave Lisa a sympathetic glance. She probably preferred to remain stolen, hidden, or, better still, unfinished, unknown, forever uncertain, travelling, drifting, simmering to become perfect in his mind's eye. He saw an adoring world. Ostentatious, superstitious, dumb, righteous, dangerous. He sneered. Disdainful, contemptuous, defiant. But it must not show; he was cautious as always. He encrypted it in mirror image, hid it in sfumato. A smile – feminine, content, agreeable – pasted in the shadows, masked with paint to please his patrons. They won't see, not really see. Now, now, that's great. A few extravagant comments if it pleases you, sir.

"Oi, s'il vous plaît Madame!" Someone behind her commanded insolently in a beautiful language, threatening to push her.

"Pardon," she smiled.

Just smile. Sari needs hers to stay positive, to shield herself from a loving world which doesn't understand. Things don't change do they? Be patient. Don't lose it, for the baby's sake.

Calm... Om...

It's okay baby. I'll do whatever they ask, smiling. These idiots only want the best for us. I'll comply, be happy, positive and strong.

See you soon.

* * *

Sari squeezes the diminishing ball of off-white yarn to size it. Enough to finish this one. Yet another toque for her girl.

"Neljä, viisi, kuusi..." She sucks in her breath quietly as she counts. This is the fifth one. The nurses, smart asses, reminded her one little hat would be one too many in Hong Kong. What do they know? All Finns enter this world with a handful of insulating headgear waiting. A baby's head must be kept toasty from day one, the first instant.

Besides, it keeps her own head occupied. She now realises how Zen Buddhism works. Scrub the latrines scrub the latrines. Year after year after year. Then – enlightenment!

"Seitsemän, kahdeksan, yhdeksän." She pauses to hold the half-finished garment up with both hands to examine, admiring again how adorably miniature it is.

Her mother Laina sits across a chunk of coffee table, the kind that can only be found in hospitals and government offices. Brown. Wooden. Substantial. Very ugly. Four square monumental legs. In case of earthquake, crawl under. How much structural strength is needed to support coffee mugs and cookies?

Laina sits straight on the sofa, hands on lap, looking at Sari, grinning with endearment. For an old lady, she has an exemplary posture. Sari finds that admirable and irritating.

She's evidently adoring the same thing Sari wishes to adore discreetly and privately. She's gratified by the opportunity to just sit there and watch her daughter count stitches. Yksi. Kaksi. Kolme. Sari knows exactly what mum's doing without looking up. She keeps her head down, pretending to have forgotten Laina's quiet, loving, and obtrusive presence.

Oh well, she only wants the best for me, just like every goddamned body else.

Nonetheless, can't you go read a book, take a nap or go for a walk? Or learn to knit? Or get diarrhoea and spend some solitary time in the toilet for crying out loud? She feels guilty for the nasty thought. *No bad wishes, not on Mum anyway.* She glances up to beam lovingly at Laina – a secret apology.

"Beautiful yarn." Mother seizes the opportunity to say something.

"They are." Sari's uninterrupted, eyes on the crocheting hook. "Bamboo yarn. Very soft and natural. Difficult to find in Finland."

"Yeah?" Laina has no idea. She doesn't knit.

BREAD DELIVERY

Laina last visited Hong Kong six years ago, shortly after Sari moved there. It was her first trip outside Europe.

Her daughter had met Song Huan in Shanghai. She was on an internship programme with a company manufacturing electronic components in China, part of her degree programme. He was an engineer from the Hong Kong office. Like most love affairs, it happened impetuously on first sight. What followed was mere formality. After Sari returned to Finland, they courted through e-mails, and he went for any training excuse the head-office had to offer in Helsinki. Two years later, in 2041, Sari moved to Hong Kong.

Her first request home was some dark rye bread. "They don't even have *ruisleipä* over there? *Voi ei!*" Laina booked her flight the next day, and stuffed a large suitcase with good old-fashioned dark rye bread. High density stuff, almost non-biodegradable. She had to sit on the lid to close it, and pay eighty euros for overweight luggage.

Before departing, she looked Hong Kong up on the map again. Of course she knew where it was – way over there; but she needed some visual reassurance. It was only a dot on the south coast of China the size of – a wee dot. Inside it lived more people than Finland. She wondered if there was still room for her.

From Helsinki to Bangkok, her stomach felt bloated with anxiety during take off and landing. Otherwise, it was smooth flying. The stewardesses were Finns, quiet and detached. The three-hour transit at Bangkok was a different matter. To get to her connecting flight, she had to cross a huge concourse. She stepped out of the plane, straight into the busiest shopping mall she had ever seen.

Wow.

Silk! Such colourful dresses in bright red orange green blue and gold. She couldn't help stroking them, smiling nervously at the salesgirl as if caught shoplifting. Perhaps a little loud but hey, what about concerts? A hint of fashion – even small doses of ostentatiousness – is okay for concerts.

Her sixty-year-old boyfriend Heikki was Music Officer Grade III (Cellist) in the city orchestra. Technically a civil servant; but deep down an artist. He loved things different, as long as not too different. He was a bit shy, perhaps fusty to some, and only truly at ease when behind his giant cello, sawing and sawing. He would be secretly proud if she showed up in one of his concerts dressed like a peacock. He would not utter a word of compliment, oh no, but she would be able to tell from the way he was quiet about it.

Electronic gadgets beeped, sang, played movies, or just made boing boing sounds. Noise, noise, noise. She was in a world-class hubbub for the first time. That's why Finland's so silent; all the noises are out here, she thought. Look at the beautiful tea sets, dishes, picture frames, leather and silk purses, elephants carved out of wood, and miniature banyan trees carved out of ivory. She could have shopped for three hours easily. But this noisy world only understood Thai, English, Chinese and Japanese. She was lost in a strange land, a stranger isolated by the language barrier; trying to overcome it was exhausting and hurtful. Laina could manage conversational Swedish and a little English when she didn't need it. Sari had taught her two identical Chinese words – "xie xie" – meaning "thank you".

Three hours were stretched into one hundred eighty minutes, many more seconds. Each phlegmatic second that wore on made her feel isolated, insecure, useless. "Why can't I remember my English?" She was disappointed in herself. "What are they announcing through the loudspeakers?" It sounded ominous and urgent. Something could be desperately wrong, and she had no idea what. She wanted to cry, her normally collected self rattled by tiredness and the onslaught of jet lag.

James Tam

ISÄ'S ASHES

Alone in a frenziedly beeping airport, embroiled in foreign noises that droned on without meaning, not even a rhythm, Laina felt dizzy.

Why am I doing this? she asked herself, travelling so far away from her cosy apartment, the comfort of familiarity, from Heikki, to be stuck in the sticky time-zone of this clamourous terminal.

All for Sari, her daughter.

She was trapped by love at the end of the planet, in a dot of a place without dark rye bread. Laina had never been anywhere that didn't have some form of ruisleipä. She couldn't imagine. Her girl evidently needed help although she had no idea what. And if Sari knew of her secretly helpful intentions... Alas.

Her baby girl was turning twenty-five in a few months, stolen by time, intoxicated with love. Wasn't that what she once searched for? Why then was she so worried? And Sari was twenty-five. Already twenty-five!

Only twenty-five!

Still young, but threatened by age; still hopeful, but desperately tired. One day, it feels the exciting beginning of a new chapter. Next day, it feels the hasty ending of an unfinished book. What a critical turning point. So brutal. Better be there for her one and only daughter, her dearest person in this world, just in case.

When Laina turned twenty-five, life was yet to begin. A quarter of a century had slipped by. Not much had happened. What was that something big she had been preparing for, while the body and spirit quietly started to wilt? A young and zestful girl woke up one morning to discover the shadow of an old woman in the mirror. Hidden, but she saw it. The realisation was abrupt, nearly shocking, and cruel. At twenty-five, she was only young in the eyes of those who didn't matter. When exactly does middle-age start? The little girl lost grip of her dream.

Dream? What dream?

She could not say. Did she have one? Most certainly, yes. It was here a moment ago, yet... With each passing day, she became less sure that she had ever had one. Her dreams had vanished like the soap bubbles her mother blew to her when she was little. So many, each with a rainbow on its skin. But she had never caught one. Blip. They never existed. She giggled.

What good is a young woman without dreams? Her surefooted steps to become somebody, achieve something or, perhaps, something else, never existed. Intoxicating love never existed. In their place loomed an uncompromising urgency, hanging emptily.

It was about time. Yes. She married Sari's father the following year.

* * *

They grew up in the same neighbourhood. He had been in love with her ever since she could walk, although he was only a few years older. Evidently an infatuation carried over from a previous life. With drained blue eyes, he watched her drift in and out of his life, like the tide, unstoppable both ways, eroding his fragile heart.

He was her storm shelter. On a nice day, she would set sail and disappear beyond the horizon, frolicking into the bright blue sky without compass or destination. When it turned dark and windy, she would rush back whimpering. He would be there – still there – staring at the horizon, waiting. It's Okay. Here, take the towel, dry yourself; have some warm coffee. She knew she could count on that much in life.

He was a book-keeper with the local supermarket. Steady, loyal and honest. Sensitive to other people and everything else, especially her. Never opinionated when he opened his mouth on rare occasions. Put all his attributes on a piece of paper, and you would have a perfect nice guy. "Too nice," she used to complain to her girlfriends.

She was a salesgirl at the music store, envisaging a career in some kind of art. "A good match," their friends said, but never elaborated why.

His reticence deepened after the marriage. A year later, just after Sari was born, he came down with postnatal depression in her stead. His love and hurt could not escape through words. Only vodka could release them through tears. The blue in his eyes started to run, making them paler. He drank more and sobbed louder.

The first Saturday after Sari's fifth birthday was a beautiful early autumn day. For a change, the weather wasn't to blame. He spent the afternoon drinking at home, weeping on and off, condemning himself for doing so. The kitchen was saturated with sad vibes and the fume of alcohol. After putting Sari to bed, Laina leaned over his shoulder and whispered with anger and spite, "Pathetic," before going to bed and putting her head between pillows. He woke her up with a severe fit of cough early next morning, and died in the hospital fifteen hours later. The doctor said it was a particularly spontaneous and fatal strain of pneumonia.

Even back then, it was pneumonia.

Laina decided to scatter her husband's pulverised remains at the lake where his parents' cottage was. "That's what he'd have wanted. I know. I was his wife," she wrote in his Facebook memorial.

It was cold and sunny. The wind was up. She took Sari out to the middle of the lake in a paddle boat. Their faces were numbed by the slashing wind. The wooden box provided by the crematorium sat heavily on her lap, giving the feeling of stability and contentment. She emptied the ashes into the water without ceremony. A gust of cold wind immediately snatched most of the sand-like remnants of the man who had loved her under any circumstances. After a lifetime of waiting and dithering, his last days had been hasty in every respect. A few heavier particles, probably dental fillings, made silent and negligible splashes.

On the drive up, she had visualised his final ripples waning softly in his beloved lake, gently nudging up to her. It was to be her poetic farewell to his unconditional love and unmitigated melancholy. Instead, everything rushed away with the wind, denying her the posthumous opportunity to have one romantic moment in their deceased marriage.

"Say good-bye to your father," she said, turning to her daughter, almost commanding.

Sari was sitting beside her, stiffened by the lifejacket, frozen. She knew what this was all about, yet didn't quite know what this was all about.

"Moi moi isä," she complied.

Laina flung the empty box away. It spun like a rectangular frisbee, landed with a crash.

"Äiti, can we go now? I'm cold."

Laina wept for the first time in her marriage. He had monopolised crying. Now that he was gone – flung off – she could cry again herself.

The next morning, they went down to the beach before heading home. Sari spotted the box in a patch of bulrushes. It had been washed ashore last night. Laina threw it back out as hard as she could, propelled by an unreasonable annoyance with Sari for having noticed the damn thing.

The wind had died down earlier. A light mist hovered above the sleepy lake. The box made a splash, shattering the morning silence. Startled gulls appeared out of nowhere, screeching like demons rejoicing at their escape from hell, causing a rare moment of excitement in the tranquil northern air. The box, as if stunned by the violent rejection, undulated dazedly where it landed.

"Let's go!" She grabbed Sari's hand and started back towards the car. Sari, half pulled along, turned to take another look at the box. Concentric ripples, gleaming softly in the lazy autumn light, rushed belatedly towards an empty beach.

ULTRASOUND GHOSTS

"Bamboo yarn?" Laina wonders out loud, nodding thoughtfully. "Can you make yarn out of bamboo?"

"Yeah, for about fifty years," Sari replies, not sarcastic.

"Very plain though." Laina tries to keep the conversation going.

Mum, you said it was beautiful a minute ago...

"I like them neutral," Sari explains, emphatically patient. "It'll suit a boy or girl."

Sari is probably the only person who doesn't know it's a boy. Laina respects and understands her wish, and keeps quiet. Better not spoil nature's intimate surprise. But are there other surprises in stock? *Will he live?* she wonders.

Sari prohibits anyone from telling her what they've deduced from ultrasonic speculation. That scanning thing was spooky. In the only session she watched, at the beginning of her second trimester, a foetus with shadily developed hands waved to her in suspended animation. Through electronic smears, an eery image reached out. *This is ancient... Where's my baby?*

It had been a part of her. She couldn't have visualised a separate life inside if she tried. But now, she saw a ghost metamorphosing before her eyes. Something from someone's previous life had entered her body, biding time, waiting to be life again. It was shedding an unknowable past, assuming a new identity, changing face, growing new bones, right there, on TV, trapped behind a glass screen. It beckoned through the monitor as if it could see her also. Hey... Mama... It was the colour of preserved meat, vampiric meat. Dr Wong should have calibrated his monitor better.

She glanced at it for a few seconds, then stared at the ceiling, eyes reddened with disappointment. "Where's my beautiful baby?" She couldn't make anything out of the blotchy phantom, not to say its gender.

"Sari," Dr Wong said with professional certainty. "Good news. Everything looks fine. The little one's developing well." He clasped his hands, then asked coyly, as if Sari was also an infant, "Now, could you see if it's a cute little boy or girl?"

"No!"

She snapped so hard and unexpectedly the doctor took a moment to recover. He then mumbled, pride wounded, "Hmm, I just thought you might ... "

"No!" Sari cut him off, warm tears mixed with icy determination in her eyes. "And don't let anyone make smart guesses in front of me. I know how to sex humans without expert guidance; when it's a human."

Dr Wong looked at Huan and shrugged. *Your wife. You deal with her,* his eyes pleaded through turtleshell rimmed glasses.

"Don't worry Kulta. I'll make sure of that," Huan promised, momentarily putting aside his fascination with the latest generation of 3-D supersonic scanners. He would have loved to spend a few minutes with the doctor on that but – some other time.

She closed her eyes, and saw it filling up her mental vision.

A spirit is being recycled... stripped down, reassembled, right inside.

* * *

Sari abhors predictions. Horoscopes, tarot cards, projections, prophecies, scans, extrapolations, wild guesses. Why not know in due course? Advance information rarely changes the course of eventuality anyway. In the end, predictions only serve to generate anxieties while things happen the way they're meant to. Didn't they have a million tonnes of data on climate change? In the end, nothing except the climate changed.

She hopes the scanning had not disturbed her baby. It's not the recycled ghost Doctor Andy Wong proudly captured with a bunch of wavelengths. Pixels. Resolution. Wavelength. Background noises. What vocabulary for the most beautiful and magical process in life. "I'll name her Sonja. Sonja Song. Beautiful like a song."

It's a girl; mother's instinct knows best. Save your gadgets. Inside, she feels calm and secure, trusting her mother, her Äiti, completely. Nothing truer than instinctual trust; that's love uncontaminated. She's kicking, turning, stretching, hiccupping, sucking her thumbs and playing with toes, killing time – no, no killing, not even metaphorically – just waiting, making time. Awaiting the magic moment, patiently. We'll see each other in due course. All in due course, when we're meant to. Not before. Soon, now.

She'll teach her Finnish. Some Finnish anyway. She cannot imagine baby talking in a foreign language. It just wouldn't sound right. Must be in mother tongue, her mother's tongue, my mother's tongue.

Right now, they are one with each other. They say this about many things. One with nature. One with the gods. One with oneself. One with this and that. Do they know what it means, how it feels, to be one with someone in body and soul?

It feels heavy.

Well, maybe it's a boy. It won't matter. Unlikely though. In her mind, she can see only a cute little girl. Her princess will have traces of her, carrying her to the future.

Lately, she's experienced a quantum leap in empathy for Laina. More than ever, she feels Mum's aspirations and anxieties, happiness and sadness. Sari has always loved Laina dearly, but also wished Mum to be... well, different. She can't say how her mother could change for the better but... Oh never mind.

Sari wants to go around the huge coffee table with her big belly to give Mum a hug. She looks up from her crochet just as Laina is getting up to go to the washroom. "My guts feel funny," she says, massaging her abdomen. "I wonder if it's something I ate."

Oh no. I didn't mean it when I wished you diarrhoea. Sorry Äiti.

BABY TOM

Officially, Sari is being cared for by twelve doctors of eight nationalities. All world-renowned, under-worked. The Medical Authority has prepared a website and twelve-page pamphlet. In the introduction, the Chief Executive and Consul General of Finland both say the Song Baby represents hope for humanity and universal love. Click "We Are Ready" to see a comprehensive checklist. The Government has done everything possible to ensure an impeccable operation. Inside "The Experts Behind" tab are virtually identical resumes and passport-size photos of the doctors in lab coats. All but two have a stethoscope clipped around the neck. All wear a confident and clinical smile.

Dr Andy T L Wong is Team Head and Obstetrician-in-Charge because he's local. Dr Nelimarkka, the Chief Anaesthetist, appointed by Finland, is supported by four specialists. There's a sub-team of paediatricians. A local professor and three international figures from Beijing, Finland, and the United States, all super bright and inexperienced. The USA sends someone to attend every birth on the planet if allowed. Then there are clinical psychologists standing by for the mother and the newborn. "How do you head-shrink a newborn?" she had asked Dr Wong. "Just in case, Sari; just in case," was the answer. The doctors are backed up by a contingent of nurses and midwives to monitor Sari round-the-clock, using up oxygen around her. The hospital is ringed in by cops and besieged by journalists. Sari is a captured alien from outer space.

The government has chartered the Maternity Ward of Queen Mary Hospital. It would have been deserted otherwise; there isn't another expecting woman within a thousand kilometres. Many people had started to question the purpose of maintaining a maternity ward, and suggested merging it with the busy department of Gynaecology, giving fertility treatment to women. Maintaining the unused maternity ward is a waste of money, they had said. The government defended it as a matter of principle, a symbol of hope. Just in case, you know, just in case. Then came Sari to save the situation.

But the underused Maternity Ward was not quite ready. Its ventilation system had to be separated from the rest of the hospital.

The government had learned its lesson from the last birth – Baby Tom's nearly three years ago. Although most babies anywhere in the world die within the first twelve months, Baby Tom's death sparked an emotional outrage, nonetheless. People bandied about the reasons as usual. Finally, the theory of cross-contamination through the ventilation system proved the most popular. The Chief of the Medical Authority would have lost his job had he not promptly bowed on TV with tearful eyes. The government is determined this time. Baby Song must not die under official care.

After that? Well, the statistics are foreboding. Worldwide infant mortality in the past three years is eighty-two percent, so far. Out of 844 births, 147 babies have lived past their first birthday. Five are yet to celebrate this perplexing milestone. If the records are extended to cover the previous decade, the deadly ratio would drop to thirty-seven percent. Better, but still astounding by historical standards.

Hong Kong had had low infant mortality for many decades. Fewer than three deaths per thousand births. But both babies born in the past five years had died within their first year. Two out of two. One thousand per one thousand by the reporting unit of the United Nation. One hundred percent.

Baby Tom slept through his life. He did not once open his eyes. He never cried or coughed, but died of pneumonia, right here in this extremely well equipped hospital, surrounded by doctors and their professors.

It was some form of pneumonia.

LIFE AND DEATH

Philosophy is mental masturbation. Sari jumped to that conclusion after a first year university course.

The professor – a Dr Pinto who lectured with a voluntary stutter and theatrical accent – was a diminutive intellectual. He spent half the course re-ruminating on a pamphlet he had written, "Existentialism and Ethics". What have they got to do with each other? Sari never managed to finish reading all twenty-eight pages. She said she had read more stimulating tenancy agreements prepared by a lawyer on time charge. Pinto wasn't to blame though. Look. Kant said this... Aquinas said that... Spinoza summed it up thus... Sartre pointed out...Wittgenstein argued... Pinto himself was only responsible for the prepositions and conjunctions linking the convoluted wisdom of a bunch of dead men.

Philosophising is a waste of time, she decided. Low level vanity. Inevitable issues are best dealt with by instincts, not obtuse circumlocution. What about acceptance? This most powerful wisdom has been lost to blindness and arrogance. To realise limitations requires clarity and humility, qualities most men lack. Huan's an exception. He likes to challenge feasibility, but accepts the inevitable the way women do. He knows helplessness when he sees it. She has never told him this makes him a good partner; men's good qualities are easily ruined by self-consciousness.

Pregnancy has changed something in her.

Her research on Baby Tom and the Infertility Crisis has planted questions in her head like multiplying viruses. What's life? What happens when it ends? She can't help wondering.

Perhaps it's the recurrent nightmares. They started the night after the ultrasonic viewing.

A baby emerges from a vast field rimmed in darkness. He turns his head frantically from side to side as if trying to fling it off, while ballooning into a giant. She screams at the rapidly inflating infant, "Look this way, Mum's here!" But no sound ever came. She's watching a silent horror movie, black and white, in an empty cinema.

In another nightmare, a ghoul seeks shelter like a vampire fleeing the rising sun. It transmutes into a cyclone, twisting into her, entering between her legs. It feels cold but mortifyingly seductive; it once made her wet the bed. Similarly, she would be helplessly muffled in dumb horror.

In the most disturbing and frequent nightmare, she gives birth to a naked mummy. Tiny, dark, desiccated. She pushes it out in a puff of light dust, with unnerving ease. It lies still between her legs, immobile like herself. She can't feel her body. Doctors and nurses, Huan, her mother stand watching by, totally ignoring her and the baby. None of them seems surprised. They watch and nod, exchanging tut-tuts and muted comments. "Get the baby!" She would scream until she wakes, drenched in cold sweat and uncontrollable tears.

* * *

Song Huan is puzzled by her uncanny existential interests, but he's willing company as long as it makes her happy. She doesn't find his indifference to metaphysics very stimulating, but his pragmatism is sobering.

Humans know next to nothing about the mysteries of life and death after working on it for a long time. Why do we exist? What's life? How is it acquired? What went before and comes after? What drives our body of electromagnetic forces and chemical bonds? So many fundamental questions... none satisfactorily answered. Not one. Not to Sari anyway.

"Why do we need an answer?" Huan asks. "What difference would it make? Would an answer make us different? Happier? Wiser? More sensible to ourselves and others?"

Most likely not, she concedes. From experience, the more we think we know, the more confused and dreadful we become.

"Can't agree with you more. So why waste time?" he concludes, hoping to end the discussion.

She agrees, but still... She tries to put things into perspective. Since our simian ancestors ventured outside mountain grottoes with stone axes and pilot fire, we've been trying to understand the origin of life. Millennia later, many are still stuck with Let there be light! Isn't that pathetic?

"It just shows that God used voice-activated switches long before us, and didn't like working in the dark even when there was nothing yet to illuminate, that's all."

She does not find it amusing, and continues her train of thought. In comparison with the meagre but measurable progress in science, we haven't scratched the surface of life's deep secrets. Let there be light would have made sense to Grandpa Caveman; but he would never have understood how digital cameras work.

"So there you go!" Huan clasps his fingers together as if praying, attempting again to conclude the discussion. "A few thousand years of no progress. So why now? Waste of time. Want some ice-cream Kulta?"

"Yes or no," Sari gives her favourite answer, ignoring the temptation of ice-cream. It was a waste of time, but not anymore. Not since she became pregnant. Not since the dreams. She doesn't want to think why. She doesn't want to admit that childbirth is again a matter of life and death, especially for the baby. We may not know what life is, but existence feels undeniable. Life can be seen and felt.

She gently cradles her tummy with both hands.

There's a carnal side with muscles and bones, and a pattern we can take for granted. Death's another story. It can't be felt. It takes over when life ends, slipping things into the unknown. If life is intrigue unresolved, death is fear unmitigated. Dark and unwelcome, philosophers can't find enough words to bring it to life, poets find it depressing, scientists can't find the funding to penetrate it. So it was left to the priests. Overcome ignorance with organised ignorance; conquer fear by concentrating it in the hands of one frightening God. Dear Lord, give us strength to spill the blood of those who don't believe in what we don't know. Amen. Something's wrong there.

"Perhaps death isn't the end of everything?" He interrupts with a suggestion, while checking the freezer. "Then it won't be so scary. Ah, here it is. How come you're the one who's pregnant, and I've got the cravings?"

"Hell, it's worse!" she says.

"What's worse?"

"Life after death. I've given some thought to that too. Eternal life is petrifying. Imagine: Hell fire for a trillion years just to warm up... or, sitting at the right hand side of God for eight million billion trillion years, then sit some more. What do you think?"

"Ooooh.... Shit."

"Exactly. Trying to choose between heaven and hell isn't as simple as it seems is it?"

"Then don't choose! It's not up to us anyway. Do you want chocolate or strawberry?" He offers her chocolate. She shakes her head. "No thank you. You're the one with the cravings."

"You guys seem to have a better sense of proportion. Someone must have noticed that eternity lasts forever, and suggested reincarnation instead: Chickens. Pigs. Dogs. Tape-worms. Horse flies. Politicians. Philosophers. Maggots. Is that what makes biodiversity?"

"Probably, from the point of mass balance." He missed her joke. "In that sense, left to the mechanics of nature, we're all unripe maggots."

"Yuk!"

"Literal truth though." He digs into the carton with a spoon. "Furthermore, scientifically speaking, every bit of our body is reincarnated. If we had a soul, a detachable consciousness, it'd get recycled in the same way, like everything else in the universe. No reason to assume we're exceptional, right?"

"No. None at all," she agrees, and imagines the chain of biological events. People – maggots – flies – frogs with meaty legs – back to people, most likely Chinese. Not Finns anyway, ha ha, we don't eat frogs. "Hey, can you quit eating straight out of the box? Take what you want into a bowl."

"Sorry," he says, and continues the same.

She thinks out loud. "Perhaps that's why we act like maggots on the planet? Nibble up everything organic, every drop of oil. Burn them off. Let it cool down, reduced. Dead. In the end, just bones and rocks."

"Frightening isn't it?" He doesn't seem frightened at all.

"Yes it is. That's why we're scared. But then we hand fear over to ignorance, which makes it more fearful; a self-feeding stupid cycle."

"You're absolutely right." He returns the ice-cream to the freezer and keeps quiet, hoping that was the end of this session. But she continues. "That's why most people don't even like to mention it. Many intelligent people plan their lives as if they'd never die. When someone passes on, kicks the bucket, bites the dust (there's a wealth of euphemism when it comes to death; anything to avoid the D-word), something must take responsibility. One needs an official reason to die even at a hundred and thirty. A Cause of Death is required by law, certified, dated, signed, chopped, then filed. Otherwise, a coroner would carve up the corpse to look for a scientific cause. *Aha, see that? Right there, in the liver.* A Death Certificate can now be issued. Everything's in order."

"Yup, that's how it works."

"I've looked up the World Health Organisation website you know."

Yes I know, he thinks. I saw you absorbed in it. "Really?" he says instead.

"They've published a list of Official Causes of Death. It includes nearly a hundred reasons including the unpronounceable musculoskeletal diseases, tetanus, falls from excessive height, war, fire, and congenital abnormalities."

"What about old age and bad luck?"

"No they're not listed. According to the World Health Organisation, no one ever dies of plain old age."

* * *

Baby Tom didn't die of old age.

He died of pneumonia although he never coughed. Perhaps his lungs were too weak to convulse. A beautiful baby with a sweet calm face; eyes resignedly closed. Such heart-breaking peace.

Shhhhh – let him sleep. Do not disturb him. He will wake soon.

But he never did. He slept his whole life, all eighty-three hours of it. The suspected cause was idiopathic. The doctors' way of saying "Uh, no idea. Sorry," in Greek. People were left to speculate. Eventually, cross-contamination became the cause of death. That must not happen again.

Sari hardly paid any attention to the news of Baby Tom when he made his brief appearance, but she had since dug him up from the internet. She studied all the public enquiry reports and testimonies. She read about the Fertility Crisis. "It's much more severe than I thought!" She studied the global infant mortality figures. The more she read, the more it seemed hopeless.

Back to Hong Kong. Two out of two in five years.

So depressing. She nearly miscarried.

There must be a reason. But nobody knows. Idiopathic. Bullshit.

Stop thinking. Stop finding out more. Quit.

She started her clinical focus on positive thoughts only. She started to knit. Keep counting stitches. Smile. If I can't resolve the puzzle through reasoning, she thought, I'll overcome it by will. For my baby.

FERTILITY CRISIS

Women often experience changes during pregnancy. In Sari's case, it was more than an insatiable appetite for the pickled herrings that she normally detested, or a nauseous reaction to the smell of her favourite liquorice candies. She also became uncharacteristically, edgily, inquisitive. Besides musing on life and death, she also became obsessed with the fertility crisis, an issue she had had little interest in before.

Like Huan, she grew up in the Age of Terrible Calamities, and had long become inured to looming threats of apocalyptic proportion. Ever since she could read, there had been a new headline catastrophe every few months. Some were fascinating; reading like thrillers. Some were so complex they seemed unbelievable even as they ravaged the neighbourhood. Infertility leaned towards the latter. Plus, low birth-rate wasn't a big deal to a generation apathetic about parenting to start with.

Now that she was unexpectedly expecting a baby, the Fertility Crisis had become critically relevant. What exactly was it? How did it start? When did it become an issue? What was its current status? Was it worse than global warming? More threatening than the recurrent bird flu? AIDS? Was it more crippling than the last surge in the never-ending energy crisis?

She googled it.

There were thousands of lively forums, overflowing with earnest explanations, learned articles, confident conjectures, zestful propositions, all seemingly derived from a different reality. She kept scrolling, and came to the conclusion that two decades of hindsight had not helped to illuminate.

Nonetheless, there was ambiguous consensus about a few things. Most people assumed infertility would continue to worsen, until the end. Sari was surprised and distressed by the widespread pessimism. The scientific community also concurred that the unknown agent of mankind's childless plight must have been lurking in the atmosphere – the only thing universally shared by every living human, north and south, rich and poor. A form of radiation? Trace chemicals? Nasty radicals? Everyone rushed to discover the answer. Many suspects were found, far too many. The search became impossibly confusing, resoundingly inconclusive. Meanwhile, a Hollywood celebrity put on a full space suit for photographers. Others attempted to isolate themselves from the rest of the planet with full face masks.

It was also commonly believed that the way humans had been living and reproducing was somehow responsible, although for very different reasons.

The religious produced a long list of popular sins. Abortion, contraceptives, homosexuality, promiscuity. Even masturbation made a comeback as being quaintly sacrilegious. Most culpable sins had something to do with sex. God had lost patience – *just how many times have I told you...* and decided to punish His depraved creatures with a brutal touch of irony. Let those who kill foetuses and flush sperms down the toilet have no more. Isn't that obvious enough?

Claims of divine punishment were often delivered with triumphant smugness, making it hard to tell whether they were meant to be taken as good or bad news. Regardless, Sari thought the whole thing did bear a resemblance to classical God wrath.

"Look at the way we live," an environmentalist pointed out. "We're planetary pests. The Earth's been infested with *Homo consumers*, multiplying and consuming mindlessly. We dig and pump stuff out of the ground, turning it into disposable items. We've always known that material balance will get us, and our numbers will destroy us one day, but have done nothing about it."

"Calling ourselves pests is to insult the human spirit," someone responded, indignant. "Every human life is sacred, unique in the universe. The human spirit marks us from other animals, and gives us the privilege to multiply and exploit the earth for a better tomorrow. Low birth-rate is a temporary issue that will be resolved with human ingenuity, just like numerous challenges before, if we'd stop trashing ourselves."

Sari didn't like to think of people as pests, now that she was incubating one herself. But she also wondered if every human life was indeed sacred and unique. No one elaborated on the relationship between over-population, an unsustainable lifestyle, and universal sterility. Regardless, overpopulation did seem to her to have been a practical concern for a long time. How come nothing had been done about it?

She searched, kept scrolling. Ah, here's one. The economy. *What?* Yes, nobody did anything about population because of the economy. The economy dictated politics; a growing populace was good for economic expansion, and vice versa.

The global community had become hooked on economic stimulants to feel alive. But the economy itself was chronically ill, rebounding erratically only when zapped with lots of money. *Print the money! Promote consumption. Buy, chuck away. Borrow more to buy more, chuck away more.* The remedy seemed incredibly simple for such a complex malady, but it often worked, at least for a while. Voila! The financial engine would again wheeze vibrantly. Consumption would start to creep up, dragging the indices along. Digging and chucking would resume. *Well done! Call an election!* Would any politician in his right mind dare to tackle the issue of population at such a delicate moment?

Besides the economy, governments were bogged down by all sorts of exigencies: epidemics, natural disasters, all the usual culprits.

"Hmm. Just like now," Sari thought. "The world hasn't changed much." But back then, people were less used to them, so made a big deal out of everything. Even the weather, newly capricious, stirred numerous debates. Some experts said the weather was *as it always had been*; other experts said it was *as never before*. Looking through archived news, it seemed there had always been a drought not far from a flood. When the flood had receded, an epidemic might hit, sometimes followed by a famine, all of biblical proportions, according to the press. When things finally quieted down for a while, everyone would rush to the stock market to speculate on which companies might benefit most from the next round of disasters... until the market crashed again.

Under such hectic circumstances, population control never had a chance to make it to the global political agenda.

* * *

The UN was a bottomless mine of idle, useless data for Sari.

According to records, the world population peaked at eight-and-a-half billion around 2020. She was yet to start kindergarten. But this figure, official though it was, was widely disputed. Some believed it was at least a billion short, even two, depending on how data had been collated and adjusted to reflect the millions who followed a long tradition of cheating the censuses.

Eight or ten billion made little difference to the big picture anyway. Whatever the number, the world was overcrowded. Oh really? Many begged to differ. Even ten billion would have been nothing compared with numerous earlier projections. For years, after generations of demographers and futurists had competed for media attention with increasingly alarming estimates, everyone had been expecting the world population to peak at twenty-five.

But...

What?

More debates between a few involved professionals as usual, just something to do.

Then came 2024.

That year, the unruly rising trend eased so abruptly it skidded. When Sari showed Huan the historic graph, he gaped. "Wow! Must have caused a panic." From almost two hundred million births the year before, the number of newborns dropped to just one hundred million.

"Just?" Huan did a quick calculation on a candy wrapper. "Line them up head to toe, and you'll get a line of babies all the way round the equator, with sixteen million left over."

* * *

There were passionate debates among and between biologists, doctors, family planning experts, economists, sociologists, politicians, journalists, religionists, bankers, socialists, insurers, environmentalists, and everyone else, for a while. Sari got lost in browsing through the prodigious amount of discussions. They all seemed insightful and authoritative, covering even the most staggering and remote possibilities. Experts continued to disagree over the cause, extent, significance, and implications of the birth plunge.

Meanwhile, the number halved again the following year to fifty million. For the first time in more than a century, zero population growth was achieved.

It continued relentlessly at this rate.

The birth-rate chart looked ominous two decades on; no wonder Huan expected panic. But archived information showed an indifferent world. A hundred million neonates were still a huge burden to an overextended planet. At the end of that year, after fifty million had died in accordance with the tyranny of statistics, the population expanded by fifty million, net. Sure, something weird must have had happened; nobody knew what, didn't care, either. Only God and a few politicians claimed credit. One for Divine penalty; the other for prudent policy.

Besides a murmur of unease about these freakish phenomena, few were truly distressed. No-one would say this, but it was alleviating news for a world deeply threatened by itself. One hundred million babies fewer than the previous year was spooky. But one hundred million new babies were still too many, far too many.

There were sporadic pockets of violence and hysterical petitioning the Heavenly Fathers over the next few years, mostly in America. After the riots were quelled and wailing at God had calmed, it was business as usual. Hardly anyone took the posterity of humanity to heart. Kind of understandable perhaps. People in the middle of a flood, with water up to their waists, furniture afloat and banging against walls, were not going to lose sleep over the prediction of a drought ten years down.

After some hoo-has, the average person returned to more pragmatic concerns. "There'll be significantly fewer workers contributing to the Provident Fund," commented an editorial in the *Morning Post*. "It may not be sustainable in the long run."

It caused an outcry.

Government was under pressure to do whatever it might take to defend the integrity of the pension system. Fund managers took the opportunity to point out that once the system had lost equilibrium, it would take considerably more effort to manage. They foresaw substantial increases in management fees. In the following year, the industry raised their fees by half a percent. Immediate concerns were dispelled.

The long-term prospect of the human race loitered around editorials and opinion columns for a while, making occasional appearances between election frauds and natural calamities. From digging into the archives, Sari could feel the subject losing newsworthiness.

Reports on the "Fertility Crisis", as it was now called, soon gave way to ads for fertility drugs. Pregnancy became prestigious and lucrative. Maternity wear was the fashion of the day. Women – some men too – wore rubber tummies that doubled as carrying pouches with a flipped bellybutton for headphone wire to pass through. "Yes! I remember that," Huan said, kind of nostalgic, when Sari showed him an old poster of a couple, each wearing a colourful Rubbertum® , holding hands, smiling very happily. "Don't look at me like that, I never wore one. They were banned in my school." Sari couldn't remember having seen one herself; probably not the kind of thing that would catch on among Finns.

Governments competed to do something about it. Tax breaks for babies and children, and benefits for expecting mothers became more emphatic with each election. According to market oriented wisdom, the problem would eventually go away if adequate financial incentives were provided.

Upon confirmation of her pregnancy, Sari became entitled to perpetual maternity leave with an inflation-adjustable allowance equal to her present salary, or HK$82,347 per month, whichever was higher. Airlines sponsored free tickets for the whole family. Buses and trains offered free rides for life. The list went on.

For as long as the baby lived, practically everything would be free, for as long as these things continued. But what if the baby died as expected?

Well, it said right there in the officiously exuberant letter from the Chief Executive, after long paragraphs of heartfelt congratulations: "For the sake of clarity, and to obviate misunderstanding, the allowance shall cease within twenty-five calendar days of the child's death." (*Why twenty-five*, she wondered.) The Government would, under that unthinkable and tragic circumstance, take care of the funeral which might attract tens, even hundreds, of thousands of mourners and spectators. Sari and Huan were not expected to object. "Please sign here then, Mr and Mrs Song."

* * *

This is 2048.

Twenty-four years after the Fertility Crisis started, world population still stands at 6.8 billion – give or take a few hundred million – but overpopulation is no longer a concern. The problem, like people, is working itself out. Median age is 63.2. People are still *Homo consumers*, enjoying their shopping. If anything, consumption has intensified, working up to a grand finale. The medical industry is booming. Brewery stocks have gone up tenfold in the past ten years; only three in every ten thousand are below drinking age. Middle-aged and childless, professionals with an interminable career ahead tend to drink indulgently. Retirement age is around eighty in most countries, so as to diffuse the pension crisis. With life expectancy at ninety for men and ninety-four for women, deferring retirement seems reasonable – inevitable in any event.

Six-billion-eight-hundred-million people, with hardly any youngsters, is the general demographic picture.

Worldwide, there have been 184,271 births since 1 January 2038 – fewer than two hundred thousand in a whole decade. At the beginning of the century, the prolific human race produced this many babies in less than twelve hours. That's not all. Out of the tiny new stock, thirty-seven percent die before they can walk.

Pneumonia, of course.

Meanwhile, the congested and sterile world continues to struggle with increasingly ferocious weather and epidemics. Mega-typhoons and earthquakes strike frequently. Magnificent human monuments and infrastructures crumble humiliatingly. Famines recur at breathless rates in Africa and Asia. Even agriculturally bountiful North America suffers periodic food shortages. Australia is a rapidly growing desert. Global warming again? Perhaps. The temperamental cycles of nature? Perhaps too. God knows.

Like super typhoons, epidemics are common. Unlike typhoons, they strike without warning. They also hang around longer, though never long enough for humans to develop inoculants.

At the same time, *Homo sapiens*, still in the billions, ageing, working harder than ever to stay advanced, productive and competitive, battling the consequences of overpopulation, worrying about not having enough babies at the same time. They plod along, numbly aware that mankind is an endangered species, most likely a self-endangered species without a saviour from the outside. They hold on to their way of life, the only way they know, to feel safe together, while dying out slowly, very slowly.

BIRTH

Dr Wong and two midwives are guiding Sari through a contraction when Laina returns from the washroom. Huan has been woken up from his nap next door by an overly excited nurse. He's presently barefooted, uncertain about his role in Sari's contraction. The obstetrician is nervous; Laina wonders if he has ever seen a woman in labour before.

Twelve hours later, in a boisterous delivery room, Song Huan, overwhelmed, assisted by soft and dextrous medical hands, places baby Song Sung – a clamp on freshly cut umbilical cord – on Sari's chest.

"What a beautiful baby.... What a beautiful baby..." she mutters, sobbing from a mixture of feelings. Joy, joy, and many others she can't name. Through the optical distortion of teardrops, she sees Laina chatting with Dr Nelimarkka at the end of the bed, drinking warm champagne which the anaesthetist had hidden in the delivery room, against hospital rules. Mum smiles proudly at her (Sari's also a mum now!) waving discretely.

Huan sits next to her, nose all red, squeezing her shoulder. "You're so brave, Kulta. You're so brave, Kulta." They both have acquired an emotionally induced stutter.

Everyone in the cramped room is rapturous, hugging and kissing. Half have tears in the eyes, a few nurses sob. These annoying characters have changed in Sari's eye. They now seem close friends, family, utterly loveable. She has not slept for a very long time, but she's not tired.

Little Song Sung cries forcefully. He's hungry, impatient to get on with life.

He'll live.

Yes, he'll live. Everyone can sense that. No doubt about it.

Sari has completely forgotten about the little girl she has been expecting for nine months and fifteen days.

LULLABY

"Mama I can't sleep. I'm scared."
"What are you scared of, Sweetie? Tommy's fast asleep."
"This house makes a strange noise."
"Just the wind, Sweetie. Same as in the old house."
"No Mama, this is different. The wind here scares me. It's bad."
"The wind's never bad, silly. Only people are."
"Listen Mama! The music stopped! How come?"
"Don't know. Maestros take breaks."
"To do what?"
"Whatever. Don't know. Don't talk about them Sweetie."
"Can you sing me a song now?"
"Mmm... OK. Just one?"
"OK. That one?"

From the far side of the ravine
blows a gentle wind.
Sweeping over the silver moon
Sailing across the purple sea
It's come a long, long way
to be in your dream.

Sleep, O baby, sleep
Only when you dream, I can come in
Only when you dream, everything's real
When the sun comes up
We'll disappear
Like the wind, gone, gone
Blowing beyond
Never to be seen.

THREE

QIGONG RHAPSODY

Qi rumbles through Ma Yili, flushing his meridian channels, warming the Dan Tian – an abdominal pocket behind the navel where his bladder and intestines are. Most people do not normally feel the presence of internal organs unless something has gone badly wrong. To Ma, that's just another thing wrong with the normal person. He neglects the body for so long, taking it for granted, until the only connection left is the emergency alarm; he only feels the stomach when it aches, rather than sharing with it the pleasure of digesting something delicious and healthful.

He can actively direct *Qi* with his breathing, which is one of a few ambiguous meanings of the word *Qi*. What else could it be? Flux of neutrinos? Expression of other alpha beta gamma bits? he used to wonder. Gradually, he gave up intellectualising it with the same cleverness he once employed to study equally quirky entities sanctioned by modern physics.

"To understand these things, you can't think forcefully," his mentor Mary Scott once said.

In the end, be it *Qi* or some ephemeral subatomic phantom, it's all in the mind isn't it? A steel door is practically empty in atomic terms. Just a bunch of electrons buzzing between a matrix of nuclei. In spatial proportion, merely a few specks of dust zipping between raison-size clusters stuck at the corners of a grand ballroom. Should the electrons freeze – if the metaphoric dust should settle – everything would vanish.

Weird? That's science... or *Qi*...

There's nothing. A door is substantially *not there* according to science, so is the physicist, Ma reckons with due humility. Not there. Nothing. Zilch. Buddha was right wasn't he? But even the brightest or dumbest scientists don't attempt walking through doors. Neither did Buddha.

Understanding is one thing, believing is another, perception is yet something else. In the twilight zone of existence, reality slips, slides and teases. The great 20th century physicist Niels Bohr said "reality" does not exist independent of observation. His contemporary, Heisenberg, told us that the reality that can be put into words is never reality itself. Were they Daoists?

Perhaps *Qigong* reshapes reality with wayward bonds and psychedelic charges, as hallucinating drugs do? After practising for decades, Ma still has no idea. It took him years to clear the meridian channels, to make room for the free flow of *Qi*. Now that he has attained this wondrous sense of void, he can let in... in... and in. Something fundamental and omnipresent, older than the universe itself, seeps into him, waking his spine, electrifying his being. Or is it the other way round? Is he dissolving into the infinite background, like a fizzy tablet in water instead?

Yes, all in the mind.

The cosmos, so very big, is no bigger than a teeny-weeny singularity. Perhaps singularity could be reconstructed in the mind, tugged behind the bellybutton. Ridiculous; but why not? If something so incomprehensibly tiny could give birth to the universe... maybe the fathomless complexity of a physicist's macrocosm could also be condensed into elemental purity, back to nothing. "In a flat universe, all the energy adds up to zero." He learned that in Physics.

It started with nothing, and will end in nothing.

"I'm nothing," he lets the thought echo. "There's nothing out there."

What can be more peaceful than me, being nothing, worrying about nothing?

How long has it been? Minutes? Hours? Aeons?

Time bypasses Ma when he meditates. But somehow, part of him knows. Dozing bus passengers always wake before their stops.

Qi radiates out of his *Dan Tian*, caressing ageing vessels, massaging aching muscles, fortifying stiffened joints.

* * *

Ma once speculated *Qi* to be the ultimate element he hoped to isolate in a giant accelerator. Ultimate – what an extreme state; a serious word used too lightly. The ultimate element must be absolutely basic. What can one say about something so elemental, other than it's the very first step from *there isn't* to *there is*? The fundamental essence of all things must be that simple; indivisible. It has to be omnipresent purity without mass, charge, spin, dimension, smell, flavour, beginning, or end...

It just is.

Shouldn't have a name. The *Dao* that can be described cannot be real... Laozi said that. Heisenberg said that. Anything with a describable feature can't be truly and ultimately fundamental can it? It's indescribable, unnameable. We exist because of a transient disruption of the primary state of affairs.

The resultant existential stir, Ma thought, perhaps still thinks, could be *Qi*. The universe, the one that we see, the big wide expanding thing out there, is the result of a disturbance, a cosmic bruise. Call it the Big Bang, whatever. It's nothing more than a temporary divergence, unmitigated stress, of the fundamental state. Like a bruise, it will disperse and heal in the fullest of time – when it all ends.

We won't be there. Nothing we own will be there. Nothing we've ever fought for or believed in would survive the healing, when the cosmic bruise settles back into neutrality.

Meanwhile, everything that exists does so at an elevated stress level. *To be* is waiting to heal, to return to ultimate basics, to be again *not to be.*

That's why things are unstable. They are unstable the moment they came into being – the moment they *began* coming into being. Status quo at any instant is not sustainable.

To Ma the Daoist and physicist, *Qigong* Master and irreligious spiritualist, the concept became self-evident after years of contemplation. Then it became far-fetched and confusing, impossible to fathom, simply weird. Then it cleared up again.

Then it went away completely, and stopped to matter.

If it is, it doesn't matter.
If it isn't, it doesn't matter.

AWAITING DEATH

Whatever *Qi* may be, it seems to be losing umph lately, deflating Ma at times like a leaky old tyre. He has to work increasingly harder at getting it going, flowing as commanded. Nebulous aches – just minor, gnawing nags hiding dormant in every human body – seem to be waking from hibernation.

Perhaps he's just being oversensitive to his body, magnifying every minute change it inevitably goes through from time to time.

"Listening to your body isn't enough. Live it, Yili. Feel it from within. One day, you might find out where your body and soul meet, and through that discover a new dimension," Mary Scott had told him. He felt like saying, *Pardon me?* at the time, but didn't. He decided to keep an open mind, and give himself time to discover.

He has taken good care of his body and spirit, and they have responded well, so far. He will soon turn sixty-nine, but he's as fit as a thirty-year-old, though he can no longer remember exactly what being thirty was like. It makes no difference. He didn't feel old, period, until recently.

Sixty-nine is nothing for a *Qigong* master. Hadn't he woken his spine, mobilised the *Ren Mai* and *Du Mai* meridian channels years ago? Clearing these meridian channels, unclogging the gate points yogi called chakras, is the ultimate challenge in *Qigong*. The rare individuals who have achieved this can supposedly live on and on, up to hundreds of years if they don't get hit by a car.

"Sounds like Father Abraham was a *Qigong* master," Young Ma had commented with a straight face, meaning to be impish.

"Who's to say he wasn't? Or that he didn't live that long?" his teacher explained. "Life expectancy is exactly what its name says. An expectation. Infants' *Ren* and *Du Mai* are not yet blocked. Compared with adults, they're nearly indestructible. Their bodies carry very little pain, and heal miraculously well, like wild animals. That's our natural state. Then we block them with anxieties, indulgences, drugs, bad food, improper walking, sitting and sleeping, and too many expectations. Abraham could have been one of those gifted individuals, like Laozi, who knew how to be in touch with his body."

"How long did Laozi live?"

"No one knows. His life and death were shrouded by myths and legends, probably intentionally. Chinese Daoists who had attained enlightenment invariably withdrew, disappearing into their own space."

Maybe Mary Scott is still alive, hiding in her own dimension? When Ma unblocked his *Ren* and *Du Mai*, she was still in touch. Her short response was, "Well done. You're born to see the way. Now forget about it. Let it be, and live well."

That's right. First, forget.

So what am I fretting about now? Death?

Can't be. Death means nothing to Ma. He had philosophically resolved the ultimate stage of life long ago. But these days, the possibility of getting stuck between life and death has started to disturb him. He would meditate and purge the thought. Done. Gone. But before long, it would creep back, mousy quiet, hook it self to a corner of the cerebrum waiting, watching, gaining weight. He doesn't fight it. *Let it sit for while, and leave.* But it doesn't. Day by day, it whispers *vulnerability* to him. "Hey, old man, life's precarious without medicare. A slip can cripple you. A burst appendix is fatal. A minor stroke? Huh, no such thing. All strokes are major. Even a bad cut can kill. You're not afraid of dying are you? But many things can make life unbearable, torturing slowly. Look, a broken tooth may hurt so much you'd have to yank it out with a pair of pliers without anaesthetic. Ouch! How do you deal with that philosophically? Another breathing exercise?"

Nonsense! But...

He wonders if he should leave this tiny community like Song Huan did seven years ago, to be alone, to wait for his own death in peace. Huan was seventy-two, only seventy-two. Old at the time to him, but no longer.

*   *   *

Song Huan was the one who started these morbid contemplations. He obviously had nothing better to do than calculating and recalculating the doomsday scenario, to pass time.

"Look Ma, according to my model, life expectancy has dropped to just over seventy, like, for me, right now," he announced one day, pointing at his own nose. "If we die slowly, it might be lengthened slightly. But that'd be cheating statistics with a bit more unnecessary pain." Ma could see agony behind his brave face.

"Thanks for the cheerful thought, Mr Song."

Song Huan was a typical engineer. He calculated and scheduled everything, including death. When everyone else was busy with random extrapolation about the Infertility Crisis, he projected how the world might wind down using just a spreadsheet programme. Ma had seen the pile of printouts. As a hopeful gesture, he had allowed for a "recovery scenario" in case fertility resumed as unexpectedly as it had ended. This prospect was now remote, as people aged and contacts became scarce. Otherwise, given the huge number of variables and the simplistic approach, his predictions had been impressively accurate.

"Substantial societal meltdown by 2085: world population falls below critical mass," was one of the remarks on his printouts. He estimated a global critical mass of one hundred million. Hong Kong would be left with fewer than a hundred thousand inhabitants. It turned out the *meltdown point* was reached a full decade earlier. Perhaps the population had dropped faster, or the social institutions were less tenacious than he had assumed. Who knows? Censuses had long ceased by then. In retrospect, Song Huan also thought he had underestimated the devastating power of what he called *Batch Impacts*: pandemics, famines, mega-typhoons, floods, and so on.

In addition, when electricity was turned off, longevity nosedived. Without electricity, the world ballooned into unreachable distances. The extant humans, huddling in small isolated pockets, rediscovered what the meaning of life had been for millennia. Water, food, sex and shelter.

Nothing else matters. This time, not even sex. Huan trained Song to be physically and mentally tough, to be ready for survival in a dying world. "Don't question. Survivors don't question. They just live," he told his son.

* * *

Shortly after Huan's seventieth birthday, he brought it up with Song for the first time: "Sung, what would you do if I got sick?"

"Take care of you I suppose. Why? Are you okay, Bub?" Song was more puzzled than concerned.

"Yeah, yeah. I'm fine, just getting old; old people get sick differently. I might become sick all the time in the future, you know."

"You may or may not," Song shrugged. "You're fit like a bull, so why so morbid suddenly?"

"I'm not morbid, just realistic. I always try to see things a step ahead don't you know?" He smiled. "Without medicine and young nurses, you can't possibly take care of me when I'm really old. We must be sensible. Your survival depends on it." Huan paused to let Song register that it was a serious message. "Know what? I'm relieved I won't be dying in a hospital with tubes coming out of every hole, and a sloppy nappy between my legs."

"So what're you going to do?" Song asked, even more puzzled.

"I read somewhere that old elephants hide to die alone. I think it's a dignified idea."

"What?" Song gave his father a loving and condescending grin – the kind that parents give small kids, and big kids give old parents. "Bub, we're not elephants. They eat bananas with the peel on."

Huan regarded his son, returned a kinder version of the same smile, and sighed imperceptibly.

Over the next two years, Huan would bring the subject up every now and then. He would focus on pragmatic issues, and simulate scenarios – what if this and what if that. What if he had a stroke, or was crippled by a bad fall, or came down with diabetes? What could Song do? What would their lives become? Song could see the longwinded nightmare his father was conjuring up but they had to face many nightmarish hazards anyway, so why worry about what might or might not happen? People went to sleep and woke up in heaven all the time, neat and tidy.

The elephantine death ritual was cited often. When Song finally remembered to look it up in the library, he couldn't find any reference to it.

"I know you'll take care of me, but we must be sensible under the circumstances..."

"Okay okay.... With a father like you, how could I not to be sensible?"

"If I become bedridden, you'll have to check on me everyday, feed me, wash me, help me pee and pooh, wipe me after I've shit the bed."

"Isn't that what you guys did for me when I was a baby?"

"Yes but you got out of the habit sooner than we wished. Your mum actually cried the first time you wiped your own ass, performing proudly for us. Taking care of a baby fills you with hope and joy, you see. That's why people love them." Huan composed himself. "Old people can shit the bed for years."

Song didn't say anything.

"Besides, geriatric shit smells a lot worse. The sulphur content and acidity strengthen with age."

Song didn't find it funny, and didn't say anything.

"Think clearly, son. Don't force yourself to secretly wish me dead one day. It'd crush your heart, and leave a nasty scar forever."

Song didn't say anything.

After a while, he got used to these discussions, and understood the issue from his father's *sensible* point of view.

But...

* * *

One day, two years later, Song and Ma returned from an overnight visit to Ma's wife at Repulse Bay. Huan was gone. He had left a note, weighted down by the jade unicorn.

Then Song vanished.

The neighbourhood became even quieter, and waited.

Song reappeared a week later in good spirits. He said he had gone camping, and met a girl. "Bub was right," he announced without elaborating. Ma thought the nonchalance was to mask his pain, but surprise surprise, Rhea appeared shortly afterwards.

Song loves his parents and talks about them often. They were the only people he grew up with. But he never speculates about the whereabouts of Huan. As far as Song's concerned, his father is gone.

* * *

Well, Ma has no reason to worry about dying anytime soon. Of course Daoist longevity could be just a groundless myth, and *Qi* an airy hallucination; but he has a philosophical fallback. He has thoroughly contemplated the superficial distinction between life and death. Physics has also helped to dismantle the illusive boundary between these two states of being something, or nothing.

If there's a spirit, a soul, inside his body, his corpse-to-be – and he believes there is – than death releases it from deteriorating flesh and bones. It is like being discharged from a rotting jail. At that point, one way or the other, the mystery of the universe will no longer be. That's quite an incentive isn't it? Almost something to look forward to.

Yeah yeah yeah, it is. But... old Huan's anxiety has somehow reincarnated in him. It must have been in gestation all along.

A Daoist hypochondriac – how embarrassing. Not cool. Perhaps his goal of seeing *nothing* in everything has backfired, turning the big void itself into *something* of a burden?

Ah. Nonsense. Just a few bad weeks, a weak spell, or some bugs playing tricks on me, and here I am falling apart, moaning and groaning like a baby.

Perhaps he is just being human, a living one. Living humans his age tend to fret about the big transition sometimes. Hopefully, it would come and go. Yes, it would come and go. Meanwhile, *Qi*, – subatomic or psychosomatic or imaginative – continues to revitalise his body and soul.

Then, come what come may. Who cares.

THE DAOIST

The fog has disappeared at this elevation, reabsorbed into the air, but Song Sung feels its invisible presence in his hair, skin, and lungs.

The coolish morning has warmed quickly. It feels like June now. He sits on the stone retaining wall above Robinson Road, overlooking the footbridge, watching Ma meditating next to a patch of string beans. Song feels hungry. The eggs and potato pancakes from breakfast have been fully metabolised to cope with the eventful morning.

The covered footbridge once served as a concourse to disperse peak hour pedestrians regurgitated by one of the longest escalator systems in the world. Things were measured against each other to see which was the longest, fastest, tallest, biggest, or most expensive. Each morning, the longest escalator carried Mid-Level residents – middle-class and middle-aged – at high-performance rpm down to Central. In the evening – *clunk, clunk, clunk* – the mechanical drudgery would be reversed to haul them back up, fully stressed. Another day's work done. Prime time TV ahead.

The elevated concourse straddles the main artery, Robinson Road. Ma converted it into his home and vegetable garden nearly ten years ago. He keeps chicken in the penthouse of an adjacent building, and lives out here himself. It's open, but shielded by the stone wall and a few buildings positioned like protective giant screens.

There's a thick layer of natural deposits at street level; but the soil is too grainy and unstable. The road drains have either collapsed or clogged, turning Robinson Road into a mini river when there is a downpour. A garden at street level would be washed out before very long.

The hanging garden is also a welcome source of supplementary water. Hong Kong has been more tropical than sub-tropical for decades. The late afternoons are drenched by predictable showers, brief but heavy. With the clever modifications Song's father designed before his disappearance, the roof drains serve to satisfy most of Ma's irrigation water needs.

The escalator carves a refreshing breezeway through the concrete jungle below. In deadly-still summer nights, sleep-inducing zephyrs from the sea would straggle up this urban fissure for a brief moment of turbulence, before vanishing into the windless night. A perfect location which blocks the wind when too strong, and channels it back when too weak. Good *feng shui*.

* * *

Song enjoys watching his Tai-chi teacher, buddy, guru, tribal elder, neighbourhood farmer and bar-tender meditate. It calms him. With eyes closed, body neutral with life, Ma looks like a statue of Buddha. But Song knows he's not. Ma has declared that himself many times.

"Don't have enough compassion in me to qualify for Buddhahood. Just like I wasn't tall enough to play NBA. What can I do?" he told Song. "I don't even know what compassion is. Even without laws, most people wouldn't murder or rape. Are they compassionate? When a kite caught a little bunny, people cry, *oh poor little bunny*. When a kite dies from starvation, people cry, *oh poor kite*, and feel happy about themselves for being compassionate."

Ma always makes sense and nonsense to Song at the same time. "What about kindness and compassion among humans for now?" Song asked.

"Humans? What humans?" Ma looked around the deserted neighbourhood. "Young man, you grew up in a world that was wilting away, losing combative energy. Mine was nothing like that. It was full of righteousness. Saints everywhere talking about human rights, justice, humanity, and liberty, not how to live a better life and be better neighbours to each other. Those same talking saints also perpetrated the ugliest crimes against defenceless people. Zhuangzi was right. Evil would never cease unless sanctimonious people die off."

"So all mercy is hypocrisy in your eye?"

"It depends. I believe Buddha himself had nearly infinite mercy. But how many Buddhas have we produced in a few thousand years?

"Well, we are all born with a degree of compassion. We are naturally merciful to different things and people under different circumstances. Like intelligence, height, colour of the eyes, we're born that way, not a moral choice, so nothing special to brag about." He adjusted his glasses; they were still smart-looking at the time. "If we listen to individuals like Buddha or Jesus, and work hard at it, we might improve humanity's compassion index. That would do ourselves some good, probably tremendous good, making us feel better inside, like taking a good dump."

"A what?"

"But like taking a good dump, it should be natural and private, not advertised, certainly not forcing others to do it with you."

Right now, Song doesn't want to advertise compassion. He needs to borrow Ma's rationalisation talents instead. He wants Ma to tell him that what he did this morning was sensible, inevitable, not cruel. He knows that would help to restore his balance, relieving him far more effectively than any metaphorical bodily function could.

* * *

Ma seems so balanced to Song most of the time, as if nothing could upset his equilibrium. He comfortably navigates between an otherworldly wisdom that transcends this trivial existence, and a brute survival instinct that sustains this trivial existence. When in harmony, this healthy contradiction means balanced Yin and Yang, cool positive tension. But every now and then, Yin and Yang would get into fights, and the positive tension snaps. He would then retreat to mend his spiritual armour.

Song actually enjoys Ma's human weaknesses more than his uncanny strength and imperturbable detachedness which can verge on being cold. But Ma seems uncharacteristically troubled by ageing lately, just like Song's father, before disappearing. Song hopes it will pass. He cannot imagine losing Ma as well.

They are good friends despite the age difference, and not necessarily because of a lack of options. Song is a good Tai-chi student though rather indifferent to Ma's obscure philosophy. He is fascinated by *Qigong*, but does not have the talent or patience for it. He is yet to feel *Qi* happening.

"Are you sure *Qi*'s not just your imagination?" Frustrated, Song challenged his teacher.

"I'm sure it is."

"Then it's not real!"

"Real enough. Everything is just something in my imagination."

"Come on. You know what I mean."

Ma smiled, and continued picking his ear with his little finger.

"How does it feel, exactly."

"Itchy. Driving me nuts."

"I mean *Qi*, not your ear. How do I know I've got it?"

"Could you describe to me how wine tastes if I have never tasted it before?" Ma sniffs his finger absentmindedly.

Song saw that Ma was serious, not just teasing, and screamed "Ah..." while pretending to pull his hair out. Then they both chuckled like kids.

Song is used to his Shi Fu being mystically cryptic. Ma loves to share whatever he knows, and is very articulate. Yet he can't describe *Qi* in comprehensible terms. Perhaps some things are not meant for words, such as a glass of fermented, wet, inanimate grape juice being described as "fresh, dry, and lively". But Ma has devoted his life to court this entity which eludes the human vocabulary, foregoing precious career opportunities; he must surely believe in it. He doesn't like the word belief though, says he finds it creepy.

"I don't believe in anything."

"OK, belief or not, you're a Daoist right?"

"Probably, when I don't mean to be. Otherwise, I don't think so."

"Ah... ."

Daoist or not, Ma's a loyal follower of life's currents. He can actually let go and drift along happily. He doesn't whine about getting wet, fret over strong currents, or bitch about the temperature. – "Just life," he thinks – He doesn't question where the flow is heading either. "Why bother if I can't change the course, and don't want to?"

His silvery crew-cut, unpretentious and rugged, is Song's amateurish effort. From a distance, it suits him well. Below his peculiarly stylish haircut is a strong but accommodating forehead. His large round eyes, open and innocent, are at the same time inscrutable in the shadows of heavy lids. They are normally gentle and soft, "gazing from the back of the sockets," as he puts it. But occasionally, they engage with a vigour that pushes one into submission or rejection. In their depth lurks an urge to question, challenge, and provoke. An inquisitive intensity has been tamed by years of meditation and philosophical musing, but still there.

His enigmatic face is obscured by a pair of goofy spectacles – a trenchant reminder of the tedious demands of post-modern life.

He accidentally dropped his glasses off the hanging garden a year ago. He found suitable replacements – ready-ground spherical dishes about thirty millimetres in diameter – in an abandoned optical shop easily enough, but ended up spending a week trying to file a pair down to fit a frame similar to the one he broke.

For days, he neglected to meditate. He hardly ate. His eyes grew red, fierce with frustration as plate after plate of top quality lens got ruined in his hands. Song and John helped, but were no better at it.

God, it seemed so easy... OK, last pair !
Oh shit ! Oh shit !! Shit shit shit!!!
One more. Just one more.
That's it.
That's fucking it.

He finally accepted defeat ungraciously, and settled for an expedient solution that John had jocularly suggested at the onset. "Just glue the disks to the outside of this, and, done!" he had said, brandishing a huge pair of ugly black plastic frames.

"It actually looks OK. It does." John tried to be comforting when Ma first appeared with satellite dishes straddling his nose. Song gaped silently. It seemed amazing how a pair of glasses can change appearance so dramatically. From sage-like to deranged, just like that. John then offered a sensible suggestion. "Now that we're no longer in a stressful hurry to relieve your blindness, why not make a few proper spares at our leisure huh? Given time, we'll find an Italian designer frame that you'll like, and do a better job than, you know, this."

For a few seconds, Ma lost his humour. Instead of thanking John for his kind thought, he snapped drily. "What's wrong with this? No! Life has no spare."

"OK, OK. Just a thought."

All that futile filing was bad for him.

Amused by this reminiscence, Song attempts a little meditation while waiting for Ma. The morning has been racing through his mind involuntarily, repeatedly, like an instantly recurring nightmare. He sits in half-lotus, and swallows saliva to suppress a rumbling stomach.

As soon as he closes his eyes, he sees the old man's greyish and opaque eyes right against his. They're in him, insisting, pleading, in the dark. He can smell them, or their owner. The dead weight of his slimy, pungent body clings to his fingers. He wiggles them gently, trying to let go.

OXFORD TAI-CHI

There wasn't any reason to take note of Ma Yili's birth in Hong Kong on 15 December 2022, near the historic summit of the population curve, just before it nosedived. Six hundred thousand other babies were born on that same average day, sharing his zodiac sign and ruling planet.

But his parents made a big deal out of it anyway.

His father Ma Yong even took the day off work to be with mother-to-be Janice at the hospital, ears red from pressing against the phone all morning. "Listen, I might be stuck here most of the day. They have tonnes of stupid wules. Text or leave message if my phone's off. I get back to you once I can. Yes lah yes lah. I low I low. But I do want to low wight away. Aiya, just do as I say lah. Okay man? Good good."

He relayed progress to Janice until her labour started. It was an important land deal. Timing of Ma's birth was bad in that sense but, oh well, it wasn't up to them. Perhaps he should have agreed with Janice and scheduled a caesarean at an auspicious hour picked by a prominent fortune-teller at a special price of five thousand dollars; but his Auntie who knew these things said that would have upset their son's natural karma.

Ma Yong was Founder and Life Chairman (his name-card title) of a profitable real estate agency. Janice was General Manager. They were madly in love with the way each other made deals in properties – commercial and residential alike. They communicated with eyeballs on the negotiation table even before they were married. In fact, that was probably why they eventually did get married.

At its pinnacle, the agency's shares traded at a price that would have taken investors more than a century to recover investment. Tangible assets included office furniture in sixty-eight sales offices. Grey metallic desks with rusty patches and rumbling drawers; squeaky revolving chairs upholstered in black plastic, laced with sharp crackles; antiquated computers with hard-disks that sounded like industrial revolutions; photocopying machines; plastic hexagonal pens with the company's gilded logo; paper; three luxury cars for the Life Chairman and General Manager; and more than two thousand telephones. Everything else was intangible, grouped under goodwill in the books.

"Hi, how ARE you doing this morning? I'm calling from Goodluck Dragon Agency..."

"Hi, how ARE you this afternoon? Oh wonderful wonderful! My name's Don from Goodluck Dragon Agency..."

"Listen," Ma Yong habitually commanded the ears of his listener before explaining his business philosophy. "Our business depends on sales calls. The more the betta, huh? A percentage would hit. Use your bwain lah. It's quantity, not quality, that counts. People who say opposite are foos or lie-yas." His modus operandi was simple, effective, annoyingly honest.

Janice and Yong Ma decided to be loving and caring parents, but weren't quite sure how. Trying to determine what was good or not for their son was a tentative process, often involving outside advisors whom they did not trust. Their confusion turned out to be a fortuitous opportunity for Ma to grow up following his own nature, amidst continuous but ineffectual parental interference.

Ma was different from his parents in every respect. It might have been some recessive ancestral genes resurfacing, or mutation. From an early age, he was subtly countercultural without making statements. His parents never noticed his well-mannered rebellion against the values they had unmindfully embraced, although they did notice a few "behavioral oddities" which included an unbidden fascination with religion and apathy towards video games.

Ma Yili was sent to boarding school in Britain when he turned sixteen because two of his parents' close friends had just done that to their kids.

After two years in an expensive boarding school in London, he was admitted to Oxford to read physics. Mum and Dad were uncontrollably proud. Oxford and physics were the only things they talked about for days, although they knew nearly nothing about Oxford, and Mum worried about the employment prospects for physicists. They held a party to share their pride with friends and relatives, featuring Yili's video phone appearance. He appeared in dirty pyjamas and scruffy hair. Nobody commented, just in case it was a trendy intellectual look that they weren't aware of.

* * *

Ma was viewing a tiny basement flat next to a disused cemetery west of campus. Basement flats were not common in the old town. This one was probably converted from a medieval cellar, or some sort of crypt associated with the graveyard.

Inside, the temperature was a few degrees lower than outside. Near the ceiling, on the wall facing the cemetery, a single window the size of a ticket booth's admitted a stingy stream of light from ground level. A single bed, smaller than the one at boarding school, was parked underneath. He liked the cool damp air, diffused darkness, and the feeling of being half buried. He found it relaxing.

He was making his fifth panoramic turn in the middle of the not quite two hundred square feet studio. The wooden beam, barely a foot above, tousled his hair. The first word that came to his mind was ghost, followed by static. Ms. Mary Scott, the landlady, stood at the entrance to give him room to look around. He was obviously excited.

"Different isn't it?" She finally said, having decided he must have spun around enough times.

"Most certainly. Haven't seen anything like this all week." His mother would have whacked him on the head for not knowing how to position for a bargain.

"A bit dark, and you're using up the headroom," she pointed out, in case he hadn't noticed. They seemed to be bargaining on each other's behalf.

"Soft light helps concentration," Ma rationalised, mostly to himself. "Any more headroom than needed just goes to waste doesn't it?"

He had already fallen into the spell of this bijou box underground. He spun around again, as if driven by a timer. There was a dwarf-sized water-closet tucked into an alcove. Next to it was a small kitchen counter with a sink barely big enough for one dinner plate. The practical inconvenience of living with these toy-like utilities crossed his mind briefly and got dismissed, unwelcome. *Nah, nothing that I can't get used to.* He jovially added a positive note instead. "Plus there's a lovely garden outside."

"Oh, talking about that," Mary Scott said, raising a finger, "I spend a couple of hours *very* early in the morning doing Tai-chi out there." She turned to regard the entrance briefly, then continued with the house rules in a gentle tone not open to negotiation. "I shouldn't disturb anyone, mind you. I'm very quiet in the morning and between eight to nine at night when I meditate upstairs. I turn the phone off. I know it can be kind of difficult for youngsters but... ." She left the "you take it or shake it" unspoken.

Young Ma had never met anyone who Tai-chi'd or meditated. He paused at the novel idea for a second. "Not at all. That's great. I love silence. Don't have a TV. Never wanted one. I listen to music on the computer rarely. When I do, I use a headphone. I'm not very musical." He grinned innocently.

"Really? You must be one in a thousand these days," she said, delighted.

"Wonderful exercise isn't it? Tai-chi. Very good for old folks you know." Young Ma commented in a British public school voice with Chinese characteristics. In the final term he had just begun to get the hang of speaking condescendingly.

"Do you practise yourself?" Ms. Scott enquired, looking amused, not judging.

"Oh a little. All Chinese eat rice, do Tai-chi and make babies, you see," he said, "Ha ha," beaming stupidly, regretting the remark right away. Too late. Two years of teenage communal life had also taught him to spill one wisecrack after another. Funny peer pressure.

Mary Scott smiled.

Not knowing how to recover, Ma sheepishly changed the subject. "Is this place haunted?"

"Yes. Indeed," the old lady answered, earnestly. "Just good-natured spirits. Gentle and quiet, with a disposition to help rather than disturb if you're respectful."

"Oh," Ma said. "In that case, I'll take it if okay with you, Ms Scott."

* * *

He would eventually learn that the eighty-four-year-old landlady had lived in China for almost forty years, and was a widely respected Tai-chi and *Qigong* master internationally.

In 1990, she quit her job as kindergarten teacher to follow her husband to Shanghai. He was a handsome banker, marathon runner, devout Christian, and hobbyist missionary. He was transferred to Shanghai on a generous package to head the fast-growing investment banking division there. His relative youth for the position deepened his faith in God and himself.

The distance from home put them in a drastically different light, an alien one. For the first time, she saw that they had very little in common. His irrepressible urge to spread the good news of investment, God, and democracy, once idealistic and boyishly exuberant, now seemed naive and trite, even bigoted. Things about him that had been amusing before now made her cringe.

It had been love at first sight not long ago.

They got married within three months of their first date. They threw a party for friends and relatives to celebrate a fairy-tale romance, and spent three years in a small but fashionable Notting Hill flat. Three years of exemplary felicity, yet Mary Scott could not recall a single memorable moment except the moving in. A pigeon had dropped a big one on her forehead when she was just outside the front door, a pile of dishes in arm. He didn't even laugh; just repeated "oh my God oh my God". Perhaps it was a bad omen.

After fourteen months in Shanghai, they parted amicably, and resumed their own journeys in opposite directions.

The marriage seemed a sidetrack at the time, but it took her to the end of the world. It was meant to be. In the next forty years, she studied under some top names in Tai-chi, and taught in highly regarded institutions. She became the first female foreigner retained by the Chinese army as a martial arts consultant.

She semi-retired back to Oxford at seventy-two, on invitation from the British Tai-chi Association to be their Chairperson, a position she kept for three years.

* * *

Up in Mary Scott's living room, Ma signed a one-page rental agreement. She shared a few old photos from Hong Kong with him. The first one was taken at the Peak. She looked in her early forties, dressed in jeans and a plain T-shirt with the character harmony at the front. A pair of old-fashioned sunglasses perched on a nest of short and curly blond hair. She was not pretty pretty, but charming with a big frown. She was annoyed with the crowd around her, and did not hide her irritation for the camera. In the next one, she was officiating at some opening ceremony with the Chief Executive of Hong Kong. He was a whole head shorter, smiling toothily, peeling back only the upper lip. The last one was taken during an interview by a local Hong Kong TV station which sponsored her visit.

"Do you know him?" She pointed to the interviewer. "He's supposed to be famous in your hometown."

Ma opted to be straight-forward this time. "No. I was still a grandfather at the time, getting ready to be reincarnated." Oh no! What a laugh a minute! His wisecracks had become uncontrollable. Mary Scott found it amusing this time.

"Of course, of course, young man," she smiled.

Young man Ma was enthralled by his octogenarian landlady. He had never met anyone so real before. Not in his parents' home; not in the prestigious boarding school he attended. She had an unassuming confidence that was captivating. It made him feel awkward and shallow, losing grip of the confidence that was the prerogative of young people, but at the same time excited and inspired. It was like being shown light for the first time. It hurt his eyes; but he intuitively knew that many interesting things would be revealed. In barely half an hour, she had shown his highly perceptive mind something he had been subconsciously searching for, without knowing what it was.

"Would you be kind enough to teach me the basics of Tai-chi, Ms. Scott? I'd pay for the lessons, of course."

"Let's see, Mister Ma. We can think about that later."

A month later, Mary Scott started to give him lessons in exchange for help in the garden. She soon discovered that the young man, underneath a clumsy elitist facade, was more talented than anyone she had ever taught. He often saw things from unorthodox angles, forcing her to examine perspectives that she had not considered before, or long forgotten. She had been too good at it for too long. Everything had become second nature, by-passing the brain.

In the beginning, Ma found Tai-chi phlegmatic, but soon realised that slowing-down heightened his awareness of his muscles and bones, which he had taken for granted all his life. Fibre by fibre, joint by joint, his youthful body was being introduced to him for the first time.

Mary Scott's uncanny strength kept Ma wondering, wanting to find out more. She normally walked with a stick, but could send him stumbling half way across the garden with a jolt that seemed frail and weak.

"Impossible! Can you do that again Ms. Scott? How did you manage? You have no muscle!"

"I have, just not as much as you. You swing ten pounds of gunpowder at me. I have only one pound but I know how to detonate."

"Ah! I see."

Her tiny garden yielded sufficient for her vegetarian diet during the summer. Ma learned many gardening tricks from her. The agnostic Mary Scott was a living encyclopaedia in Eastern and Western philosophies and religious history. Her hobby-horse was the witch-hunt. She told Ma gruesome stories about how hundreds of thousands of innocent women were humiliated and tortured at length by "God's Wicked Eunuchs on Earth" before being roasted alive. She always finished off with "So, hallelujah!"

"But the church did a lot of wicked things. Why are you particularly upset about witch-hunts?"

"Perhaps I can't help thinking a woman like me would have been roasted for sure. No doubt, in the name of God. Maybe I even was in a past life."

In addition to fluent French and a scholarly knowledge of Sanskrit, she spoke much better Putonghua – the official Chinese dialect – than Ma whose mother tongue was Cantonese. "Hong Kong Putonghua is the only accent that even the speaker can't understand. Quite a linguistic phenomenon," she teased. She was a great calligrapher and good cook, still teaching and writing part-time at her age, and regularly she contributed articles on Daoism to magazines. Through her, Ma's mind was opened to Laozi's transcendental wisdom and atheistic spirituality.

"I can't believe such ancient teachings are so consistent with modern science!" Ma was thrilled with his discovery.

"Why shouldn't they be? The world hasn't changed much, has it?"

To Mary Scott's delight, mentoring Ma over long pots of Pu Er tea soon became a stimulating exchange. She was enjoyably challenged by the young scientist over a subject which, like many things she once found stimulating, had lost vigour over time. His exasperating probing, sometimes innocent, often acute and incisive, forced her to revisit a lifelong erudition afresh, giving it modern relevance, making it more complete in her mind.

A timely exercise, she thought.

ULTIMATE PARTICLE

After his Master's programme, all was set for Ma to continue with his doctorate. He would soon leave his fingerprints on the LHC – Large Hadron Collider – a twenty-five kilometre particle accelerator underneath the border of France and Switzerland.

It was the longest accelerator in the world, a breakthrough, but unfortunately rather too long for something so complex. Something was always wrong somewhere down the line.

When it was not being repaired or maintained, scientists would use the rare opportunity to bang subatomic particles head-on at fantastic speed. *Bang. Puff. Ziiiipp... Yes!* It was regarded as an exciting and privileged opportunity.

The sophisticated banging approach might have seemed brutal to some. But the underlying principle was simple and appealing. If particles collided hard enough, they would break down into ultimate particles that scientists called Higgs bosons; as good a name as any. To help the common mind, journalists nicknamed it the "God particle". God's name was again used to make things comprehensible to those who would never understand otherwise.

Ma was deemed good enough to manage some of these bangings. A renewable grant was in place. Everything was moving in his direction, except perhaps his subconscious.

One Sunday, after playing with some energy calculations in his den, he lay down sideways on his bed. The morning sun was dribbling in through the window. He stared at the uneven wall, a few inches from his nose, creating a humid spot with his breathing. That same spot must have been plastered and painted numerous times over past centuries, by people who were now dead. He wondered what its original stone texture looked like, and how it was built without machines and electricity. How was anything done without machines and electricity?

The wall appeared solid and terminal. It gave him a defined space, shielding him from the outside. But lying beyond it was more, much more. He was lulled into a reverie.

A hundred metres away lay a matrix of dilapidated coffins at about the same level as him. Once upon a time, the last dribbles of the interred had leached out of them, percolated through soil particles. After mixing with ground water, they seeped towards this house. They flowed around and underneath, heading for the river. In his mind, he followed the flow of diluted carrion juice, from the graves to the house, from the house to the river, to the sea. Along the way, some of it rose to the clouds, drifted off to faraway lands. "We see only what's in front of us," he heard his own voice in his head. "Beyond lies much more. Each of us is connected to everything else. Just look!"

He got up, went out to the garden, feeling drowsy, stumbling a little. Spring was in the air but the sweetness of the season was scrubbed out by an interminable drizzle. He had no idea how long he meditated. He experienced deep level *Ru Ding* – the trance-like state Mary Scott had told him about, for the first time.

A bird gliding through timeless space...

"It must feel awfully lonely," he had commented.

"You might find out one day," she had said.

Now that he was experiencing it for the first time, he was unaware of the outside world.

Mary Scott watched him from her window.

He emerged from his gliding trip drenched, and went straight to his notebook as if trying to put a caught fish into the bucket before it flips away.

He jotted down quickly:

"To find the ultimate particle by banging things harder is like trying to measure infinity with longer tapes. What's 25 km to nature? We're like ambitious ants carrying a 'giant' ten-inch branch to survey the Great Wall. An impressive, remarkable undertaking, but only to ourselves.

We won't catch the Higgs boson. Zhuangzi said "the universe is no bigger than the tip of a fine hair." That's science, modern science. The ultimate particle exists – yes AND no –

everywhere, in everything, by the trillions and trillions, right at the tip of a down hair, forming a continuum through time and space.

To pursue the infinite with a finite life and limited intellect is futile, mad. That's it!"

He underlined "That's it!" twice. No, he would not spend the rest of his life arranging for tiny particles to crash.

He sensed nosey medieval ghosts jostling around him, trying to take a better look at what he had just written.

* * *

Ma told Mary Scott, whom he called Shi Fu – teacher – the next day. If she was surprised, she didn't show it. She smiled gently, encouraging as usual. "Yili, I don't understand anything about what you do, although it sounds very exciting. But your decision sounds good, probably more interesting in the long run. I could see it coming."

For the first time, he noticed Shi Fu looking old, more easily tired than before. She was almost ninety. It saddened him; but he was too excited by the moment to be melancholy.

That afternoon, he was in his supervisor Doctor Roberts' office. A Nobel laureate who had stopped smoking for the sake of his lungs, but continued to suck on an empty pipe for his image. He always appeared absorbed in something far more important than whoever was speaking to him. Those who didn't know of his Nobel prize would have guessed by watching him think.

After listening to Ma, he put the wet pipe back into the pocket of his tweed jacket, and stared over Ma's shoulder into the distance. They were sitting opposite each other, separated by a mound of books and papers on the professor's desk. After a few odd minutes, Dr Robert said absently, nodding to himself, "Hmm. That's right. Yes. That's right."

Ma endured another minute of awkward silence, then mumbled, "Thanks Dr Roberts. I'll finish the paper in the next few months, before going." The professor carried on nodding. "Thanks," Ma repeated, then got up and left. As far as he was concerned, he had served notice.

"It's time to graduate," he explained in an e-mail home. His father's response was abbreviated and characteristically perplexing.

Got ur msg son. What changed mind? Listen! Always think twice. We hv bn practise calling U Dr.! Mum and I golfed mainland last wk. V. hot but wonderful. Called ur mobile but off as usual! Hv they cut line? We discussed with Auntie Pauline. She thinks what U want in the end is gd for U are independent. But I think dedication also important for young people. I tell this to salesmen every day. Listen! Give up is easy. Who cannot do? Letting go not so easy. U know what I mean? :D (a blinking yellowish smiley face) *U hv 2 degrees fr Oxford. Mum says we break even –* :D (another smiley face). *Come home soon? Remember to think twice.*
Luv U
M&D.
p.s. Topped up ur a/c. Ck. bank balance.

M&D for his Mum and Dad, probably to save computer memory. So many things that he had not questioned before appeared increasingly surreal.

Later on, when he worked for big corporations and the government, he would write truncated and ambiguous e-mails himself. He had learnt that brevity reflected position in the corporate food-chain. Enigmatic messages also served to hide bad sentence structures, cover up spelling errors, and give the impression that he was busy with more important things. Always appear to be busy with something else more important was his first corporate enlightenment. His standard response would eventually become "noted. brg. ma," all in the lower case, with due respect. After he joined the government, it would shrink further to "noted", or pure bureaucratic silence.

He was happy that his account had been topped up though. Good boy, Father. Good boy.

Paul Jones, an American who shared a lab with him, was the only person who showed surprise. "Wow! Fuck me man," was Paul's exuberant response to every piece of news, including this one.

Six months later, Ma Yili started his job as Research Scientist with a medical equipment company in Singapore. He wanted to stay away from Hong Kong for the time being.

CONFESSION

Something's clucking in his head.

When emerging from meditation, Ma takes a minute or two to recognise his chickens' impatient rat-tats. He gives them water and lettuce each morning before dawn, but doesn't let them out to forage until he's done his morning routine. There are hungry dogs around. In the post-modern world, chickens are precious; they come before eggs, bringing fertiliser, then meat.

He rubs his palms, massages his face in their warmth, then takes his glasses out of the Ming dynasty redwood chest. It said circa 1500 CE on the display tag. He didn't pay attention to the price for he had no money, and the antique shop had no keeper. It was a treasure box of a plain design, hand-made to perfection. The airtight lid closed with a silent hiss, like a sigh. It must have kept many treasures and secrets over the centuries. Secrets tend to make one sigh. Ma has no secret to keep, just his glasses, keeping them from being pushed over the bridge by accident again.

He unfolds his legs, breathing into the creaking of his knees. He doesn't know how he comes out of meditation. One minute he would be suspended between time, oblivious of himself and his surroundings. The next moment his awareness creeps back, then he remembers the chickens.

He sees Song on top of the stone wall, eyes closed, shrouded in anxiety. Before he manages to sneak away, leaving the young man alone, Song opens his eyes. "Morning, Shi Fu."

"How's birthday boy?" Ma says warmly. "Hungry for bean salad and fresh soya milk? I picked some mushrooms yesterday." Food never fails to calm Song, Ma knows. He might become fat, very fat, if he stops running one day.

"Is it safe?"

"Just watch me eat if you're afraid."

"Oh heck. Won't be the first time. I'm famished. I only had three eggs and half a dozen potato pancakes for breakfast." He skips down the steps. "I need counselling and rationalisation, your expertise. But let's eat first." Then he remembers. "Rhea thanks you a million for the eggs and chicken."

"How's she doing?" Ma bends over to pick string beans and shallots.

"Fine." An imperceptible pause before helping with the beans. "Kinda moody lately. Like me. Maybe she's reached yet another milestone she's set for herself. Who wouldn't be moody though. That wretched mansion; it's like living inside blue cheese."

Ma gives Song a curious glance.

"What's that?" Song refers to the trumpet on the chair, something that he's not seen before. "Taking up music?"

"I spotted a few young monkeys snooping around the other day. Found that" – he points at the trumpet with his nose – "at one of the flats. Thought I'd use it to scare them off."

"You might need a gun to do that. The gibbons are probably expanding too fast at the Botanical Garden, so the young are seeking new turf."

"I know. It'd be a disaster if they got interested in mine. Can you let the chickens out and clean up the coop while I cook?"

* * *

Song finishes giving Ma a graphic description of the old man. It sounded more horrible in his own words than in his memory. He holds the plate up with both hands to lick – a theatrical gesture to mask his unease. Ma's attention drifts to Song's pants for cerebrospinal fluids.

"I didn't get splashed if that's what you're looking for. I didn't do it." He puts the plate down. "Yum. Thanks. I couldn't. Not after he stared at me. He freaked me out."

"What happened then?"

"I don't really know, to be honest." Song clasps his hands before his nose, as if praying for better recollection. "I think I did something terrible."

"What do you mean? What could be worse than manslaughter?"

* * *

Song changed his mind in the last minute.

Perhaps it was not really a change of mind. Maybe subconsciously he never intended to execute the euthanasia plan. The old man's stare jolted him out of his shock reaction. He did not have the stomach for it. Neither could he take his eyes off the old man's. Something had been nibbling at them. Flies? Beneath his decay was an earnest plea. Pathetic, powerful, captivating.

I'll live. I will. Give me a chance.
Come closer, take a look.
Here, Sir. See? I can. Please ...

He suddenly lost all strength, feeling deflated, wanting to collapse next to the man. Mercy-killing is not my kind of thing, he realised.

He found a piece of canvas canopy in the nearby parking lot, and dragged the old man off the road on it. The man was slippery and pungent. His fingers felt a gaunt man, just bones and rotten skin; but dead weight is heavy.

He then ran home, grabbed a bottle of water and a few tomatoes, and took them back to his patient who was by then fast asleep, or fainted, or dead. Song did not attempt diagnosis. He dragged him further behind the building, looking back at the path as he did so. When everything was in final position, he said, "You okay here?" Without waiting for an answer, he ran home again to wipe himself down and change.

Ma has listened with shallow breathing, appearing undisturbed. "You did what you could. So what's bothering you now?"

"My conscience," says Song. "Soon as I got home, I woke to the fact that my concern had been selfish – chillingly selfish. All I wanted was to get out of the situation, whatever it took! Oh how I wanted a long hot shower.

"It wasn't compassion that drove me to help. I only felt disgust at the time. I was annoyed at the shit luck of bumping into him. I don't think I did anything wrong, but I was a cold-blooded hypocrite. I feel horrible about myself."

"Come on," Ma says, sympathetic. "Why are you so freaked out by a dying man? You're an expert in corpses. We've seen some really messy ones. We've barbecued a few squishy ones that could no longer be picked up." It sickens him to recall the awful task. The repulsive smell stays in the hair, skin, nose, for up to a week, no matter how much he shampoos and washes, and rinses his nostrils with his dainty neti pot nasal irrigator.

"But he wasn't dead." Song gets up to stretch. He picks a pod and eats the soya beans raw. This is early, he thinks. Maybe global warming is still with us. Raw beans taste absolutely foul but he habitually eats a few to get Ma going. It has become their ritual. "You'll end up with pancreatic tumour." The warning comes predictably.

"No one will find out if I do," Song points out. "I know I have no reason to feel guilty, and I don't, really, but do, kind of. Nobody could have helped him, and there's nothing left in his life except a desperate wish to hang on. But – "

"How do you know he wants to hang on?" Ma interrupts.

"I was going to say exactly that! I don't. Maybe he wants to die and I could have helped! But I chickened out. Worse, I prolonged his agony instead. Water. Tomatoes... ," he utters disdainfully.

Ma watches Song performing self-analysis and criticism, and lets him carry on after a reflective pause. "The water-and-tomato trick didn't do much for my conscience. I feel terrible, probably worse because of that. I've never felt myself a hypocrite before."

"Why not?" Then Ma notices that Song was not up to teasing. "OK. Be kind to yourself. You did what you could, and you were confused."

"Yes and no," Song says, reflexive. "When I dragged and dropped him to trash, I had a clear objective in mind."

"And that was?"

"To hide him from view, from the path. I kept looking back to make sure he'd be well hidden. I don't want to see him again. I don't want to find out what has happened to him the next time I go past. So I left him to die, slowly, although, I'm sure, it wasn't my intention at the time. I'm sure." Song trails off into a defensive mumble.

There is a self-conscious courage in people making confessions. Confessions are hard to start. Once underway, however, they tend to go on, and become melodramatic. Having finally let it out, Song feels better though still gloomy. He was eager for some form of pardon when he started, but no longer. He leans over the handrail, pops the last bean into his mouth, and drops the pod over the bridge. It falls weightily for a surprisingly long time, as if in suspension, before landing on the foraging chickens, startling them. A big hen realises that something good has fallen out of heaven, and taps it up with a swift peck.

James Tam

GENERATION ZED

Ma contemplates Song's brooding profile, trying to sort out his conflicting dispositions. Doesn't he always?

Part of his friend is made of sensitive genes passed down by some melancholic figure higher up the family tree; but most of his soft spots have been fortified by nurturing. He has been trained to be mentally and physically tough since a kid, brought up to be a ruthless survivor, a savage wannabe. "Always move on, son. Survive! If you stop to think, the will to survive dies." Sometimes, this polarity makes him more complete, a tough guy with a soft heart. At other times, like now, he is torn apart by the tension. Unlike an argument with others, internal conflicts do not work you up. They drag you down, quietly, making you empty, vulnerable. Whichever side wins, half of you loses.

Evidently, the incident this morning incited a civil war in him. Helplessness assaults his soft side, and hurts the pride of his hard one, provoking a barrage of emotions.

There is guilt. He feels bad about being so damn clear-headed when he dragged and dropped the man off to die unseen. He needs to digest the heartless victory of his acquired callousness.

He is also annoyed, even angry, pissed off at the bad luck of the encounter. Bad luck is portentous. It seldom travels alone. God knows what's next.

Then there's sadness. Sadness grips him deep, although he is good at not showing it. The stranger probably reminds him of his father. Is this the same fate Old Man Song faced? Faces? What about his own destiny? Was he to die alone, in a planet of one? Being healthy and the youngest, he might just outlive everyone. Is he old enough, now that he's forty-two, to be troubled by this desolate prospect?

What else could Song have done though? Ma tries to assess his friend's options. Take the man home to nurse him till death? Out of the question! In the past, he would just have called an ambulance and gratified his conscience. "Yes, a stinky old guy's dying by the gutter of Old Peak Road near Tregunter Path. Uh, Okay. I'll wait, but please hurry. I have a meeting in an hour." No such neatly-packaged Samaritan convenience anymore. He had to evaluate, weigh, and decide, right there. He had to exercise compassion with cold-blooded clarity. Not easy. Whatever he decided would have created doubt afterwards.

This tall and handsome middle-aged man is trapped into being the kid of mankind forever. One day, he might double as the oldest man alive as well. If I had a kid, Ma thinks, he would be of similar age. *Good thing I haven't.* Raising the last human would be a heartbreaking task.

* * *

Those born in the 2040s were called Generation-Zeders, ominously referring to the final letter in the English alphabet. The last trickles of humanity were made celebrities by birth, by a prosperous and troubled world run by hyperactive and sterile grown-ups. Everywhere Song went, he was swamped by doting folks willing to pay a million just to pinch his cheeks. Sari and Huan soon gave up taking him to the park.

Every day they received tonnes of presents. Money, flowers, toys, letters, chocolate castles.... People made bewildering offers for his hair, old clothes, blankets, toenails, and more bizarre articles such as used nappies and urine. According to widely circulated formulas, baby piss can be brewed into a magic potion to restore fertility in women, promising to solve half the infertility problem. When direct collections were not possible, extraction from nappies could be considered as substitute.

Try this. Take fifty millilitres of urine from an infant under one, mixed equally with infusions of red clover blossom and nettle leaves prepared overnight, finish with a squirt of lemon and a pinch of rock salt. Drink at room temperature once before breakfast, once after dinner, for at least five days before ovulation. Then, copulate, of course. After ejaculation, lift her bum high into a shoulder-stand to keep every drop in, and wait. Tick, tick, tick. Duration unspecified.

Did it work?

While the women drank lukewarm piss, their men waited with lifeless sperm (under a microscope, they looked like flood victims in aerial photographs), wondering how to avoid kissing when it came to the copulation step. In any event, Sari and Song Huan never even considered selling a drop of Baby Song piss. All the products in the market that bore the Song label were counterfeit, but they did not bother to complain.

Hysteria and insane adulation eventually died down, but it took years before Song could blend into a much smaller world. He has never experienced "normal" life. He never will. The definition itself had long expired, and was changing every day.

For a Generation Zed-er, Song had an exceptional upbringing. His parents were painfully aware of the harm the loving world was eager to inflict, and did their best to fence him off. They brainstormed and simulated the future world, and prepared their son for the imminent change of reality.

Most other parents were intoxicated by their instant fame and fortune, unwittingly letting their families to collapse under exasperating privileges, ruining their precious kids. Many Generation Zed-ers committed suicide during their teens, often in a gruesome manner, as if to shock and take revenge on a world that they ended up loathing.

Want to see me dead, right? Here, watch!

Evolution from the Stone Age to the twenty-first century had taken thousands of years. The return trip has taken only a couple of decades. Within that period, Song had to part with all the things he had taken for granted from birth: airplanes, cars, telephones, internet, running water, flush toilets, ice-cream, chocolates, reading-lamps... and, finally, his parents, somewhat prematurely in different ways. Song grew up without peers. His parents were much more than Mum and Dad. They were everything to him.

His life has been a long line of losses. There is always something else next. Perhaps that is the nature of life, but in his, there is never replacement. Regardless, be tough. "Remember son, always move on. And don't ask why. Survivors don't ask existential questions." He wonders why.

Bountiful leftovers – sturdy shelters, warm clothes, tools, knowledge, imperishable food-like substances, and medicine with expiry dates brought forward by legal advisors and marketing managers – make physical survival in 2090 easier than in the Neolithic Age. But psychologically, sitting back to accept regression is much more agonising than struggling to make progress.

The Family Flintstone could derive strength from two sources no longer available to extant humans: the future and ignorance.

Mr Stone Age neither knew nor cared where his race was heading. The question was beyond him. Survival was a precarious game, demanding total concentration. He followed his instincts – raw, sharp, and fresh – down the chancy path of selection. He reproduced whenever he could – so what if someone's watching – and passed on these instincts. Posterity gave him additional willpower to go on. Just go on, naturally. When he felt helpless, he would cry and howl, pray to the sky, a strange rock, the silent moon, or wandering wolves. *Feeling better? Yes.* He stomped back into the brutal and hopeful unknown.

In 2090, primitive hope and an unquestioned future have been lost. Atavistic instincts have been conceitedly neglected for generations. Can they be rekindled still? Civilised humans had no use for instincts that gave humans survival advantage; instincts were barbaric, to be outlawed if possible.

When Song feels low, confused, sad, or endangered, he does not have a god to turn to. Knowledge has deprived him of this expedient comfort. He must get out of situations himself, all by himself. He is alone, moving on, like cosmic debris. He must not stop to wonder what for... it would sap his survival will, his father told him. Under the circumstances, it could be detrimental.

* * *

Ma watches Song pinching bits off a leaf of *bak-choy*, tossing them absentmindedly to the fluttering birds below.

What about me? Ma wonders. How come I don't feel sorry for myself the way I take pity on him?

Perhaps because he had had enough of advanced civilisation, and welcomes a calmer and quieter world? Maybe he feels his generation was the last of a few that were guilty of putting Song in his wretched situation?

Unlike Song, Ma has lived through a full spectrum of human follies, from technologically-driven hyper-delusions to those of the post-modern Stone Age. At his age, it is unlikely that he will be the last one out, though he knows there is no guarantee. A bad case of dengue fever or cholera could kill everyone else, leaving him to shiver alone. He had thought modern amenities superfluous when they were around. "People take hot showers and sleep in air-conditioned rooms everyday," he used to lament. "Do they ever feel the privilege? These things bring joy only in the first few days, then become part of the energy bill, nothing more." Now that they are no longer available, he would scream with joy if he could take a hot shower, drink a cold beer, or just enjoy a summer night's sleep in air-conditioning, out of the whirring clouds of blood-thirsty mosquitoes.

When the world shut down, Ma was in his early fifties. About time, he thought. Civilisation had long flown off at a tangent in all directions, ignoring common sense, deriding mass balance, disregarding obvious limitations in a tiny planet. The world had become derailed and had plunged into wishful-thinking, frivolous wishful-thinking. Delusion, realism, and cynicism had become interchangeable and indistinguishable to most.

He had cunningly exploited this mental chaos at work.

Everything sounded too good to be true, and was mostly untrue: universal justice, human rights, zero discharge, people power; yes to global warming, no to global warming, transparency, globalisation, sustainable development, free economy, free press, free expression, free worship, free lunch.

In olden days, imperial sycophants pandered to the whims of a few lunatics. Twenty-first century lickspittles pandered to collective chimeras, inflicting long-term damage with unprecedented vigour. Denial seemed an outstanding human talent. If reality was not brutally twisted by a few despots, it would be fatuously distorted for the majority, by the majority. People in power – be they a few hoity-toity royals, a bulldog of a despot, or the democratic *hoi polloi* – ended up behaving the same.

There were real and imagined crises of prodigious scale and complexity. Nobody understood, so they left them to politicians with a four-year vision and grade-nine science. Excesses were universally worshipped. Globalised people shared a straightforward desire for more – simply more. Ma remembered his father's mercantile wisdom. "It's quantity, not quality, that matters." He was dismayed how right his old man had been.

Rich nations were fatally dependent on suicidal growth and consumption. Poor nations strove to become the same. There was no turning back. Humans were being chased down the cliff by the hungry tigers they had raised. Keep running and jump; or stop and be eaten.

His generation was the last of a few that worked hard to destroy. What baffled him most was the lack of a rational motive. In strangling the future, they stuffed themselves fat, and were constantly unhappy about something. They were too stupid to be called selfish. They gained nothing by destroying the future for their children. But, if the world were not ending, Ma wonders, would Song's generation have continued to make the same mistakes?

Ma could see some kind of an end approaching. The laws of physics told him sustainable development could not last. The way it is ending is perhaps unexpected, but to him not puzzling. Statistically, human existence is a miracle. Once existence has happened, eventual extinction is certain. If not because of this, it'd be because of that. Only a matter of time.

He tries to imagine the cause of universal sterility. The atmosphere is a proportionately *thin* crust of the planet, like the skin of an apple. Something that humans had been jamming into it for decades, perhaps centuries, suspecting no harm, accumulated quietly. Parts per trillion became parts per billion. Parts per billion became parts per million. Obliviously, breath by breath, our mysterious and fragile reproductive systems were nibbled at, eaten alive by our own waste. On top of that, lunatics had been manipulating the ionosphere for decades, turning it into a weather weapon.

One day, it snapped. Something unidentified had transgressed an unknown threshold, expediting an industriously devised self-extinction. Well, Ma thinks, unsentimental, what do you expect?

Nonetheless, watching Song and Rhea shuffling along at the end of a vanishing line of humanity saddens him. Perhaps longing for posterity is after all a potent instinct that can't be suppressed by rationality.

* * *

"Look who's here!" Song sounds more cheerful.

John Johnson jogs towards them along Robinson Road. Although only a few years Ma's junior, he looks a young athlete from this distance, with big springy strides. He yells excitedly up to them. "Guess what I saw this morning, boys?"

"Oh, no! Not another one," Ma mumbles under his breath, rolling his eyes into an 'oh-my-god' face, forgetting how goofy it looks behind those glasses. A laugh spurts out of Song. "Don't mention it to John, will you? I don't feel like more discussion."

"Sure," Ma says. "Enough of that for one morning. Plus he might run up to resuscitate him, then we'd be in real trouble."

Song gives a wry chuckle.

"You know," Ma looks into his eyes, sincerely sympathetic. "I would have done the same thing, except I wouldn't have bothered with the water and tomato. You had no choice."

"Thanks," Song says, feeling lighter, grateful for his verdict.

FOUR

TEARS IN SHEK O

Rhea dries her hair vigorously with a towel, standing back from the window just enough to be in the shadow, while watching him collecting firewood on the beach. She's been watching him for days, a little more than fifty hours to be exact.

She hasn't learnt anything from this stealthy observance, except that now she's hooked. What would happen when he leaves? She can't bear the thought. The last three days has been a whole mini-lifetime, a new one. He can't just go now, she thinks, right away embarrassed by the possessive tone in her head, which she suspects isn't quite together this very moment.

He seems much better today, but still sad.

Sad people are harmless anyway, right?

Yes they are. Yes they are...

No other possibilities could be entertained right now.

Since his arrival, she has been spending her days watching him, and her nights crying for him, or because of him, she doesn't know which, or why. She only knows the maddening dullness of life – one that had been reduced to mere living – had suddenly been lifted. He has saved her from the death grip of desolation. There are more than just salty waves and wandering ghosts out there. There's him – a living person, a young man who has filled her indistinguishable days with suspense and surprises, even emotions – intense emotions. Imagine!

She is confused and scared. An indulgent kind of confusion that one snuggles up to; a titillating kind of fear that tickles. Yes, she still exists. She's alive, not just living. Everything seems real again; it feels so unreal.

*   *   *

After this morning, she no longer worries about him killing himself in front of her eyes, framed between two wooden slats of the louvred shutter. He may be a little schizophrenic (who isn't?) but no, he won't hurt himself. In fact, even from her distance (probably because of that?), his presence conveys hope and security. He does not seem the kind that would hurt anything.

The sight of him strolling along the beach at sunset resurrects the butterflies in her stomach, butterflies she thought were long dead, digested and flushed down the toilet with a bunch of cellulose.

"This is ridiculous!"

She reprimands herself again for this ludicrous state of mind, for smiling coquettishly at the mirror like an adolescent. "Loneliness has driven me insane!" she mumbles out loud, pacing the spacious sitting room. "Rhea, you're crazy. Nuts. Mad. Pathetic! Get a hold of yourself. Calm down!"

But she knows that, if she does not act now, she might wake to find him gone in the morning. In his place would be an empty spot, just sand and the waves, again.

* * *

He appeared in the late afternoon two days ago. There had not been anyone on the beach for many months. He looked young. How's that possible? She wondered.

He started a fire before dark, and grilled something for dinner. After eating, he sat by the fire, seemingly enjoying his solitude. Rhea was about to go down, or light some candles to make her presence known.

All of a sudden, he started to cry.

Oh no, not just crying. She shuddered; goose-bumps rose on her neck. He wailed for half an hour, then stopped abruptly as if his vocal cords had snapped. The waves continued with their swishing, insensitive. He threw some sand over the fire, and lay down next to its cindery remains.

Everything turned black in a few minutes, collapsed.

Rhea realised she had a candle turning soft and slippery in her hand. She did not light it. She locked the doors – something she hadn't bothered to do for some time – before going to bed. She could hear his crying in her head.

Is that real? Has he stopped? Is he asleep?

Is it possible to sleep after crying like that?

So many tears...

She put her head between two pillows, and cried herself to sleep.

* * *

She woke up with a headache. The pillows were damp, like the air. She rushed to the window. The sun had started to glow below the horizon. He was not there; only his lone backpack on the towel, next to the ashes of last night's fire. Was it really last night? Did I sleep? Everything seemed to have lost orientation and continuity.

Twenty minutes later, he came in from the choppy sea, long wavy black hair straightened by the water, exposing a pair of big ears. Rhea noticed the proportion of his muscular body. He must indeed be a young man, she thought, and blushed.

How she wished she had a pair of binoculars.

This must be the only sea-side villa in the world without one. Her maternal grandparents – Gong Gong and Po Po – perched above the promontory in their majestic villa, hated looking out of the windows. The sight of breathtaking Shek O Beach vexed them. They never swam, or took walks along the shore. The feel of tacky sea breeze and wet sand in his shoes drove Gong Gong berserk; strolling barefooted was disgusting, a disgrace, out of the question. That stretch of sand also attracted noisy tourists like flypaper to bugs: barbecuing families, running children, and teenagers with ghetto blasters. *These people* – their collective pronoun for the rest of the human race – were loathsome even from their protective distance. Zooming them up optically would have been unthinkable.

This was their seaside villa. Their main house, similar in size and layout, was in Repulse Bay, another beach town barely fifteen minutes away. It also looked straight out to sea, with an awesome view which Gong Gong bitterly called *million-dollar pitch-darkness*, which was what greeted him by the time he came home from a full day of work he didn't need to do, and social intercourse with people he despised, seven days a week.

He was rich, ranked twelve worldwide by magazines, therefore generally regarded as successful. People lined up to suck up to him. They invited him to chair this and that committee or charity or advisory board. He once enjoyed his prominence; but found it increasingly detestable as he aged. But he did everything he could to defend it. He even filled his final years with more of it, perhaps to show he still could, and was not about to fade away to die. Never.

The main house was also without binoculars.

*   *   *

He prepared breakfast out of cans and jars.

After breakfast, he wandered to the far end of the beach and disappeared. He returned two hours later, and approached the scarp underneath Rhea. To her relief, he did not climb the steps to explore. He was about fifty metres away. She tried to hold her breath, her pulse, her thoughts, lest they blurt out loud.

He's Eurasian... like me.

More surprisingly, he looked in his late twenties, at most early thirties. She had not met someone younger than herself for a very long time. She had not met anyone for a very long time.

He was restless in the afternoon, trying tai-chi, yoga, meditation, reading, swimming, walking, reading, napping, then back to meditation, each lasting about fifteen minutes.

Such a short attention span for a man like him... Like him? What do I know what he's like?

The tide was rushing out when the sun set gorgeously behind the hills in the opposite direction. Rhea seldom took notice. She had lived all her life in houses with beautiful sunsets, nearly every day. Before she was even old enough to admire their beauty, it had become tedious. This evening was somehow different. Golden reflections shimmered on the receding tide, giving off sparkles she had not seen before.

The young man finally settled down. He sat cross-legged at the edge of the water, a towel over slouching shoulders. The last trace of daylight had vanished. Gong Gong's million-dollar pitch-darkness had returned.

The waves lapped lazily against the rocks, making soothing swishes. Rhea once loved that sound. At Repulse Bay, the waves were far away and mostly silent. In Shek O, they linger on after the day is done. That was one of the reasons she moved here. But she had since found it exasperating; that swishing sound day after day. What incessant futility!

Should I go say hi?
Should I ...

A startling howl.
He started to cry again.
Oh no...

The air was instantly filled with the same heartbreaking wail. Rhea pictured his mouth wide open, epiglottis trembling at the centre. A wounded lone wolf. The sound of a heart being ripped out, and crushed.

If I ever had to cry like this, I wouldn't go to the sea.

The sea makes a mockery of human tragedies. The indifferent waves never take note of our sadness. Tears run into the sand and leave no trace. I'll go cry in the mountains, find a cave that echoes. Rhea was frozen by an eerie moment of poetry.

She turned away from the window and stumbled to bed as if intoxicated; trembling. She buried her face in the damp pillow, and started to cry. She did not want it to stop. She wanted to stay up all night to cry and cry and cry. But she finally fell asleep.

Tears continued to flow in her dream, into the pillow.

* * *

Che bella cosa e' na jurnata 'e sole,
n'aria serena doppo na tempesta!
Pe' ll'aria fresca pare già na festa
Che bella cosa e' na jurnata 'e sole! ...

What a beautiful thing this sunny day,
The air serene after the storm!

Rhea woke to O Sole Mio with its original Neapolitan lyrics. She sat up with a start, shook her head, rubbed her eyes, and tiptoed to the window as if she might otherwise be heard.

"You must be joking!"

A translucent glimmer in the morning sky foretold another hot and sunny day ahead. He was standing on the edge of the water, naked, facing the emerging sun. His legs were wide apart, like the Vitruvian Man with a slight backbend. His arms were stretched out high, fingers extended, in a grand embrace of his audience – the sun itself.

* * *

He's a different person today – lively and positive-spirited.

He spent the day swimming, resting, reading and writing. He napped for more than two hours after lunch, then cartwheeled across the beach. Either he's discharged the sorrow that choked him, or has broken at last. Whatever the reason, there is something new in him that makes Rhea want to sing, scream, or hop.

All afternoon, she debated with herself about going down.

Just go. You have no choice now anyway.

What nonsense. Go down those steps, and you'll be asking for humiliation, or something much worse... You'd have only your stupidity to blame.

What humiliation? What worse? He's harmless, a fellow human for Christ's sake. Trust your intuition, if not judgement.

Well, go then. You've been fantasising for two days. About time you meet him face to face, and find out what it's like for a woman in your situation to deal with a mentally unstable man on a deserted beach. By the way, he's naked.

Rhea! It's now, or never.

Okay. Okay. Now then.

She checks her closet, and frets. She did not move anything from Repulse Bay. The wardrobe here is a lavish collection of brand-name fashion. Shockingly, nothing suits the occasion. In fact, nothing seems to fit any conceivable occasion these days. She picks a white cotton hippie dress. It'll look good with my long black hair on the evening beach. It's too revealing bra-less though, especially for meeting a naked man for the first time. But a bra doesn't work either, so dowdy. Damn. Forget the bra, take a shawl. She pulls out a cashmere shawl from India, and tries it over her shoulders. Yes. A bit warm but...

"Oh my hair!" she screams.

It has been rumpled into an unwashed heap for days while she suffered the unknown tragedy of this stranger. She has not brushed her teeth or taken a bath either. She runs to the outdoor pool and jumps in, not caring about preserving the reservoir for drinking use right now.

James Tam

RUNAWAY

When Song returns home from an overnight visit to Repulse Bay with Ma and John, a note, weighted down by his father's favourite piece of antique, the jade *qilin*, awaits him on the desk.

He reads it again and again. *That's it? That's all?*

He replaces it under the paperweight. He feels his breathing becoming heavy and slow, not sure if it's calming down or giving up. He starts to pack as if by instinct. Five carrots, two firm tomatoes, two drumsticks from the big jar of rendered chicken fat that Huan preserves cooked meat in, three sweet potatoes, a bag of macaroni, a light camping pot, one big bottle of water (there'll be streams wherever he ends up going), and a can of ancient black bean dace.

An extra shirt and pants in a waterproof bag. Toothbrush, toothpaste, soap, a big wad of tissue paper, matches and a few disposable lighters. Diving knife, chopsticks, and a big towel. A book about wolves gets thrown in; he picked that up from the bookstore last week. He wanted to better understand the mystic and cunning beasts that dogs are reverting to. Pens and notebook. No plan or order; just throwing things into a knapsack.

On the way out, he walks past his fancy mountain bike. His father's is gone.

He needs to run, forever if he could. He has no destination in mind. There isn't any point running all over Hong Kong to look for his Bub. His father has planned his disappearance well; nobody can find him.

Just run.

* * *

He's jogging much faster than usual. Something's burning inside, driving all cylinders. His unstoppable feet take him in the direction of Repulse Bay where he came from early this morning. The rest of him follows. His father's voice rings in his head.

Geriatric shit smells a lot worse than infant pooh.
Secretly wish me dead... Don't...
It'd crush your heart... forever.

It is a warm and sunny day, not a speck of cloud in the deep blue sky. He is thoroughly soaked, and has to refill the bottle three times before reaching Repulse Bay.

Don't force yourself.
Think clearly son.
Don't force yourself...

At the normally deserted beach, a small group of old folks are having an afternoon out. What a surprise. A man with a flowing beard is playing erhu, pulling an uncharacteristically light tune out of the melancholic two-string instrument. A woman who looks in her early seventies sings merrily to it, hands locked in front of her stomach like a soprano. Her crystalline voice belies her age. The youthful melody comes out effortlessly, slicing through the thick hum of humid sea breeze.

In a faraway land
Lives a beautiful maiden
Everyone who passes her by
Turns his head for a lingering glance...
A lingering glance...

They regard each other, proud of their performance. Humans and monkeys seem always to know how to entertain themselves even under dreadful circumstances.

They have a geriatric audience of two men and a woman. The men sway in half-doze. The woman claps silently, mutely out of sync, moving her lips to sing along.

The singing lady waves for Song to join. He normally would have spent half a day singing and chatting with them, giving them news of the outside, reporting that nothing has happened.

But he is not in any mood to socialise. He waves back, tries to look friendly, and runs on. How ironic, he thinks. Hardly anyone left, yet he has to keep running to be alone.

When he reaches Stanley, he still does not feel like stopping, and continues all the way to Shek O Village on the other end of Hong Kong Island.

He wanders into the local grocery store to check it out, and is surprised to find a few cans of spam and sausage waiting on the shelves. Evidently, rich folks in this part of town are not so desperate. Most supermarkets were emptied out long ago although it is still possible to discover odd bits on top of high shelves or hidden away in the corners. Most people did not live long enough to consume half of what they had grabbed. Apartments are therefore better stocked than supermarkets. But scrounging abandoned homes carries the risk of bumping into the owner, covered in maggots. It would ruin the appetite for days, defeating the purpose of food hunting.

Mega-warehouses remain the most reliable source of well preserved food-like substances from the past. Due to their relatively remote locations and sheer size, initial looting hardly dented their immense stocks. Without cars, looters could not carry much. The bountiful godowns would remain an emergency food source till the end of human time.

* * *

After dinner, he breaks down. He cries, and cries, like never before, then collapses from exhaustion.

He wakes before sunrise, and goes for a swim. Swimming in the dark spooks him. Right now, strangely, he craves a long swim in the dark.

It feels good. He is not scared of the black water this morning. The glints of the deep dark sea soothe him as he crawls out. The hypnotic sound of water sloshes gently about, as if whispering their commiseration.

He keeps going. *Yes, keep going, son.*

His right leg cramps, so he floats on his back to wait it out. The predawn sky is lighter than the water, with a few morning stars.

On the way back to the beach, the sun rises behind him.

All day, he feels like a zombie. The glaring beach seems surreal in comparison with the dark sea. His thoughts are involuntary, broken by blank spells. They come in fragments, then disappear at random.

Äiti loved the beach.

He has not thought of his Mum for a long time. He was eighteen when she died. Forgetting made things easier, and teenagers are good at that. People die in epidemics; that's what epidemics are about. Death was everywhere, reported on TV like an international football league, keeping people informed of the latest scores. The only option was to detach oneself, objectify, and deny.

Don't think about that. It'll make me sad.

But only top meditation masters can tell the mind to stop thinking. Ma says he can do that.

He attempts meditation and all sorts of distractions. None works. Memories surface like gas bubbles in a swamp. At sunset, he surrenders and lets go. It erupts into a melodrama. He asks the sea questions. Why? Why are you doing this to me? Why am I so lonely? So terribly lonely? He bursts into tears again, relieving the pressure in his chest. He wails to unravel a knot.

He cries like a baby. Suddenly, he realises how ridiculous and unreal his situation is, and laughs out loud, then cries even louder.

He runs out of tears. The pressure in his heart has lessened. He whimpers like a wounded puppy. He has never cried like this before, or seen anyone crying like this. It feels good. It unclogs him like chemicals unclog an old drain pipe.

Everything starts to flow again.

Talking to the sea is dumb but relieving. No one is watching anyway. He needs to talk to something. Circulating thoughts in the head only magnifies questions and suppresses answers, creating deadlocks. The sea is a patient listener, totally indifferent.

After the tempest, clarity returns. Empty, fresh, clear. The cloud in his head has dispersed. He can see his own thoughts coming and going.

At the cottage in Finland, by the lake, where the family spent their summers, they watch the mid-night sun. He's a little kid, on Äiti's lap. The smell of sauna; the tea-like fragrance of birch leaves splashing water on the scorching rocks tickles his nose. Contentment is that simple... that vulnerable.

He's about five, perched high on his father's shoulders to watch the fire-dragon dance in Tai Hang. This is Mid-Autumn Festival. The dragon is made of incense. The smoke hurts his eyes. He looks down and sees his parents holding hands. He feels a burst of happiness and sniggers.

He's running up the Peak with Bub's goofy friends.

The plague has claimed Äiti. Did it really happen? Bub has vanished. He's worried, but he waits, very patiently. He realises he can wait a long time. Somehow, he doesn't want the waiting to end. While waiting, nothing is final. While waiting, he can postpone all other problems. His breathing is shallow and light, waiting.

Don't stop. Keep waiting.

He wonders, finally, where his father might be, right now.

Warm tears flow again, but tenderly. Big drops roll down his cheeks, silent and gentle, no longer angry. Some of it drains inward; he swallows.

He sits by the water all night, going through whatever comes to mind. Let them come. No more thought control. Everything is allowed.

Come. If you don't come, you can't leave.
If you don't come, I can't set you free.

His first taste of ice-cream was a shock. He shudders. How he loves to taste it again, so sweet and cold in the mouth.

His parents are mad at the people swamping him in the park. He's shocked, a little scared of Mum's angry face.

Memories he never knew existed file out of hiding like long-lost friends straggling into his father's memorial. They take him by surprise, make him smile, and cry once more.

Haaaa... That feels good.

For the first time in two days, he realises that sand fleas have been feasting on him. He is itchy all over.

The sun is rising. Beautiful. Magnificent.

He takes a deep breath, springs to his feet, and sings at the top of his voice.

O Sole Mio...

It sounds quite good.
The sun, glowing happily, seems to agree.
"Bub, you're right."

ENCOUNTER

Song squats naked, fanning the fire.

For the first time in days, his head is clear, thinking only of food. The mental storm had swept clean the dark corners of his memory.

Simple peace never lasts. While enjoying the uncomplicated pleasure of anticipating a lousy meal, a woman enters the corner of his vision. A woman? And from what he can make out, a young woman!

Holy shit.

She's in white and orange, standing at the north end, pretending to be looking out at the sea, obviously to avoid direct confrontation with his nudity. The lurid remains of the sun, low behind her, make her fiery orange. His heartbeat picks up abruptly; exhausted adrenaline and hormones are again on red alert.

He pulls the towel and wraps it around the waist, then ostensibly returns to the kindling. He would have jumped to scream hi to the fellow human but... she's an impossibly young woman.

What difference does it make? A great amount, somehow. He sits on his heels, continuing to fan too vigorously. His poor head is again somewhere else, reeling, wobbly.

She notices him kind of dressed, and strolls over. Song watches her approaching. Impulsively, too rash and irrational even to call it presumptuous, he sees her entering his life. It is taking forever.

"Hi," he greets her. "Human?" He stops fanning, sweat beads ooze from his forehead and upper lip for multiple reasons.

"Only part-time these days." She smiles politely. "I live there." She points with her chin. Both her hands are lazily occupied with keeping the shawl around herself. " Just got back from a trip and saw you here. Haven't seen anyone around for months, so I thought I'd come down to say hi."

Uh! Do people still take "trips"? What a dumb thing to say Rhea! Oh well.

"What a pleasant surprise. Hope I haven't alarmed you. I've camped out here for a few days to enjoy the magnificent sunrise," says Song, immediately conscious of having talked too fast and smoothly, sounding almost a stranger to himself. "By the way –" he struggles to find his own voice "– I'm Song Sung."

"Oh sorry. Rhea. Rhea Rhella." She doesn't offer her hand. He is too way-down-there for a proper handshake.

Song resumes flapping the piece of cardboard at the fire.

"Did you say Song Sung?"

"Yeah. Song like the dynasty. Sung like the pipe instrument, in Chinese. It should be Sheng in Mandarin but they spelt it Hong Kong way. I know, it sounds like a Song is Sung. More fun I guess. Perhaps a bit ominous too?" He gives his most charming grin, then turns to regard the hills behind, catching Rhea's eyes en route. The sun's gone. A few wisps of grey clouds remain, rimmed in crimson orange.

"It'd be even more dazzling if it sets over the water," says Song.

"Then it'd have to rise behind the hills."

"You're right. Can't have it both ways." He forces his attention back to the fire. "I saw the most memorable sunrise this morning. It was... mind-blowing." The fire gains strength. "Here we go." He puts the cardboard down and looks at Rhea. "Like to join me for dinner?"

"What's on the menu?" She leans to examine the small pile next to the fire, clutching the shawl closer.

"I had chicken drumsticks preserved in schmaltz like French confit, only better, but I finished them last night. Just to let you know I normally eat with more class," Song explains meekly. "I've only got spam and canned sausages left." He holds the cans against the fire and squints to read. "May 2071 and February 73. Hmm. Not really in their prime but... The spam's fresher. You're the guest, you can have that."

"Uh, you've just made me vegetarian."

"That bad?" Song grimaces. His mood is improving by the second. He's talking faster than usual. "Macaroni? But boiling water with this fire takes patience. And the pot's too small. Wait!" He reaches into his backpack to take out three sweet potatoes. "Almost forgotten. Home-grown!"

"Perfect," she smiles sweetly. "Invitation accepted." She actually loves sweet potatoes roasted. She takes off her sandals, and sits down across the fire. "It feels strange to see someone here."

"It feels strange to see anyone anywhere. I've been a lone ghost here for days."

"I've been a lone ghost here for months, and months." She then reflexively regrets lamenting her loneliness to a strange man, and adds in a nonchalant voice, "Well, who isn't a lone ghost these days? Where do you live?"

"Robinson Road, near the Botanical Garden."

"What? That's a long way. Did you take the bus?"

"Ha ha. Not that bad. It normally takes me about four hours. But I was on nuclear power this time, and set a new record of three hours and a bit, I think. I don't wear a watch but I know my time when I run." He opens the spam and sniffs it. "A little bruised and grimy; nothing that fire can't purify."

"Sure you want to eat that?" Rhea looks concerned and disgusted.

Rhea never eats these "virtually non-biodegradable food-like substances." She does not need to. There is a sixty-square-metre pantry in the villa stuffed with daintily preserved proper food. (Whole legs of Parma ham and blocks of cheese flown in from Italy, for example, and a dazzling collection of salty fishy morsels and preserved veggies and flower hearts in cans or jars.) Much of it has moved on with time and the help of oxygen and moisture. They have been partially consumed by mould, or become desiccated; but enough were left to meet Rhea's occasional craving for a nostalgic treat. The wine and liquor shelves can easily satisfy the most fastidious alcoholic for a lifetime or two. All that within fifteen steps from her kitchen table, but she mainly eats fresh produce from the neighbourhood golf course, grown by Zhu Yi – Auntie Zhu.

Zhu Yi's in her mid-sixties. She grew up in a farm in mainland China, came to Hong Kong thirty years ago, and got stuck working as a domestic helper – a servant according to Gong Gong, who was too rich to bother with politically correct euphemisms – for Rhea's family. She loves Rhea like the daughter she never had. "Romance's not in my karma," she had told Rhea. Rhea commented that she made it sound like a great blessing. "*Aiya*, Wheea –" she never could pronounce Rhea – "to someone like me, it is."

She now lives at the Shek O Golf and Country Club, once colonial and ancient, with two women who also served rich families in the area, also without romance in their karmic composition.

Most of the golf course is now a young forest. The fairways, with the exception of the 18th hole, have been swallowed up by trees and wild plants. The resourceful ladies turned the final approach, next to a picturesque brook, into a farm, and the clubhouse into a barn, with a growing population of chickens.

Rhea who had previously not given any thought to where potatoes come from is now a seasoned farmhand. She helps the old ladies out regularly. Sometimes she would stay in the barn. She loves the Ladies of The Brook and is grateful for their company, but their nice and simple ways, unpretentious contentment, cheerful and aimless small talk, and suffocating attentiveness, would all start to bug her after a few days. She would have to escape back to the villa, to be alone. After all, they are from a different universe than hers.

The ladies found a pig in the village, possibly a surviving pet. They kept it fenced up in the fairway bunker for a couple of months to fatten up before slaughtering. It was a squealing event that kept Rhea away for a whole week.

* * *

"You ran all the way here to watch the sunrise?"

"Actually no. I had no plan when I started. Just needed to keep running, to escape I suppose, and be alone."

"Hope I'm not intruding."

"No no! Not at all. I no longer need to be alone. In fact I was starting to feel lonely. You showed up at the right time. Perfect, really."

"What happened?"

"I lost my father."

"I'm sorry... You know, I lost my parents too. Maybe I never had them. And they're probably not even dead yet."

"My father's not dead either. And I may not have lost him. I don't know."

"What about your mum?"

"She died long ago. Plague."

"Oh... . . "

* * *

"Did you ever go to any Project Future events?"

"You mean those government Gen-Zeder parties?"

"That's right."

"Just once or twice when I was really young. Can't remember anything. We preferred to stay away from government activities."

"Giving excuses for being antisocial?"

"Well, I needed survival skills, not public pampering. My Dad also tried to keep me out of the shrivelling school system. It was funny. I was encouraged and helped by my parents to play truant, everyday if possible."

"Lucky you. I wish my parents had done that. We would have met if you went to those functions though. But I was a big girl when you were still wearing nappies."

"Hey, I've been told I wore only designer nappies you know, all monogrammed and sponsored."

* * *

"Are you Eurasian?"

"My mother's Finnish. But I thought I look pure Chinese."

"Says who?"

"Everyone I know. My skin, hair, eyes."

"They must all be men. You look 100% mixed to me."

"Is there any issue with logic here? Once you're mixed, nothing's a 100% anymore is there?"

"Are you trying to confuse me? Didn't know I'm talking to a mathematician. Now what's the chance of two Eurasians meeting in Shek O, in a deserted world, huh?"

"A hundred percent, obviously. Can't change that fact now, can we?"

"Mathematically okay this time?"

"Absolutely!

"You said your father's Greek?"

"Sort of. His mother's from Algeria. Also a mix of god knows what. You know, I sometimes hope all that mixing's good, makes me stronger, like cross-pollination right?"

"I doubt it but I like the idea. I need every excuse to feel strong and special these days."

* * *

"They sent you to boarding school in Switzerland when you were thirteen!"

"Sick, isn't it?"

"I didn't say that. And you studied International Relationships!"

"Very useful, isn't it?"

"Sorry, I didn't mean it that way either. Just that it sounds so... fascinating."

"Just say *bizarre*. I could tell your lips were getting ready to say it."

"You speak French?"

"Oui monsieur, plus German, Italian, Greek, English and Chinese."

"All fluently?"

"All rapidly; none perfectly."

"I only speak three languages. Now I feel like a mute."

"That's all they ever taught me, languages..."

"Come on! You must say something with these languages too, I imagine?"

"I know a lot about shopping and music, I suppose."

* * *

"You're lucky. You've got wise parents. My mum was a compulsive international shopper. When she came home from the Champs-Élysées for a brief stop, before going to Shanghai, she'd first give orders to the servants for five minutes. *Put this here, put this there. Be careful with this.* Then she'd give me the same phoney hug she gave the dogs."

"...."

"She called me and the rest of the world 'Love' or 'Darling'. *Hello love! How're you doing, Darling!*"

"What about your father?"

"He didn't exist. He spent his life pretending to be busy and useful to strange women, and avoiding his family. I'd seen him maybe a few times more than Haley's Comet after I was about six."

"…."

"I was much closer to my grandparents, especially my mum's parents. Even as a little kid I found them more human but…money had ruined their lives and destroyed their children. They realised that when they were old. But too late. They treated me differently, with more time and care, like a kind of compensation. But they were always unhappy about everything."

"Hmm, never knew it's so much hassle to be rich."

"It is... . Actually, it is."

* * *

"You always eat like this? You really seem to enjoy every bite of that spam, you know."

"You see, every meal could be the last. Understanding that makes food indiscriminately delicious even without wasting time on fine cooking techniques."

"That's an interesting theory."

"And we are what we eat. Of course you've heard that before. Food become us, every bit. Some may stay until we die. This is the only chance to see and taste a potential part of yourself. Don't you think it's a rather intimate process?"

"I'm afraid what you've been eating is only good for shit, Mister!"

"Fine! But all faecal matter remains a part of me until I pooh right? If you say I've made friends with Song Sung, you can't possibly exclude the slithering tube of faecal matter inside my gut can you?"

"You're gross! You should have studied scatology."

"What's that? A branch of theology?"

* * *

"For a thirty-five-year-old man, you talk about your parents a lot."

"Do I?"

"Don't take it wrong, just an observation; perhaps a bit of envy as well."

"This is a special day too. My mind's been fully occupied by them. I grew up without anyone else, no other kids, no school mates. They are my world, my everything... I mean, they were...

.

"I've been very emotional for a few days. Hope you understand."

"I know. I've been crying too."

"You too?"

"...."

"I won't apologise for crying though. My Mum – see? here I go again! – Mummy used to say people who're afraid of emotions can't be trusted. There's nothing wrong with expressing one's feelings, sharing them with those who are willing to listen. If we apologise for crying, we should say sorry for laughing too, right?"

"What about anger? Should we apologise for losing our temper?"

"Probably. Never thought about that one before."

* * *

"If you have ONE big wish, what would that be?"

"A l-o-n-g hot shower. I'm sick of baths. I miss a good steamy splashing."

"Oh I'd love that too! Even a short warm one would be great!"

"You'd be welcome to join me, to save water you know."

"Ah, ha ha."

"What about an apple pie à la mode?"

"Yum! A glass of cold milk?"

"Or just ice? A bucket of ice would be nice."

"I hate eating ice by itself. That's it? Shower and ice for your one big wish?"

"Not a lot more really. I might sound a bit of a saint but I've never wanted much. You?"

"I'd like a baby."

"WHAT?!"

"I want a baby."

"You serious?"

"Why? It's nature. All women want babies at some point."

"But you're not supposed to confess that to a strange man!"

"Oh pardon my impertinence, Sir! What was in your sweet potatoes?"

"Even if you have a baby, by a miracle, it'd grow up all alone on this planet."

"There'll be others."

"Get real lah, Missee!"

"Yes. There will."

"How do you know?"

"I just do. Woman's instinct."

"OK. Even if there were to be others, how would they meet?"

"Like us."

"Like us... ?"

* * *

"Can I make a confession?"

"Confession? Oh I love them by others."

"Promise you won't be offended?"

"Depending what it is."

"I've been watching you from behind the windows for two days."

"Ah, I somehow suspected that to be the case, Ms Rhella! Did you like the show?"

"Uh... not really."

* * *

"What do you do up there all day?"

"I spend a lot of time at the golf course farming with the old ladies. Otherwise, I day-dream, and play the piano."

"You're a good player?"

"Mmm... as good as it gets for semi-professionals. I used to perform in small concerts and big parties for friends, for my grandparents' charity things, stuff like that. No one dared to criticise anyway. They all told Gong Gong I was a genius."

"See, being rich isn't all bad. You can be a genius."

"But I *am* a genius!"

"OK then. Genius. Don't you think music's strange?"

"You mean beautiful."

"Yeah, beautiful, but strange that it exists in every culture, from fishing folks to mountain tribes, from the equator to the Arctics. It's not really something essential, if you think about it; not like, say, language. So how come every culture has it?"

"Because it's essential."

* * *

"There had been no starry nights like this in Hong Kong for a long time."

"Busy people had no use for darkness."

"So beautiful."

"Do you believe in the stars?"

"You mean horoscopes?"

"Kind of."

"Only good predictions. But I read somewhere that everything on this planet, everything in us, supposedly originated from out there so... I wouldn't be surprised if we've retained some mysterious connections."

"A good friend of mine is a physicist. He teaches me Tai-chi too. He said the exact same thing except that everything's a temporary disruption of the original state, like ripples on the water. All will calm down one day and vanish!"

"Hmm. Meanwhile, what's the chance that some atoms in our bodies knew each other on a distant galaxy billions of years ago, and shared electrons?"

"Infinitely small but not impossible. I like the idea though... kinda seductive."

"Ha ha. Stop daydreaming Mister. It's late now."

* * *

"What about destiny. Do you believe in destiny?"

"I believe everything's predetermined, maybe down to the molecules."

"Doesn't sound like you somehow."

"Why? Should I be sounding like some macho guy who's got fate by the balls?"

"No, but you said you've been brought up to just get on with life."

"Yeah but it's my destiny to be the way I am, you see."

"But if everything's been decided, what are we here for?"

"To play it out. The sunrise has been determined but it's still fun to watch, plus we don't know how determined actions interact in the long run. There's another point. If there's no fate, then there's no room for sympathy."

"Mmm..... Strange theory I must say."

"If fate's in our own hands, then all misfortunes are just, and could have been prevented with a bit of hard work and other admirable human virtues, right? Why then should we be sympathetic or charitable to anyone who's too lazy to improve his own fate, making it perfect?"

"Why? Because the expression of sympathy impresses God, and increases our chance of going to Heaven; that's why!"

"Ha! I like that. Great strategic consideration. Did you attend a Catholic school by any chance?"

* * *

"Do you like cognac?" Rhea asked. The fire is dying; the air is warm and sticky. The sweet potatoes were good. Rhea had one; Song ate the rest.

"I learned to like cognac not too long ago, but we're used to the best, since it's free. I'm spoiled," Song says with smart-ass satisfaction.

He senses the arrival of a critical moment. But for the past few minutes, he's been holding back the urge to go to the toilet, or a spot behind the big rock he calls the toilet for now. The anticipation has caused a tremor, stirring up his inside. Some clumsy instinct is trying to alert him for what he already knows might be coming, tightening up his guts, speeding up peristalsis as a result.

Goosebumps appear on his arms. He can no longer focus on what Rhea's saying.

Hang on! Suck in *Qi*.

Oh shit.

He's just made it worse, charged it pneumatically like an air gun.... And he doesn't have pants on. Just a beach towel around him, a light colour beach towel for that matter.

"Gong Gong has only the very best. There's a roomful. A case of Chateau Margaux 2060 too if you like wine, and..."

"Rhea, can you excuse me for a minute?" Song interrupts, bending slightly at his waist; pathos on his face.

"You OK?"

"I'll be back in a moment." He rushes off ten paces, then hobbles back, grimacing with embarrassment. He bends down to grab some tissues from his knapsack, then duckwalks quickly back towards the rock, folded over. A fleeing Quasimodo.

Pants! Should have grabbed my pants. This is the best time to put them on with dignity. Oh well.

* * *

When Song remerges, Rhea is standing by the fire. She clutches her shawl with one hand, holding the sandals with the other. Her face, barely illuminated by the dying fire, radiates an introspective delight. Her eyes, staring at the embers, glint with feminine instincts: coy and bold, determined and cautious, amused, loving, calculating, ruthless, full of dreams. Capture, now! Women's dreams are fragile. In the post-modern world, they are even more ephemeral and uncertain. But at times of crisis, when men have stopped dreaming, women must go on, keeping his alive as well...

Song's feelings are much more straightforward right now. She's gorgeous! He kicks some sand behind like a dog.

"Washed your hands?"

"Sorry, sorry, sorry."

"Why apologise over basic human needs?" Rhea asks with mock challenge.

"Sorry for keeping you waiting. It didn't flush."

"Should we put some water over it?" She looks at the cinders.

"Yes."

He makes a few trips with the little pot, until the charcoals turn dark and limp. The only light left comes from the crescent moon, and the thousands of stars looking over its curvy outline.

"Shall we go?" Song clasps his hands in a – well, let's see, everything taken care of – tone, a little too nonchalant.

Rhea's silent. Sure.

He puts one arm around her waist. She leans lightly on him, and they stroll towards the Villa. The crescent moon makes a smiling face above. Stars are twinkling, winking. All wonderful things from our childhood come back to life when people fall in love, however old they are.

Song can see Huan smiling; it's his own smile. Today, for the first time, he feels his parents in him, now that they're no longer with him. Every little idiosyncrasy has a genetic shadow. His father must have kept running the same way when Sari died.

Yes, we're all a continuation of others, Song realises with a refreshing sense of clarity. That doesn't make us less individual. No. Chapter two is a continuation of chapter one, not a part of it. This is how the story continues. No matter how unique we regard ourselves, we're just descendants of some amino acid molecules which coagulated a few billion years ago. Our genes link us to the distant past, and allow us – well, they did – to live on into the future. So much magic. Impossible things happen all the time. And now, against all odds, he has a beautiful woman in his arm. Rhea feels so good against his chest. He feels warm blood running wild in him.

She looks down at their steps, trying to synchronise like kids do. There's an erection behind the towel.

Oh dear. Men should always have pants on. They can't hide what they have in mind as well as we do...

"Can I say something?"

"Yes?"

"Hmm. How should I put it. You're the first man I've ever invited home this way. We've only known each other for a few hours. I don't want you to think I do this regularly."

"I know."

"You do... ?"

"I can tell from your eyes."

In darkness?

Rhea looks up, trying to judge his sincerity. Men don't hesitate to lie in this situation, and women don't hesitate to believe them. She can't see his eyes in the dark, but feels sure that he's sincere.

Song's precocious tumescence is becoming terribly awkward and embarrassing, unfairly distorting other noble and upright feelings that he has, or is developing as a matter of urgency, for Rhea.

Oh you fucking thing. I should have remembered my pants.

Rhea glances down at it again, trying not to laugh with secret satisfaction, or to allow silly doubts to spoil the moment.

All of a sudden, Song lets go of her and unfurls the towel in one big dramatic gesture. He flings it over the shoulder, and walks on ahead theatrically like a triumphant Greek god returning from a fantastic celestial massacre. His penis leads the way, pulling him along, bouncing like a mini plank at the bow of the galley. He starts to sing O Sole Mio in a deep and powerful voice.

Rhea laughs so hard she doubles up, holding her stomach. She hears her own laughter reverberating in open air. What an unfamiliar sound – her own laughter. It must have been a long time. Or is this the first time ever?

GUJI'S ENCOUNTER

She sits on the parapet wall on the roof of her low-rise apartment, bare feet dangling on the outside, oblivious to the danger of plunging down six floors.

She lights another cigarette. Pale blue smoke rises towards the metallic crescent moon, crossing the dark space in between. The smoke makes her head light. She's rising like a fish fascinated by the silvery hook overhead. So inviting...

She has never smoked before. There is no previous experience to tell her how dried up the tobacco is, and how horribly stale it tastes. She just puffs away, one after another. She has the urge to do something "bad" tonight; smoking is as close to it as she knows. Her tongue, numbed by the strange assault of oxidised nicotine, feels slimy and heavy, twice the normal size. But it's the only thing that feels substantial right now, weighing her down, tentatively safe from the lunar bait.

"Does life happen in here? Or out there?" She asks herself a strange question, and chuckles lightly. She's never thought of that before, and is not going to think about it now. There's nothing left. Everything has been extinguished. Not that there was very much to start with.

For almost sixty years, she has been like the condensate collected by the battery of dehumidifiers in her parents' home at the Peak. A distillate of nothing. Pure and tasteless, just something sucked out of thin air, day after day with a whir – the same monotonous whir, to be dumped.

A different whir, sometimes by Beethoven, sometimes Mozart, sometimes Saint-Saens, occupies her head. Like drunken party guests from a different time-zone, they brazenly disregard her wish to end the party, to go sleep.

No! The music must go on, louder and softer.

Quiet !

No way. A different tune comes on instead.
It's Mozart again; that eerie requiem.
Oh please... turn it off
Just for a little while... I beg you....
Eternal rest grant unto them, O Lord
What about me O Lord...? Why not unto me?

She was cursed by music at the age when Mozart first started composing. It took her down an obsessive path of no return, then humiliated her for her lack of genius. Then it punished her for trying too hard. Now it haunts and torments her with unprovoked vengeance.

In the beginning, her piano lessons were nothing more than a cultural supplement to family riches. Her father, a successful investment banker, was keen to demonstrate an interest in things outside the money circle. A grand piano, on top of it a small vase sitting on a lace mat, makes tasteful furniture in the living room; and lessons from a good teacher were affordable. Her parents even gave her what they thought to be a musical name. Melody. Melody Mok.

Unfortunately, Melody was instantly obsessed by music. Madly, all she wanted was to listen, learn, play and talk about music, neglecting everything else. She told everyone she would become a concert pianist one day. "What if you can't?" grownups teased her. "I can. I have the talent," she would answer. Cute. As a matter of fact, she was talented, but not enough. Having a little talent can be a big curse. She also tried way too hard, too early.

Gradually, talent and ambition gave way to agony, bitterness, and disappointment. But the melodies continued, involuntarily, incessantly.

The music could no longer be stopped.

Her head has been subjugated by men – recognised geniuses. Their ghosts have made her their concert hall and cabaret. Movement after movement, they torture her with their masterpieces.

See? Melody. Easy does it. La di da!

But not to you huh? Ha! Not to you! Not to you!
Ay ay ay, not you! No! Not... .

She pulls out another cigarette, long and thin, spotted with brown stains. She tries to light it. The wind is up without her noticing, strewing clouds over the thousands of stars that dotted the sky earlier. Her long black hair – blackened again by dye for the first time this afternoon – flows across her face, fluttering roughly, feeling like linen rather than the smooth silk that it once did, smelling of ammonia. The wind smears her into the night sky like a wet painting, merging her with darkness.

Flick flick flick – the lighter won't work. She throws it into the wind, screaming. "Useless! Useless!! Useless!!!" The cigarette drops off her lips, and rolls off her lap. The background chorus reaches a crescendo.

She closes her eyes, and sees the lighter tumbling through the air. A few seconds later, it lands with a pedestrian click – barely audible.

Shattered. Motionless. Settled. Peaceful.

Grant them eternal rest, O Lord,
May everlasting light shine upon them.

She wonders how it would feel.

* * *

"Ah! You startled me, little girl. I could have fallen off!"
  "Sorry."
  "What are you doing here?"
  "I live here."
  "All by yourself?"
  "With my little brother, Tommy."
  "I've never seen you here before."
  "We've been hiding."
  "Where's your family?"
  "All dead. Long long time ago."
  "Poor girl."
  "Can you be our Mama?"
  "Of course I can Sweetie. I'll be your Mama."
  "What did you throw away just now, Mama?"

"A lighter. A useless lighter. Dead now."
"What's that noise?"
"It's music, Sweetie. Just music in my head."
"I don't like this song, it's scary."
"I don't like it either."
"Can you play Twinkle Twinkle Little Star?"
"I can but it's not up to me right now."
"Oh... Is it up to him, the man with curly white hair?"
"Sometimes."
"He scares me."
"Don't mind him, Sweetie. Let's talk."

FIVE

BATTLEFIELDS

John Johnson ingests a mouthful of soya milk, circumventing the left molar, then gingerly sucks at the cavity to clear phantom drops that he knows may not be there.

Ma and Song watch with an empathetic grimace. John's misfortune is no laughing matter. It reminds them of the vulnerability of their own mouths. They subconsciously tighten their lips, as if to guard the teeth closer. Ma sucks at his own teeth in solidarity.

After telling Ma his encounter with the old man, Song is now eager to hear John's story. So far, all he hears is the slippery sound of an empty tooth, and Ma's sympathetic echoes.

The filling came out about two weeks ago, provoked by nothing more than gentle breathing according to John. He felt a grain in the mouth, and picked it out with his fingers. A teeny bit of tired alloy, stained and ugly; but the hole it left behind felt disproportionately huge. "Ha," he said to Ma, tonguing it for the first time. "I think I've got Tycho in my mouth," referring to the lunar crater. Ha, that was the last time he joked about it.

A moment later, his tongue returned to Tycho of its own accord. Since then, it has not stopped. It has become obsessive-compulsive – thrusting and dabbing all day and, John suspects, all night in his dreams as well. Whatever he eats seems to end up in Tycho, and gets stuck there as if it had extra gravity. His tongue would poke it involuntarily, attempting to dislodge it, but would end up jamming whatever it is further in. He would then revert to suction. Gentle, desperate, luring, noisy, disgusting suction.

While the urge to suck is unstoppable, John knows how precarious the operation is. There may be only a papyrus-thin layer of enamel guarding a raw nerve-fibre directly linked to the part of the brain responsible for unbearable pain. Like a land-mine, it waits to be triggered into a tragedy. Only a matter of time, an unwitting step, a trip. What if he does that in a dream, sucking it with undue force? The premonition makes him cringe.

John Johnson's been through a hell of a lot. His life's been a continual transfer from one battlefield to another. He escaped his parents' failing home to become a soldier in a brutal war; survived a spiritual struggle with God; and emerged unscathed from the cannibalistic savagery of the corporate world. He'd lived through financial tsunamis and epidemics, and has been coping with the slow death of humanity without losing hope or composure. He is a man of mettle, a tough guy. He never could have imagined that a tiny cavity would drive him to such humiliating despair.

* * *

John grew up in Fort Lumber, Kansas, population 8,377, usually rounded off to ten thousand by the residents. Remarkably, the little town held three Guinness records, including the most McDonald's cheesy quarter-pounders eaten in three minutes. His parents' home on the outskirts was a happy one. A buttress of rock-solid family values; a down-to-earth version of the American dream.

His father was operation chief of a small security company, the largest one in town, in charge of six guards and three armoured vehicles. The guards, each with a bushy moustache and friendly potbelly, waddling with affected vigilance, looked identical in uniform. The armoured vehicles were similarly alike. Grey, metallic, angular. From family pictures on the mantle-piece, he could see they were Dad's favourite backdrops. Here's happy days against the Ford Aurora circa 2026. Here's the three of them beaming next to a newly painted Great Wall Carapace-X.

A vehicle was behind each and every photo on display. A men-only photo was taken in front of Uncle Wally's truck. It was John's first hunting trip. He was clutching a second-hand 12-gauge shotgun Dad had bought in an internet auction for his 13th birthday, his initiation into manhood. From the way he held it, you could tell he was tense about appearing relaxed, and deferred to the more experienced weapon. It had done more, been more, taken life before. John hadn't. Not yet.

Mum worked at the animal clinic, maintaining records, sending bills, counting money and depositing cheques for the vets. The family spent Sundays at church where everyone from "their neck of the woods" was. They shared innocuous jokes and updated each other on gossip if any was in circulation. Life followed the hypnotising pace of inertia. Fort Lumberans complained about the lack of excitement, but counted it a blessing in the same breath. Every now and then, there would be something real to gossip about, like the medical progress of a cancerous neighbour. Most of the time, they'd just get entwined with ready-made drama in TV soap operas. Occasionally, they would mix the two.

After service, they took turns to set up a barbecue at the park next to the church. Everyone brought hot dogs, burgers and salads. Most of them were fat and jolly, addressing each other as hey big guy or hey big gal. Someone would be on a diet, eating only pretzels. Light beer in coolers waited in the car trunks while the big guys worshipped. Later on they would be drunk straight from the cans slipped inside styrofoam sheaths imprinted with a beer logo. The kids played video games or threw balls or kissed behind the bush. Even the teenagers did not mind being with their parents on Sundays. They were nice people, one big family in a small community that John loved dearly. If he had one ambition, it was for things to stay that way forever.

He was unexpectedly good at school. Unexpected because neither Mum nor Dad were remotely academic, and in all fairness did not expect their son to be. "Now that's evolution," Dad concluded, proud of John. "The Grace of God," Mum corrected him, frowning lovingly at him for mentioning the controversial E-word. Undeterred by good grades, John wanted to join Dad's security firm one day, to be just like him. Failing that, he wanted to pilot the local sightseeing plane which sprayed insecticides when there were no tourists, or be a preacher. Any of these options would have made him a happy man. But life followed its own path. Suppressing ambition was no guarantee of success.

Out of the blue, their happy home was incensed by unrequited love. Dad had been having an affair with the receptionist at the company, a Nancy whom Mum renamed "The Fat Slut" after she had flung shit at the fan. Oh well, men have momentary lapses but *Christ*! it wasn't a momentary lapse. It had been going on for five years although Dad insisted it was only four and a half. Nancy finally got fed up with Dad not agreeing to divorce Mum, an intention which he had never had and, to be fair, never declared unequivocally. Anyway, Nancy decided it was time to make things ugly. "Enough's enough. Fair's fair. I have my principles," she said.

Mum was crying at the top of her voice, screeching to breaking-point. "You fooled me five fucking years for God's sake! You have the fucking nerve to come home and kiss me after you suck that obese cheesy cunt for five fucking years for God's sake! What kind of fucking animal are you, for God's sake!"

Dad was whimpering, hardly audible. "It's not what you think, Hon. I'm sorry, Hon. Won't happen again, Hon."

John had never heard his Mum swear before. She was a good hymn singer. (So was Nancy. They were in the same choir.) She had a sweet and delicate voice. For someone who never swore, he thought, she had got the hang of it rather spontaneously, with remarkable facility. As fluent as if possessed by the devil. He found it sad and scary.

John was also disappointed in his father, but kept quiet about it. He could tell Dad was deeply sorry. Being a young man himself, he kinda understood Dad was in a way a victim of this man thing. But Nancy? *Oh dear.* Mum was ten times nicer. And five years? He couldn't quite get it. Maybe Dad was actually a coward? He didn't want to think any more about this. In any event, he didn't know how to explain this *man thing* to Mum. She also wanted to forgive after a while, but did not know how. Every time she discussed it, she would unknowingly make it harder for herself to get out.

"Why don't you give him another chance, Honey. Let him come home and start over, like pressing the reset button on a computer." John heard Mum's good friend Pat saying.

"What? No, Pat. No. I can't. He betrayed me. Betrayed my love."

"C'mon, you know he loves you. Men are just weak. He probably didn't mean it. Why can't you just forget and forgive in God's name."

"No. I can't. It's a matter of principle."

"What principle Wil?"

"Fairness! Love! Loyalty! We're Christians, Pat."

He was seventeen. For the first time, he wanted to go away.

He joined the Marines the following year, shortly after the terrorist attack of September 2044. Some fundamentalists tried to launch forty-one simultaneous attacks as a crude commemoration of the occupation of Iraq forty-one years ago. Why forty-one? God knows. Out of forty-one suicide bombs, only two were successfully damaging. The rest were just gross. Nonetheless, the sad reality that these things don't just go away and be forgotten was disturbing. They said ancient peoples have long memories; but everyone was ageing, becoming ancient, haunted by memories and principles.

"We'll return a hundred fists for each and every assault at freedom and democracy. God be our witness!" The President vowed, his approval rating doubled from 18% overnight. The gods were again out in full force, taking their respective sides. Oil had become even more critical than forty-one years ago. Conflict was unavoidable.

"Think positive, Mum. I'm gonna be a warrior. Someone's got to defend the country against these lunatics, right?" he explained after everything had been decided. She wept, looking much older than a year ago.

Dad had moved to a shabby bachelor suite downtown. John told him over the phone. "I feel bad son. You'll understand one day. Be cool kid." Then he said, "Love you son," and choked up.

"Hey Dad, I'll be fine. Just give Mum time." He wanted to cry too but held back. It didn't feel right. He was his own man now, soon a warrior. The idea was becoming more real by the minute, now that there was no turning back. He was heading for boot camp – scared, sad, and excited.

* * *

Being a warrior was nothing like what John Johnson had in mind. It was a brutal transformation, kind of basic. He was first broken down into raw components – sweat and muscles – then rebuilt with push-ups and duck walks. He marched about in sand and dirt, and proved himself man by taking psychological assaults and juvenile abuse from his officer like a dog.

Sergeant Murray had a permanent glint of venom in his eyes. His front teeth protruded like a cow catcher on an old-fashioned steam locomotive, pushing his upper lip out so much it cast a noon shadow on his chin. His engine hissed maliciously when he bawled at his grunts, his "pussies and faggots." Occasionally, he would call John "fruitcake", a puzzling insult reserved for him alone. That little sinister aberration, with John spotlighted, deeply troubled him. He would have a nightmare every time after Murray had called him fruitcake.

John the fruitcake had to holler back "Yes Sir! Thank you Sir!" while Murray sprayed a lukewarm aerosol of spittle at his face.

John felt he had failed as a warrior. Every warrior he had seen in movies had pride and honour. He had lost both since becoming a soldier. Warriors have formidable enemies and heroic fights. He had neither. Soon after arriving at the battlefield, he even lost sight of who the enemies were. After three years in the Middle East, he also lost his smile. He still laughed, even wildly sometimes, but never smiled.

He had learned hatred in its pure form. It sizzled in his chest, and spread to every cell. He loathed Murray, but was afraid of him. He dreamt of chiselling his teeth out, one every other day. He hated everyone and everything in the Middle East. The underground resistance who planted roadside bombs, martyrs who blew themselves up to save their country, or go to heaven, making a mess. He hated their men and women, their boisterous markets that wouldn't take a break to let the war happen, their food which tasted good but... even a piece of naan bread filled him with disgust and horror. He hated their kids who stared contemptuously at his convoy with sad eyes. He hated their cute little babies who would grow up into contemptuous little kids, then men and women. Every thing was poisoned, yet it was his job to add more. He hated his fellow soldiers; he hated himself and the way hatred was consuming him.

After returning to the States, he visited his divorced parents briefly. He told them he needed to find God, and was going to Florida to do Religious Study. He hadn't really planned it. It just came out like that, and instantly became a decision. Getting out of his military contract was not easy but he succeeded. His had a convincing religious conviction.

It felt like God's will at work.

*   *   *

God might have willed John to move to Florida, but He wasn't there Himself to receive him.

John gradually cured himself of hatred, and started to smile again, but his loneliness intensified. Unlike his hometown church, or the military, something human was conspicuously absent in religious academia. Soldiers had esprits de corps, and they knew how to make fun of even the most tragic circumstances. In theology, a dense pall of anxious faith blanketed everything.

Most of his fellow God seekers were baffled by the sinfulness of society, pained by human weaknesses, and overwrought by undefined yearnings. How can humans, originally handmade by God, be so remote from perfection? They wondered, but dare not ask. They were disappointed with people, secretly including themselves. *What a lousy design!* But they could not criticise the Architect. They contrived to love His defective creatures nonetheless.

Compressing human nature into an unquestioning faith pumped them up like pressure vessels, threatening to blow any minute. Everywhere he turned, he saw ecclesiastical suicide bombers. Blind, self-righteous, remorseful, rapturous, aggressive, lost, sad.

He became depressed.

During darker moments in the Middle East, he would pray, and see light ahead. Now that he was in a God circle, he had lost his ability to pray. He did not know what to pray for. Gradually, he did not know who to pray to.

One Sunday after Church, he sat down to write. The sermon earlier was about faith and love, again, given by a maniac. On the way home, he questioned himself about where human judgement, inadequate as it was, entered the picture of faith. Where should one draw the line between insanity and religious conviction? Why would the freedom to worship be a noble principle if it made no sense whatsoever?

I better put it down in writing, he thought. I'm too upset and confused to think. Writing things down gave him the distance to be objective. After an hour, the sheet remained blank but for a single sentence he had doodled over and over. "Would Jesus be Christian if he was alive now?"

His answer filled six pages.

For the first time, he focused on the human side of Jesus. What a remarkable human he was: A rebellious and revolutionary thinker in a corrupt and brutal world. He was full of imagination; probably inherited that from his mother. What about the religions founded in his name? If Christ had stayed on Earth after the Resurrection, and lived on with his people, would he have donned a tiara (assuming the Vatican would elect him Pope rather than crucifying him again)? Would he have sanctioned the Witch-hunt? Crusades? Inquisitions? The persecution of Galileo and many others? Would Jesus go on air now, more than two thousand years old, wearing makeup, joining hands aloft with Superstar Evangelists to praise the Lord and ask for a donation?

His answers were no, no, no, no, no. No way.

Jesus was not that kind. Not to John anyway. Was that faith? Or the opposite? He wasn't sure, but sensed Jesus' approval.

Jeez, if Christ himself wouldn't be Christian these days, why should I, John Johnson?

He switched to marketing.

It was a desperate and unplanned move. His pragmatic nature told him to accomplish something, now that he was on campus. Unexpectedly, he enjoyed business school. It was steady, predictable, and promising – everything he had been missing. He also met his future wife, Sue, in Marketing 101.

At the nadir of his life, he started to climb.

* * *

John graduated in 2053, at the age of twenty-five, and joined a large oil company as executive trainee. A few years later, he was sent to Beijing on a promotional transfer. He was living with Sue at the time, and suggested that they might as well get married so that she could come with him on company expense. She agreed.

John enjoyed expatriate life in China. He believed in working hard. For the first time, something he believed in smiled back. He started his days early, and worked most weekends from home. He travelled frequently – at first all over China, later on back and forth to the States as headquarters started to notice him.

To kill lonely time, Sue tried to learn Chinese but it's so alien. She went wine-tasting with other expatriate wives who couldn't tell Coca Cola from Burgundy. She learnt yoga, twisted her back, and had to walk with a cane for three months. She explored

China by herself and fell into an open sewer in the unlit countryside of Guizhou late one evening, when John was in Houston.

Finally, she tried leaving him, and succeeded.

It worked out well for both. They were instantly relieved and happier. Sue found a new man and new life back home within a year. John focused on working. No hard feelings.

In 2068, John moved to Hong Kong to take up the post of Manager – Regional Strategy at the Asian Headquarters. He liked his new home right away, but never expected to spend the rest of his life there.

EXTINCTION

John jogs along the Eastern Corridor from Central to North Point most mornings. At sixty-two, his knees are still strong and bouncy, the one good thing he got out of boot camp.

He picks the harbour-front freeway mainly because of safety. Most inner roads are hollow underneath, and have caved into underground chambers and pipes, creating giant pot-holes. Their surfaces are covered with fallen debris from looming buildings which continue to let go of windows and air-conditioners without warning. Being next to the water, the freeway is well drained, periodically flushed by typhoons. The concrete is badly eroded, but strong enough to support the negligible weight of a human for a long time to come. Long enough for me anyway, John thinks.

He turns around at North Point with military precision. He looks at his platinum Rolex Oyster Perpetual to check the time. He does not like its look, but was impressed by the price tag of more than half a million. "Wow. No way." He tried it on in the abandoned shop, and has been wearing it since.

Twenty-eight minutes later, he's back at Central, sitting on his cast iron bollard at Queen's Pier, drinking from a water bottle. He's an animal of habit. If it's up to him, he would keep everything the same, in good predictable order, forever.

The osseous skeleton of Kowloon's vacant skyline sits on the other side of the harbour. What went wrong? How did a vibrant community disappear just like that? And what next? There's always something next, isn't there? Good or bad, always. He refuses to roll over and accept *this is it*. No. Never. Not him. John Johnson does not surrender; he always finds a way out. Every last human is now a warrior, with a duty to keep trying regardless of the odds, to the last minute. He mentally gives himself a pep talk.

But keep trying to do what? Repopulate the planet? Men and women are now fewer and farther between, and old. Besides, he hasn't the slightest clue why everyone is sterile. Being totally clueless bugs him. Ma doesn't care. That bugs him ever more. "So," he would say, sarcastic and apathetic as usual, deriding John for agonising over an impenetrable mystery that's none of his business. "Genesis II – Return of the Consumers – produced and directed by John Johnson. Don't waste time!"

"So I can join you in productive meditation?"

No. He would not give up; he should not. He must try to understand. To try to understand is the most remarkable quality of the human spirit; it deserves respect and protection, not derision. Once we understand, then we might find a way out; we just might.

He and Ma have gone through it enough times. Sure, on the grand scale of things, extinction is inevitable. John understands that. Out of a thousand living things that ever roamed the planet, nine hundred and ninety-nine are long gone – thoroughly dead. This is a spooky place. Death Valley on the Milky Way. Fine, mankind has been around for only a little more than one pitiful minute, if the age of Earth is put into a twenty-four-hour time-scale. He has heard all that before. We're downright negligible, okay, and extinction seems unavoidable, natural, even expected. Certainly not surprising. But wait! No. Not okay. Maybe we're not negligible! Human consciousness is evidently unique. He knows what Ma would say. "But we know nothing about consciousness. And what's unique? What isn't negligible in the grand scheme of things?" That's why there is no point debating semantics with Dao Master Ma. It kills time, though.

What John can't dig – that's how he put it to Ma – is the way in which we are disappearing. So damn puzzling. So helpless. And dragging on for so unbearably long. No Armageddon. No mutually annihilating nuclear wars or collision with a pulverising meteor. No divine floods that submerge the Himalayas. No invading aliens surfing on UFOs. No resisting heroes from Earth. No warriors. No final judgement. "You mean no retrieval of fetid good souls from decomposed bodies to restore justice?" Ma smirked.

No. Nothing like that. Just no more babies; cut off from the future. Human production terminated, like a dated model. Obsolete. *Sorry Sir, we don't make this anymore.*

Homo sapiens – Sons and master Species of Planet Earth, left to die like a beached jellyfish. Isn't it pathetic? Except flies and maggots, nothing else notices – not to say cares – about the death of mankind. We are sorely not missed. If anything, other earthly life-forms appear pleased by our departure. How humiliating. Unfair. Pathetic.

Ma thinks humans had squeezed the environment too hard for too long. Indeed we might have. But what has that got to do with fertility? We had no choice! We were stuck in a closed system. All living things eat and shit; so why are humans the only ones to bear the consequence? And didn't we try to make amends? To restore balance? Didn't we try harder than all the other animals put together?

Looking back, it does seem naive of us to have hollered "Save the Planet! Save Mother Earth!" In the end, Mother Earth is indifferent. She spins and glides regardless, tripping round the sun, oblivious to the absence of her human passengers. She never needed any rescuing. Mankind, on the other hand, is suffering a dreary extinction. One at a time, we are leaving a planet that was once ours. Somewhere along the line, we must have misplaced ourselves in the big picture. We were the ones who needed rescuing.

* * *

Normally, ageing prepares us for death. Today, a tooth gone. Tomorrow, one ear blocked forever. Then the legs go wobbly, kidneys turn gummy, friends become dead, mind goes blank, and the heart stutters. Bit by bit, things go kaput. Then we die.

Sardonically, the human race is approaching death in reverse.

Long-lost beauties are trickling back to tease us with a wonderful tomorrow that we might not see. The air is fresh, the water sweet; the sky is starry and the sea crystalline, teeming with life. No more round-the-clock news on murders, wars, rapes, elections, bankruptcies, corruption, economic chaos, plagues and famines. Earth is becoming lovelier by the day. Even humans are benefiting from the disappearance of their own race. What a wicked design. For the first time in decades, John wonders if God actually exists, with a personality as described in the Bible.

The most ironic rediscovery is people themselves. People can no longer help one another the way organised societies did. That's a pity. But when they do, it is more personal and rational. Difficult circumstances have brought them closer in an honest and open way. His small circle, for instance, would not have come together in the old days. He and Ma, he suspects, would have despised each other based on their equally fixed but opposing principles. Previously unbridgeable gaps between people like them have closed and disappeared.

Fundamentally, people remain who they are. Looming extinction has not changed their beliefs, values, personalities, preferences, loves and detestations overnight. Obstinacy is a durable human quality. But the situations that engendered disagreements have all but vanished, leaving them holding on to their principles like commandments cast in ice tablets, melting into irrelevance. Have they ever been relevant?

As the hyperactive world dies down to prehistoric quietude, humans become likeable, even to humans. Villains are extinct, or purged from the hearts of the beholders.

HOLE DIGGING ECONOMY

Being Manager (Regional Strategy) of the world's second largest oil company made John feel purposeful and privileged. The rental value of his office alone, in prime Central, was so ridiculously expensive he could brag about it at cocktail parties. "Can you believe our office rent has gone up to $260 per square foot? – Per month, not year!" How could anyone not be awestruck by spending power like this?

When he was not eating business lunches, he would take a sandwich to Queen's Pier. It was only a couple hundred metres away, but it would take him nearly ten minutes to walk, pushing and elbowing through the human traffic jam.

He would always sit on the same bollard, at the edge of a gushing stream of people. Anxious boats and impatient ferries criss-crossed at above speed-limit, blaring maritime profanity at each other. All that filled him with raw energy. Sometimes, his favourite bollard would have been taken by a fishing goon. It would annoy and puzzle him. He liked fishing, but the harbour had nothing but minnows, bugs and plastic bags to offer, all smelling of diesel-oil and sewage. In spite of this, some spent their day-off dipping a line into the murky water. "Caught anything?" he once asked. "Na." Just as he expected. Is this some form of Oriental mysticism? he wondered. Zen Buddhism? Undercover cops?

He would leave the mystic alone, and return to his tuna or roast-beef sandwich. For lubrication, he would drink pop zero. It tasted foul, and made his tongue brown, but it contained no energy. Zero. He could have drunk one after another and not got fat.

Lunch-hour was not necessarily unproductive. Scurrying pedestrians made deals over the phone with food in their mouths,

155

catching up with objectives, swallowing, agreeing. John liked that most about Hong Kong. It worked rather than whined. Hongkongers were always planning and working on something, any something, to make money, or just to feel busy. Given a choice, John realised, however, they preferred luck over effort. The city was obsessed with lucky and unlucky numbers, from car license plates to telephones. Four was inauspicious because it sounded like "death, or fail" in Cantonese. Floors containing the ominous number sold slower. So developers skipped them all, along with the 13th floor, with due respect to European preference, making all buildings sound taller than they actually were. One could actually live on the 50th floor of a thirty-five-storey building after the numbering had been adjusted to avoid having floors with the number four or thirteen. After the third floor came the fifth. One floor above the twelfth was the fifteenth and so on. But the Chinese had learned from experience that good fortune was unreliable, so they backed it up with hard work just in case. A sagacious bunch.

Honest to goodness work ethic. That was what made his old country tick, before con men jammed the clockwork with greed and deceit, and fiat money. . . Oh well, that was capitalism. Not perfect, obviously, but the best system we knew. It was intrinsically fair. Be good, work hard and take risks; capitalism gives you a chance. The higher the risk, the harder you worked, the higher the reward – all fair and square. John agreed wholeheartedly the first time he heard of it in business school.

Expectedly, his buddy Ma Yili thought otherwise. "Capitalism was the most feudalistic and unfair system in human history," he proclaimed, probably just to bug John.

Unfair? Perhaps. All systems are unfair to losers. But feudalistic? John's jaw dropped.

"Yeah." Ma swirled the claret in his goblet, observing the legs. "You know what this is? Long-chain fatty alcohol and esters."

"You have a wonderful way to make everything sound disgusting, Ma."

"Now, enlighten me. What's wrong with hereditary aristocracy?"

"Well," John started cautiously. He knew that every Ma question came with a snare. "Feudal lords passed on their title, wealth and privilege to heirs who often were imbeciles. They had done nothing to deserve the service and loyalty of the men and women who served him. I'm sure you have no problem seeing the injustice in that."

"No, I don't. But I also fail to see how it was different from an imbecile who'd inherited share certificates from Tycoon Daddy, who had done nothing to deserve the wealth, privilege, and a deciding influence on the career and livelihood of thousands of employees. Samie same lah. No?"

John screwed his face into a dramatic grimace, trying to think of a counter argument.

"Actually," Ma continued. "Capitalists were way worse. Feudal lords maintained their own thugs to fend off hungry peasants and devious rivals. Modern lords were protected by the State and its communal force, funded by the tax-paying middle-class whom they ripped off. The modern system was much more unfair and exploitative if you ask me."

"That's why I'm not asking, Ma."

* * *

"Work's everyone's primary contribution to the common good of a society. Work's a fundamental measurement of one's ethic and competence against his fellow men," John stated, ignoring the déjà vu. He must have said something similar numerous times, in one of their recurrent debates. Tweedledum and Tweedledee had deliberated everything below and above heaven to pass time. Fine wine and old age had raised their tolerance for repetition, and fortified passion over issues that had long become irrelevant.

"What?" Ma was incredulous as usual. He detested civilised jobs. Mere drudgeries for the sake of maintaining hyper-activities in an overpopulated world. Just a way to chain superfluous humans down to a stupefying routine. "There's only one reason to work: to make a living. Assigning moral value to it is absurd. Is a tiger which follows a longer route to find prey, or kills more than it needs, more ethical than others?"

Work was a sensitive topic. John had been a workaholic, deriving near-spiritual fulfilment from his job. Ma had been a phenomenal work dodger – a "parasite" was the kindest word John could come up with. "Lean back, suck blood, enjoy your cleverness, then laugh at your host." Actually, Ma was worse. Parasites did not laugh at their victims. Ma took pride and pleasure instead of guilt at having fooled the system. "You're a swindler," John said, pointing a finger at his best friend.

After Oxford, Ma spent three years in Singapore working for a medical equipment manufacturer, first as Product Development Scientist, then Senior Scientist. He was subsequently transferred to Shanghai to head their Research and Development Department. With two promotions in five years, he was rising like a corporate balloon when he resigned, ostensibly to become a freelance consultant. To consult in what? He could not say. To some, he would say he needed to find his own space. Most of his business trips were visits to Daoist historical sites or famous kung fu teachers.

In 2056 he ran out of money, and returned to Hong Kong. He found a job with the Environmental Protection Department. It happened to be the first positive response to his prestigious degrees and glamorised CV. His destiny took another erratic turn; Ma Yili became an officer of the environment.

A job's a job; career was not on his private agenda. He had kept a cool distance from his parents since Oxford, and needed an income. Once inside the bureaucracy, Ma had disappeared like a mouse set free in a warehouse. His ambition was clear and simple: to minimise work, and avoid attention. He wore comfy Clarks loafers like everyone else, and slipped them off noiselessly under the meeting-table like everyone else.

According to the official record, his single biggest mark – he left none other – was being Team Leader of a project entitled, "Zero Waste in Ten Years", an initiative of The Hon. David Dib Fu. The Hon. Fu was an elected councillor who suffered from seborrhoeic dermatitis. On a bad day, he would be covered in dandruff, looking like an apparition in the middle of a snow storm. He was unstable in the head in both a dermatological and a psychiatric sense. Nobody wanted the job. They knew it would go nowhere more erratically than other projects that were heading nowhere according to plan.

Ma volunteered.

A long-term assignment with an impossible goal. No imaginable contingencies or tangible yardstick to measure elusive progress. Lots of categorical failures in other international cities to copy from, then benchmark against.

Perfecto! The memo delegating him the project arrived much sooner than normal. Ma whistled, and tittered like a bad guy in Batman.

Loads of papers from other governments around the world were readily available for cut-and-paste confection. Ma would sprinkle a touch of local flavour himself. "This is the MSG, the most delicate ingredient," he explained to his deputy Peter, whom he handpicked for a general lack of intelligence and initiative. "Too much, and you'd spoil the dish. Too little, you can't cover the original flavour. After MSG, we'd top it off with a few sensational keywords that are controversial and easy to pronounce. Some Councillors would sniff them out, and start an interminable debate. The longer it is, the wilder the derailment, the better."

"Really?" Peter looked painfully puzzled.

"Really. Peter. It works every time."

"Really?"

Time flies, really. Ten years had elapsed. Ma had unblocked his Ren-Du Meridians in the meantime. The Hon. Fu had become bald, making his dermatological troubles more exposed. Strangely, his pathetic appearance had made him more popular with niche voters. When the project team prepared for a small tenth anniversary party, Ma realised that the numbers were catching up with them. To avoid embarrassing queries from amateurs, he suggested changing the project name to "Zero Waste in Hong Kong – A Long-term Goal in Sustainable Development". The steering committee thought it brilliant, and adopted it immediately, without public announcement. "It's a small technicality," the Chairman decided. "Let's not make a fuss."

Since the project's inception, urban trash had increased by six percent after discounting a higher moisture content. Ma's team reported to the Council Environmental Committee thirty-two times, produced twenty-two working papers, six voluminous reports, three city-wide campaigns and eight workshops. According to Ma's private tally, their activities had generated twenty-four dry-tonnes of garbage. "Not bad," he showed Peter. "Could have been a lot more right?"

"Really?"

* * *

Ma recounted how he recycled and reused overseas reports year after year, exaggerating for John's sake.

"They would have made me Departmental Employee of the Year had I been willing to betray my principle of invisibility, and bothered to fill out the tedious application," he bragged. "I understood the grading system better than most."

"How was that different from" – John paused to find a diplomatic word – "theft?"

"Each and every way," Ma replied insouciantly.

"The Government, your employer, the taxpayers – shit, I was one big one – paid you to do a job. You didn't. You deliberately didn't! but continued to get paid …"

"Plus an assortment of rightful benefits." Ma interrupted.

"Yeah. You got paid, with benefits, but failed to provide the service society expected. You also infringed copyrights. If that wasn't theft, what is?" John thought about his tax money.

"Don't you worry about copyrights. I always rearranged my reference material to reflect a local context, and acknowledged everyone in the bibliographies." Ma winked. "And hey, society didn't know what to expect. At least that's what it said to me through its elected representative. You can't accuse someone of stealing something if you have no idea what that something is can you?"

"What?!"

"Come on!" Ma was more sincere. "Do you think I, a nobody, could have changed the system? Fu had the popular mandate. When he wanted something done, no matter how ludicrous, we had to do it, or appear to be doing it. The majority of voters didn't think. Zero waste, no more garbage, good idea, let's go, they said. My project, in the hands of an unthinking and hardworking bureaucrat, would have consumed a hundred times more resources, and produced much more garbage. Luckily, I was there to contain damage. I took the project to its inevitable endpoint with minimum consumption and wastage. I did Mother Earth a true favour by reducing unnecessary work, as was my sacred duty as an officer of the environment. Remember the Three-R Principle? Reduce, Recycle, Reuse. That's what I was doing!

"And what's the alternative? To wholeheartedly work my ass off on some idiotic sound bite that was impossible to achieve?

To nullify gravity and invalidate mass balance in accordance with Hong Kong Government procedure and policy? To loyally do my official part in the perpetration of stupidity and hypocrisy, and help it grow? Would that be better for society, and make me more noble in your eyes?" Ma raised his eyebrow, then relaxed his face into a wide grin.

"That's oxymoronic polemic man," John mumbled, shaking his head. He went through the rationale again, in search of weaknesses or fallacies. Something had been cleverly twisted, he was sure. It was not the first time he saw Ma attacking unquestionable principles with ridiculous notions put in reasonable words.

"So, Mr Ma ..."

"Don't call me Mister because you don't agree."

"OK, shit-head," John smiled.

"That's sounds much more like you, John."

"So, there were no meaningful jobs in this world? What do you suppose would have happened if everyone sat on his ass picking his nose all day like you?"

"Uh, I didn't pick my nose all day." Ma paused for thought. "Jobs are neither meaningful nor meaningless, although I know what you mean. Small-scale farming? Education? Basic medical services? They are kind of necessary in my subjective view." He then raised his glass. "And the making of this stuff, of course."

"That I couldn't argue with you." John returned a toast.

* * *

Ma got up to replenish their glasses with more *Louis XIII*. They toasted each other again. "Can I give you an illustration?"

"Oh, I've got room for one more."

"Imagine, some nut with a few bucks decides to dig a hole in the middle of a field because, well, he's nuts. Then someone equally compulsive fills it back up. The Hole Digger's pissed off. He hires more hands, creating employment and a following. They research, develop, innovate, and use machines to dig bigger and deeper holes faster. The Hole Filler in response hires engineers to develop machines that back-fill at a matching pace. While this obsessive behaviour flourishes and technology progresses, we have an emerging economy, with dedicated facilities producing increasingly sophisticated machines for

Digger Inc. and Filler Inc. Two more lunatic tycoons are in the making.

"These facilities need technicians, labourers, engineers, financiers, quality controllers, marketing people to persuade others to dig and fill, accountants, package designers, insurance agents and logistics backup. They all need food, housing, clothing, education for their children, entertainment and so on. The government hires more people to hover around and watch.

"Meanwhile, farmers are short of labour; young people prefer the more challenging and fulfilling jobs offered by Digger and Filler. More efficient farming is needed to feed the expanding middle-class. Now, put Digger Inc. and Filler Inc. on the stock-market as conceptual growth stocks and presto! Watch these cylinders fire, driving a vibrant economy teeming with ambitious and stressed-out people holding meaningful jobs. All that, for a part-time hole in the ground, financed by the market. *Ha, haha!*"

"You're so full of shit," John laughed heartily. "I give up. I've had enough of your fallacy for one night. This Louis *EX*-something makes my head spin anti-clockwise. I'm gonna dig a hole now. Goodnight pal."

"Goodnight John."

ABOUT GOD

John was wandering in the neighbourhood when he first saw Ma and the gang working on the hanging garden.

"What are you guys doing?"

Song Huan explained they were diverting the rooftop drainpipe to a storage tank. "Good idea." John introduced himself and volunteered to help. By then, it was again okay to be friendly and helpful to strangers, even in Hong Kong.

John liked Huan right away – an old-fashioned gentleman, his kind of guy. Song's relative youthfulness was refreshing. Ma was witty and amusing, but a bit overbearing in a paradoxically insouciant manner. Their acquaintance felt awkward at first, even slightly tense at times. But they had no one else of similar age and pigheadedness to talk to. Gradually, they became best friends, but continued to suspect a hidden mutual contempt temporarily misplaced.

* * *

They were having after-dinner coffee and cognac to celebrate the first harvest of Ma's hanging garden. It was autumn, but the temperature was still up in the low thirties, and the bugs were cocky. It felt like midsummer except for the occasional spell of dry northerly wind. Autumn's arrival was yet uncommitted. After some enterprising discussions of how they might, encouraged by their anticipated success, expand the hanging garden, Huan started to yawn. Song left with his father. John and Ma chatted on.

"Old Song said you did a lot of work overseas?" Ma was serving John his *first* one-for-the-road.

"Almost everything." John then gave a quick summary of his career, from foot soldier to executive. "After all that, I'm now retired without a pension."

"But you own half of Robinson Road." Ma gestured panoramically with his hands. John followed them to regard the neighbourhood and smiled. "True. All that prime property, without a market."

"That sergeant of yours sounded nasty."

"Oh, he was the biggest asshole I've ever met. The way he treated the Ali Babas was... unspeakable."

"What'd he do?" Ma asked too quickly, then realised he really did not want to know.

"I'd prefer not to talk about it. Unspeakable." John's tone had darkened. "Perhaps his loudmouthed moralisation made him more creepy. Infinitely more creepy."

Ma nodded without commenting. They fell silent for a moment, then John said, "Looking back, Murray wasn't all bad. He made me determined to get out. Without him, I might have stayed. I didn't know what to do next. My life would have been very different if I had stayed in the Marines. It's strange how one thing leads to another."

"Life's like that isn't it, a series of connected unknowns."

"At the time, it felt like stumbling from one disillusionment to another. Whatever I believed in always turned out to be different, something disappointing."

"Don't you think that can be relieving?"

"What do you mean?"

"Disillusionment. Losing faith in templates. Destroying expectations. Doesn't it feel kinda good with a big sigh?"

"Easy to say now. But I was brought up to have faith. Beliefs were my headlights on a dark highway. Losing them one after another was scary."

"You still believe?"

"Yeah," John said without hesitation. "I still believe in God although I ceased associating Him with the holy books long ago. Someone has to create and regulate this vast and strange universe out there."

Ma smiled politely.

John continued: "And – I know it might sound crazy – I believe the Fertility Crisis will somehow come to an end. I think humans are here for a purpose; God wouldn't dump us just like that."

"Mmm," Ma grunted. He wanted to keep his mouth shut but failed. "You surely must have thought about who created and manages God, and who created God's creator."

"Sure, I have."

"So who are they? One at a time please!"

"What's a muffin made of?" John sat up and asked.

"Pardon me?"

"Just tell me what muffins are made of!"

"John, I don't eat that crap. Why? Sawdust and pig fat?"

"Close enough. What if I tell you they're made of flour, eggs, sugar, water and other items. Would you be happy with that answer?"

"Sure...," Ma responded dubiously.

"Why don't you ask what flour, eggs, sugar and water are made of?"

"Because ..." Ma was going to say because he *knows* what these things are made of, but quickly realised it would lead to endless layers of the same question; an infinite onion.

"So, you know what I mean." John winked, pleased like a prosecutor who had successfully trapped his victim in cross-examination. "Big or small questions, we have to stop somewhere. Correct me if I'm wrong Ma; in Daoism, don't you stop just as arbitrarily and accept that whatever is beyond is unknowable, so you leave it unnamed? Dao can't be named, period. Fine, very sensible.

"I'm doing the same. Only I call it God because that's the name I grew up with. *My* God is just as unknowable and omnipresent. Perhaps the only difference is that God cares and Dao doesn't. I want my God to care, so He does!"

"So you have God at your command."

"You said that. I didn't." John theatrically crossed himself.

"But as you said, God has been institutionalised; and a lot of damage has been done in His name."

"True, but that isn't my God. Those weren't God's problems – just human follies you see. All good ideas are eventually corrupted by man. That's why I decided Jesus Himself wouldn't be Christian. Look at all the sorcery and superstitions that've grown out of Daoism and Buddhism. Although they weren't fanatical or organised, do you think Mr Laozi and Gautama would have recognised their own teachings in practice?"

"Good point," Ma conceded. "But there's still one fundamental difference."

"Which is?"

"Daoism and Buddhism recognise an infinite mystery lying beyond the limits of human cognisance. An absolute deity, on the other hand, blocks our way forward. God's a dead end. That's why theistic superstitions tend to be fanatical. Other than that, I fully agree with you."

John was pleased. This supercilious Ma fully agrees with me? He used the opportunity to shift the focus on Ma instead. "I suppose you've never believed in a god?"

"Oh I have. Very much so, in fact. I was extremely God-fearing in my younger days; the same God as yours, before He changed His will as to my faith."

* * *

Ma's parents, like most Chinese, were religiously pragmatic. The gods can be good and powerful and all that, but why bother worshipping them unless it brings some potential benefit such as money and health in return? Isn't that the fundamental reason for having a filial relationship with godheads?

Most of the cultural rites they knew were purportedly Buddhist or Daoist, or eclectically both, all funeral or festivity related. Put three sticks of incense in an urn, bow, ask for a blessing – two if they're simple – ceremony concluded. Eat the offerings, and hope for a favourable miracle.

Each of them had been to different brands of Christian services, mainly weddings. Some girls became Catholics so they could have a romantic church wedding rather than one officiated over by a monotone civil servant with bad breath, wearing a polyester tie. In church, Yong and Janice Ma would rise and kneel with an anticipatory instinct sharpened by years of speculating in the market, and chat merrily through the sermon as befitting a happy occasion.

Had someone told them Buddhism and Daoism were atheistic philosophies, they would have been baffled. "What's atheistic?"

They knew Islam was another major religion from the Middle East, all the time fighting with Christianity. That was the extent of their religious knowledge.

Nonetheless, they shared a number of attributes with the pious. Humility was one. They were humble before god, any god. "God rules the universe. We are powerless and at his mercy so just pay respect!" Charity was another. When requested, they would donate at the going rate whether to a church, temple or mosque, provided it was tax-deductible. "All religions teach people to be good. To support with a few dollars is good for karma." Then they had hope – the linchpin of any faith. They hoped for big wealth, good health, and enhanced karma in return for the donation.

Whether god was male or female, Jewish or Greek, Indian or Chinese, temperamental or dotingly loving, was irrelevant. "What does it matter? Not up to us to decide or change so why waste bwain juice?"

"Treat gods like emperors. Show respect and keep a safe distance, especially when so many claim to be the one-and-only, and you're not sure who'll win," his mother advised on a subject she preferred not to discuss. She was worried by her son's recent religious fervour. "Be open-minded. Don't put all eggs in same basket. What if you pick the wrong god? You get punished! What for huh?" It dawned on Ma that open-mindedness was more than a virtue. It was also a hedging strategy when it came to betting on an unknowable Divine.

Like many religiously indifferent parents in Hong Kong, they had sent Yili to a Catholic school. The Catholics' grip on the education system had been established in the colonial days. The British were not Catholics, but after a terrible storm wrecked Macau, in the second half of the 19th century, the Macanese flocked to Hong Kong, which then became well-stocked with nuns and priests.

Ma's school was operated by the Salesian Brothers. Attached to the school was an urban monastery fenced off from the depraved world by rusty chicken-wire. Everything was old and dark, mysteriously other-worldly. The green opaque windows, permanently closed, captured young Yili's imagination. A reinforced concrete crucifix – the sacred icon that puzzled Ma later, when he had become sceptical ("Why do we worship the torture gizmo that killed Christ?" he would eventually ask Father da Silva who taught him science) – loomed above a low marquee, overlooking a dusty courtyard and a traffic jam six feet on the other side.

Ma wanted to be inside one day, to be privy to Divine Secrets, studying arcane scriptures behind closed windows, chatting with God. He decided to join the priesthood as soon as he could.

In the meantime, he felt the burden of Original Sin. Alien guilt tormented him. He could not sleep. He would stay up, kneeling by the bed, mumbling "Hell Mary, full of gwace..." (it was only much later, with better English, that he realised his inadvertent blasphemy), slipping a plastic rosary through growing fingers. Bead by bead, he discharged his abstract guilt, petrified and insomniac.

He wanted to get baptised; it might help him sleep.

Mum was worried. "Have you noticed the dark circles around his eyes? What if he becomes a priest and lives in temple? Then we have no grandchildren," she told her husband. "You better talk to him."

"Don't worry lah. Leave it to me," Ma Yong promised, looking confident and cheeky.

"OK to baptise of course," he told his son later. "But not before you get your Dwiver's License."

"Huh?" Ma Yili was confused by his father as usual.

"Say pahdon. Not huh!"

"Pahdon?"

"Religion is deep." Ma Yong paused to nod contemplatively. "Deeper than dwiving. If you can't dwive, you're too young to pick a god. Huh?"

"But ... "

"No BUT lah, only a few years. Twy weading my car magazines first, okay?"

Time passed slowly in those young and graceless days. Meanwhile, Ma was corrupted by the Church's historical adversaries: science and girls, *inter alia*. Irrelevant questions bubbled devilishly in his mind.

After Father da Silva's lecture on Newton's Laws of Motion, Ma merged his newly acquired scientific knowledge with biblical scenes. What would be the velocity of the Ascension? He mused. Did Jesus take off like a rocket? Or majestically like a king? His quick calculation showed that the dignified approach would have taken many hours for Jesus to disappear from sight.

Did any of the Apostles leave halfway? It would have been rather tedious watching the Lord rising for a whole day wouldn't it?

On the other hand, Christ taking off like a rocket would be so unthinkable....

Ma was becoming annoying – as teenagers are prone to be – to his Catholic mentors. His soul was drifting further from salvation. The drift soon turned into a flight.

* * *

"Where I came from, you'd be shot for that!" John laughed. "You can't take the Bible literally. I loved my church; all my friends were there. They were good folks, genuine, much more Christian than the ecclesiastical crackpots I later met in theology." He paused to bask in the nostalgia of his childhood community. "So you got rid of God, and replaced Him with Science?"

"It wasn't quite that sophisticated. I was just going through a smart-ass phase. You know what it's like." John felt like saying "You mean you're past that?" but kept his mouth shut on a straight face. They didn't know each other well enough yet.

Ma continued, "Perhaps, for a little while, science was my new God. But I soon realised the more I learned, the more questions I faced. The mystery wasn't resolved; it got deeper instead. I had kicked the church out, but only pressed the reset button on God."

"I know what you mean. I did the same. I saved God in my heart and chucked the rest. So what happened when you pressed reset?"

"I felt empty, unfulfilled, and horny."

"Horny ? "

"Yes. God was toying me with puberty at the same time. I had to manage pimples and girl fantasies while going through a spiritual crisis. Imagine."

John chuckled.

"Anyway, science did not become my new God. My old God was multi-functional. He gave me a blind sense of purpose, which was a lot more reassuring than a clear sense of no purpose. But now that my eyes were open, I couldn't go back. I was stuck."

"So what happened?" John urged like a kid.

"Gradually, I invented my own prayers. I needed them. I was too used to them. Hooked you might say. So I concocted my own spiritual methadone."

John laughed again. "Did it taste like orange juice?"

"I re-established my spiritual bearings with a mixture of science and exercise. Cycling and swimming were my early meditations. Eventually, when in Britain, of all places, I learnt Tai-chi and *Qigong*, and discovered Buddhism and Daoism from my Scottish landlady. Know what, before then, I thought Buddha was one of the Indian gods.

"Slowly I found a renewed sense of awe, a wondrous sense of peaceful awe that keeps me in perspective, humbled but not depressed. I quelled anxieties without stopping to reason or search. I now have a personal understanding of God that's magical, intelligent, peaceful, and beautiful rather than dogmatic, ridiculous, tempestuous, and scary. I finally had God tailored to suit my nature."

"Interesting," John said contemplatively.

"And, you know what?"

"What?"

"Lately, when I look in the mirror, I can see a halo around my head."

"Don't worry. Just senile cataract. Try Vitamin B12 or reincarnation."

QUEEN'S PIER

Fishes have a memory of only a few seconds; John could not remember where he had read that.

"Bullshit," he thought, as he watched the flurry of activities around the sunken barge. The supposedly forgetful creature evidently recognised his looming silhouette, and associated it with a tiny shower of ancient crumbs. They were warming up their fins and jaws for the imminent contest.

John was sitting on his bollard at Queen's Pier. He came here each morning after the run to read, feed the fish, then drop a line when lunchtime neared. When he did not feel like fishing, he would daydream, or give the bollard a coat of paint. It was the only object in all of Central that still gleamed with artificial vanity.

Fifty metres away was City Hall, a few ugly square blocks from the 1960s. It escaped redevelopment because by the time conservation had become belatedly fashionable in Hong Kong, most old buildings had been dumped into the harbour to make land. Having survived the process of elimination, the City Hall became a classic by default. Dead things have fates too. John now stored his fishing tackle at the reception hall.

The harbour, once a receiving body of millions of toilets, was crispy blue, teeming with wide-eyed and unsuspecting life. A colourful fish called Green Coats was John's favourite. It had a parrot-like beak adapted to crack sea urchins, and silky smooth flesh under flamboyant turquoise scales. Post-modern fish may not be forgetful, but they sure were dumb, ready to bite at anything. A piece of yarn or a strip of plastic would make good baits. Like the trawlers that used to scrape the harbour's barren floor a few times daily, fish had become similarly plentiful, desperate, and stupid. There was after all an advantage in being an endangered species yourself while other edible ones thrived.

He dropped the last handful of crumbs and rubbed his hands. The fish leapt for them, making slippery flip-flop sounds. They reminded John of the stock-exchange floor, with brokers bumping around like pinballs. John found the submarine bustle hypnotic, like campfire. He could watch for hours.

A giant shadow flitted past. The barge fish vanished instantly as if by magic, then reappeared just as fast. So fast, that John was unsure if anything had happened at all. A giant fish? Momentary blackout? Shadow of a huge bird? He looked up. A few kites glided haughtily by, looking down at the world, searching for rats. None of these. He looked out towards the sea, and caught a blinding reflection of the morning sun.

Then the shadows returned. This time, they surfaced, and splashed.

"Ooooh... "

A pod of dolphins leapt about thirty metres ahead, Chinese White Dolphins, pink in colour. Before he recovered from the shock, they had circled back. Five, perhaps six, seven? They jumped and dived in perfect synchronisation, clicking, squealing.

"They're so happy...," he murmured.

*　*　*

"It wasn't an accident," John concludes, still visibly euphoric. Tycho has been momentarily forgotten. "They spotted me and turned to check. It was deliberate."

Ma wants to remind him of Tycho just for fun, but decides against it. John needs a break from that empty molar. "Wow," he says instead. "Dolphins in Victoria Harbour – our world-class confluence of sewage and injected chlorine. Don't know what to say. Too bad the Environmental Protection Department isn't here to claim credit."

"That's right." Song seems more excited than John. The dying old man's eyes have finally been purged. "They're super smart. They must have recognised that you're human, a long lost friend or... enemy, whatever. So they jumped to say 'hi'."

"Or to squeal *catch me if you can,*" Ma added.

"That's exactly what I thought," says John. "You've heard me grumbling about human extinction before. To me, human consciousness makes us unique. Unlike the gazillions of beings that went before us, we deserve special consideration. When I saw the dolphins this morning, it dawned on me that we might not be so unique after all. They seem to know something we don't. I wish we understood their language. We could have learnt something that'd make a difference."

"John, if they knew something that we don't, and we understood their language, we still wouldn't have listened to a bunch of fish. Otherwise, we'd not be human."

"They're not fish," Song corrects Ma, who returns a *duh* face.

John continues. "Like a simple and wise guy with a big heart, they're not holding grudges against us for what we did to them and the oceans. They probably pity us instead, and leapt to say 'hi' for old-times' sake."

"Hello?" Ma waves both hands in front of John's face.

"I know I sound like a sentimental fool now but, it was… it was… awesome. If you were there, you'd be the same. I guarantee."

"It's experiential Shi Fu, your favourite explanation for everything. Understand?" Song turns back to John. "So what did you do?"

"What could I do? I waved after them like a dumbfounded kid at the Ocean Park, refusing to leave after the show. I felt like weeping but couldn't. Don't ask me why."

"Why?" Ma asked.

SIX

SLIPPERY STIFFS

Stiffs are tricky to handle because they are stiff for only a short time.

They soon become stinky, sloppy, and slippery, fouling up the whole neighbourhood. Nothing smells remotely as bad. After a close encounter with the rotten kind, the aftertaste of death would cling to the nose, clothes, hair, skin for days. Ma's nasal irrigation is helpless against the morbid odour that has penetrated the moist lining of his own throat, lungs and guts.

For a while, most bodily remains were disposed of by family members, next door neighbours, or friends, in a timely fashion. Gradually, deaths have become more lonely. The first such forlorn body, or what was left of it, was discovered by Song. He was scrounging for provisions in an apartment block half way up the Peak. Just something to do, like shopping to pass time. Led by the unmistakable odour, he found the bloated old lady seeping into a fine sofa with beautiful floral appliqués. The sight of her mucous drips crawling down a piece of furniture was gruesome. Yet he was neither sickened or upset. He surprised himself.

He left her undisturbed, and reported back to the tribal elders.

"What stage is she at," asked John. There was a hint of excitement in his voice.

"Stage?"

"Yeah. A corpse decomposes in stages. In the beginning, it's a little puffy and bluish. You might see maggots crawling underneath the skin already. Then the guts become bloated. The tongue sticks out, and the eyes may start dribbling down the face. It'd be covered in maggots by now. You can hear them munch if it's quiet. Sounds like someone masticating oatmeal with their mouth open. Then –"

"You're making this up."

"No! I know my dead bodies, Ma. I was a soldier."

"Sure. You guys only shot at people from a kilometre away."

"What are the other stages?" Song's curious.

"Ah, the next stage would be final. I think it's called putrefaction or liquefaction, something like that. We called it the frothing finale. As the technical term suggests, the body becomes kind of liquid. Brain juice leaks through the nose and ears and eye sockets."

"I don't think she's that advanced, but she seems to be dripping a bit. I'm not sure."

"Then we'd better hurry. It doesn't take long to get there in this climate. Two to three weeks max from the last breath is my guess." John regarded everyone. They stared back at him, silently electing him leader of the task force.

"Bub?" Song turned to his father, who had been listening silently with a grimace.

"Sure."

"You don't have to, old man. There's enough of us." John smiled to Huan.

"No, I'll come."

"Okay then. Bring lots of towels. We'll need them."

*　*　*

She turned out to be a Stage Two according to John's assessment. After examining her from a respectful distance, they held an emergency meeting outside in the parking lot.

Whew!

Huan supposed that there would be more of "these" in the future so why not find a dedicated spot where they can stock up firewood for cremation. A neighbourhood crematorium.

"Good idea!"

"But wait, the problem is transportation. Stiffs aren't stiff for long. They become soft and slippery like an overripe tomato. If you grip hard, your fingers will go through them."

"Get out of here!"

"What about burning right where we find them. Carrying firewood would be easier than moving a slippery corpse?"

"Good idea, engineer!"

"What if there are others in the building?"

"In that case, we'd better leave the task to whoever is living there who can't smell."

"They could be immobile."

"And alive? Come on. Fine, we'll first check for others in the building just in case."

"What if the fire gets out of hand?"

"We can make sure it doesn't. What do you say, engineer?"

"Sure can."

"If it does?"

"Big deal."

So, the committee decided on in situ cremation. Move a few pieces of flammable furniture next to the body. Cover her (it?) with cloths and blankets, add starting fluid, then...

"Should we give her some kind of ceremony?"

"What ceremony?"

"A prayer, farewell speech, incantation, any rite of passage you know."

"I think a three-minute silence would do."

"What about one-minute?"

"Yeah one minute should do. We hardly know her. Just a gesture. She stinks."

"Come on! Be respectful."

After observing a one-minute silence, they said "be on your way," ceremoniously, struck a match – wham! – and left.

They hung around outside for a while. Black smoke billowed from the windows. It looked oily, and smelled like cooking bacon.

On the way back, John shared a little more of his expertise, to break the silence. "You know what's the most gripping experience in handling corpses?" he asked, pun intended. Nobody seemed interested. "The hands," he said. "The hands," he repeated.

Song looked at him inquisitively.

"Soldiers, doctors, and people in death-related professions can carry a severed head, swing it by the hair, toss it around for fun. It takes getting used to of course, but cruelty helps to objectify. Kicking it like a football makes the job easier."

Ma raised an eyebrow at John. Huan looked ahead, intensely pensive, apparently not listening.

"But you can't grab its hand as if you're shaking it." John nodded earnestly at Ma. "The icy fingers send a chill through the spine of even callous soldiers. I'm not kidding you."

"Unless she's someone you love," Huan said. He had been listening.

* * *

The old lady did not just turn into smoke and ash.

She visited Song Huan that night, and invited him back to the apartment for tea. She served green tea, plainer than water, at room temperature – the temperature of a cold room.

"Would you like some biscuits?"

Before he could reply, she had already offered him one on a small dish. A cool and pinkish biscuit, like raw pig skin from the fridge, was pushed under his nose. Huan was too polite to decline. She was pleased.

The biscuit started to melt in his mouth. The starchy dollop started to slither, wriggling, struggling, drowning in his saliva.

Maggots!

He closed his eyes, and swallowed quickly, just managed not to gag. The frail lady seemed the sensitive type; she would have been saddened or offended if he had spat it out. She smiled, looking happy and kind, as if pleased that he had passed a crucial test. She reached forward to grab his hand. Hers was cold, like Sari's in the hospital, but much skinnier. It had no flesh, just shrunken bones in frozen skin, like his Mum's favourite chicken feet pickled in white vinegar. There was always a jar in the fridge.

Her grip sent a sharp chill up his spine. John was right.

Her eyes started to run, drooling down her cheeks. She wiped it with the back of her hand, apologising in a bubbling voice. Her throat was dissolving. "Please don't mind Mr Song. It's just the way things are. Don't mind… "

Huan woke in a cold sweat. He could taste the biscuit at the back of his throat. He dreamily mumbled the first thing that came to mind. "I don't want Song to see me dead. Don't touch my body," then fell asleep again.

He woke up decided. He would die alone when the day came, if possible.

LETTER TO SON

Sung,

I've revised this letter so many times it tires me to look at it now. My eyes can hardly cope with the copying, and my fingers hate it. I write slowly, as you know. What bothers me most is that repetition eats away my feelings. Feelings are precious to an old man, you see. I've only discovered that in the past few years. Sadness has become numb; so numb that it makes me grumpy, scared, and pained, rather than sad. And, believe it or not, a good laugh is the only thing that brings tears to old eyes. Funny, eh?

Some feeling is lost with each revision. Something that meant a lot to me a few months ago no longer matters. It's like that something has died ahead of me in the time that has passed. Perhaps I should have kept the first draft. It might have been jumbled and confused, but raw and real, with one more year of life in it. But that would not be me would it? I had to edit, edit, and re-edit, until, finally, here it is, lying exhausted in front of me. Yet, it's not done. I must give it this one last round.

Last year, I started this letter with "Sung, I don't know where to begin," and got stuck. I now know where to begin, but have no idea how it might end. I originally planned to depart eighteen months ago, but kept postponing. I told myself I needed to prepare you better, better and better, for a life without me. I'm finally running out of excuses, and tired of lying to myself.

When you were born, I was about your age now. What a surprise. I believed in statistics and predictability. I detested surprises. As an engineer, my job was to identify variables, pin them down for management. Miracles don't exist. But somehow they do. You were born.

You can't imagine how much you brought us. You enriched our lives with laughter and innocence while everyone sat and waited to age and die. You added a whole new dimension to my life; a dimension I had never imagined.

Yet, sometimes I wish I had used a condom. It hurt me to watch you growing up without friends, dreams, or aspirations. The future that awaits you is static, terminal. But how could I have known that we weren't sterile? Your Äiti never let herself be examined; but I had been sperm-counted twice for fun and charity, and been duly certified "low and phlegmatic" on both occasions, like everyone else. That said, had we known we weren't barren, we'd probably have tried harder. The end result would have been the same.

Fortunately, you were an exceptional kid, even in your teenage years. But that pained me more. Can't ever win can we?

When you were four-and-a-half, eager to grow up, everyone was at some age and a half older than you. I was forty-and-a-half; Äiti was thirty-four-and-a-half; your friend Johnny was nine-and-a-half. You were puzzled why he was older, but with a birthday *after* yours, in November. He was a rare Generation-Zeder, unspoiled. A pity that he succumbed to the plague so young.

When you turned five, I asked teasingly what you wanted to be when you grow up, now that you were *already* five. You said, "I want to turn six first." Yes, one step at a time; that's what we had been trying to teach you, but you were evidently more talented than I thought.

Your silly little moments still make me smile. Remember your first candy? We withheld candies until you turned five. Not easy; the whole world was eager to pamper you with everything at its disposal. On your fifth birthday, I had the honour to present you with your first candy. A liquorice drop from Finland. I can still see your face. It made your Äiti sob. You were a lucky boy. Most kids had long lost the privilege of being excited by candies at a much younger age.

I'm babbling, but these memories are all that I've got left. They give me strength, and a purpose in the past tense.

Your fever at ten worried us even more than your first year. Your temperature hovered above 103. Your throat swelled so much you had no neck. I could tell the doctors had no idea. They put you in a glass room, like an exhibit in a mausoleum, and wiped you with alcohol every hour. We watched. Your Äiti prayed to God, whom she never believed in. She offered to trade her life for yours. Good thing God wasn't doing any trading that week. Not yet anyway. On the eighth day, you woke up with normal temperature, shivering. By the afternoon, you were normal again, as if woken up from a good rest. Nobody knew why.

Now, I'm not supposed to get stuck in the past. Let's focus on the future instead. You have many challenging years ahead. I might have a few of my own left. Increasingly, our problems will diverge, and I don't want mine to become yours as well. That is the main reason why I must leave. However, while preparing for it, I've come to realise something else. I need to set myself free, unchain the ghost inside, before I die. I can only do that alone, as soon as possible.

I like things predictable, don't mind them being boring as long as they don't change. I probably got that from my Dad, or developed it from his early death. But fate has been most perverse. We live in a dramatic epoch, to say the least, and we are right in the epicentre because of you. Nevertheless, for years, I tried to maintain an orderly life in an unravelling world. I've been a dutiful sailor on a sinking ship, doing my utmost to stay the course, adhering to the operation manual amidst great chaos. I've been being myself, I guess.

When your Äiti died, everything died. But I hung on. In the hospital, I didn't feel sad, just exhausted, thoroughly exhausted, too exhausted to let go. I was so blank and calm, it scared me. I wished hopelessly to wake from a bad dream. She'll wake soon, I told myself, or I'll wake to see her making breakfast. But I had no vision of the kind. I was no good in fooling myself. She was dead. I could not pretend otherwise.

I didn't cry. When I left the hospital, I went for a very long walk. Perhaps I would cry when alone, I thought. But I didn't. I don't know how long I walked. I suddenly noticed I was dead tired and hungry. I came home with a roast goose, remember? You had cried, for me too, I knew. I was almost envious.

For weeks I lived in a daze. I was intently undisturbed; as if carrying primed explosive. I didn't cry at the funeral either.

All these years, I have not dreamt of your Äiti, not even once, until a few months ago. We didn't talk, just being comfortably silent together. She made me porridge. I woke before eating it, and cried. It felt really good.

Maybe my heart has finally come out of a coma. Now I want it to live. I want myself to live, to drift, for once, without any anchor, before too late. What have I got to lose? You might think I'm too old for this self-searching game. I certainly thought so. But I have a clear realisation that I might have lived my whole life according to my conception of others' expectations. I'm suddenly desperate to find out if Song Huan has been my true self, whatever that means. Do I sound like a teenager? The difference is a teenager has time, I don't.

Sung, I'm neither scared nor sad, just ready, eager to go, in a positive spirit. We've been much more than father and son. We've been best friends and companions as well. Nonetheless, we must part one day soon. Rather than letting it take us by surprise, or torment us with a protracted farewell, let's make it happen by design. I assure you this is the most sensible way; I've given it a lot of thought in the past two years. The heart will hurt, yes, but it will heal. You're not an emotional coward like me. You're more like your mother. You know how to let things out, leave them behind, and move on. You've always been a truer person than me.

How I wish you had a woman, a mate, in this lonesome world. It's a pity the few girls who came and went were all impossible. Remember that pretty little thing from Chongqing the government tried to pair you up with? What a nightmare! A typical Generation-Zeder. A bit too old for you too, wasn't she? Unfortunately, my generation not only ruined the physical world for you kids, we also spoiled you rotten, poisoned your spirits. What thorough destruction... Well, we tried to raise you "normal" in a world that was anything but. I sometimes questioned whether we did the right thing, making you the odd one out in a tiny crowd.

I wonder where the other Generation-Zeders are. Did they all commit suicide? Move away? Anyway, I hope you'll find a woman you can go through the coming years with, even a bitch! Maybe you should move to the mainland, where there must surely be more people left. Do I sound like a father nagging his son to get married?

Know what, son? That's enough. I can go on like this forever. I've done that many times. But this one's for real. I must get going. So should you. Our journeys can't wait.

Don't worry about me. I have a good plan (as usual, ha ha). I know exactly where to go, where there's good food and safe shelter. I may feel lonely sometimes, but getting old is a lonely experience anyway, even surrounded by people. When I'm out of here, I'll do whatever the moment calls for. I'll be free. I'll cry when I should, not years later. I've been too serious, so I'll try to develop a sense of humour too. (Was that funny?)

Thanks again, Son. Thanks for making my life complete. The rest is up to me now. Thanks for being you. I love you; you know that. Remember what I said last week? You'll always find me and Äiti in you. You will.

Bub

* * *

Huan puts the letter under the Ming Dynasty jade qilin, and heads for the door. His bike and backpacks are waiting.

Fifteen minutes later, he is back. He sits at the desk, takes out another piece of paper, and hurriedly scribbles:

Sung,

It's time to leave. I've been preparing you for two years so don't say you haven't been warned! I have to go one way or the other. This is the best way to go, and the time is now. We must live according to the circumstances. We're survivors, right? I'll be fine. I'll be happy. You too.

Nothing can separate this family. Look inward, and you'll find me and your mum, always.

Bub

He folds the original letter twice, and inserts it into his back pocket. He places the note under the qilin, and looks around the room one more time.

"Bye," he says, then turns to leave.

CROSSING NEVERLAND

Having finally loaded the two backpacks into the sampan, Huan's hands and legs were trembling mildly.

For a nice sunny day, the sea was unexpectedly choppy at the Sheung Wan Public Pier west of Central. Underneath a deep blue sky, frivolous whitecaps in the harbour aggregated into ferocious surf by the time they reached the jetty, thrashing the small boat against barnacle-covered steps, making it groan like an irritated bull. He had moored it there two weeks ago.

He sucked at the cut wound on his palm. The blood tasted salty. Barnacles had cut his knees and hands but without them, the mossy steps would have been impossibly slippery. Lowering two camper-size backpacks and one lightweight mountain bike onto a bobbing vessel had turned out to be too much for his creaking knees. He felt old – much older than an hour ago when he left home.

He considered quitting. Come back next week, even tomorrow, better prepared. He could still get home and unpack before Song returned but... "Come on, I'm not a quitter." No. Not before, not now. Not this time. This was a one way trip. Stop looking for excuses. "Oh well, I've never been a water person. All will be fine, once I've reached the other side."

He looked over at Kowloon, avoiding the water in between. How he wished the tunnels were open, so he could bike underneath the harbour. But the tubes were flooded within a few weeks after power generation had ceased. Many were surprised. "If they'd divided the volume of the tunnels by the daily amount of water sucked out by the drainage pumps, they'd have expected it. It's that simple," he had told his son.

This little boat would do just fine.

After a century of reclamation, Kowloon should be half an hour away max, with the agile sampan. He untied the stern, held the line in his hand, and stepped in. He landed a bit too hard with stiff knees. The little boat rocked petulantly in response. He extended his arms to balance like a tightrope walker before squatting down, very slowly, to wait for it to calm.

"Happier now?" He talked to its pointy nose, as if it also had ears.

He pulled the bow-line loose, felt the oars in his hands, then told himself encouragingly, "Yep. Here we go!"

Away from the pier, the water was less rough. There was nothing for it to bounce and re-bounce against. The boat suddenly seemed willing. It sloshed assuringly, as if purring to its new owner. Puffs of white clouds hung fluffily above, giving perspective to the flat blue sky, listlessly watching the lone sampan bobbling. The once hectic and magnificent Victoria Harbour looked petite and rustic, like an unexplored lagoon. "Neverland!" he exclaimed – a contrived attempt to cheer his faltering spirits with a childhood memory half forgotten. "Where did Neverland come from?" He could not recall. A beautiful place anyway. A fairy tale.

He rowed backward, facing Hong Kong. Everything looked impossibly clustered. How did it fit in so many people? The anxiety that had gripped his stomach all morning had eased. He was feeling better, quite good actually, on the surface. Inside, he was hollow. In the centre, his heart hung heavy, dense and cold, hardly beating.

He directed his mind back to the journey ahead, and remembered his mantra for Song. "Look ahead. Keep moving. Don't think." He had just started his first unplanned adventure, not that he thought a planned one would make any sense. A new life, new excitement, new chapter – the final one? – awaited him. Just row on. He took a deep breath, and sighed. "Yippee. . ."

He rowed north-east towards Tsim Sha Tsui, back-tracking slightly. The jetty there should be more spacious and in better condition, he hoped, trying to remember what Kowloon had looked like.

In barely twenty minutes, he had crossed the harbour, heading for the quay. The water turned wild again, worse than before. The vertical seawalls bounced the waves back and forth, compounding their strength with each cycle. The boat squeaked and rocked like a fearful animal.

"Woh, woh, cool. It's okay."

He approached the western steps. Compared with Hong Kong side, the platform there was much higher, the steps thick with algae. He couldn't jump on. He considered swimming the last twenty metres with the boat in tow. It might have been the safest way, but he would be wet and defeated. No, not so soon. He had just started his adventure.

"Come on, fishermen my age used to hop on and off like grasshoppers. Don't be chicken." As he was convincing himself, a big wave slapped the sampan sideways. He gripped the gunwales by reflex, and let one oar slip through its lock.

"Shit!"

Struggling with one oar, it took him another twenty minutes to get hold of one of the timber dolphins that guard the side of a pier against the ships. He tied a rope around it, and half crawled half dived onto the slippery steps, the other line in hand. He saw his nervous fingers in front of his face, clawing desperately for purchase. He ended up soaked anyway. Slowly, he stood up on the landing, trying not to tremble, unsure of what next. The peaceful mood that had accompanied him across Neverland had vanished.

He only noticed the line in his hand when the boat tried to jerk it from him. He tied it to the handrail, and bent down to grab the backpacks. *Don't be stupid, you can hurt your back this way.* A long pole with a rusty hook at the end lay not far away. Sailors had used it to catch ropes thrown from the ferries. Fishing the heavy backpacks up turned out to be more difficult than expected. Everything had turned out to be more difficult than expected so far. One of those days.

Now, the bike.

The pole was useless for that. Gingerly, he lay down on his stomach, prostrating on a slimy step. Wet algae squished against his chest. He felt a sharp pain in his right knee. He extended both arms, trying to reach. Suddenly, the boat attacked – *Slosh! Bang!* – It jumped up at him.

He got up to tighten the rope, taking up as much slack as he could, and got back down again. He grabbed the front wheel with one hand at last, and started lifting. At that instant, a surge of waves rushed in, like besieging bandits. The boat, propelled by the frothing waves, thrust at the bike, knocking it against the side, splashing Huan with oyster-smelling water. The wheel turned, pushing the spokes against the fork, catching his fingers in between.

Ouch!

He let go in time.

The bike crashed down on the prow. Huan did not hear it bang. It hung there for a brief moment, as if in suspension, then tumbled off.

Not much of a splash either.

Huan watched his favourite bike sink, dispersing fish on its descent. It touched the bottom after a few long seconds, then settled as if it had always been there. The bike had reached its final resting place ahead of him.

Having done its job, the boat quieted down, undulating gently, innocently. Huan got up painfully slowly. He towered over the boat, staring at it venomously, eyes narrowed into slits full of hate, then spat at it.

"*Fuck you!*" he hissed, then slung the backpacks onto his shoulders, and turned towards Nathan Road.

DOGS

Huan was pushing a wheelbarrow down Nathan Road. The damp backpacks sat weightily in it.

Once a main thoroughfare of the Tsim Sha Tsui tourist district, lined with shops, shops, and shops, the boulevard had become a long line of ruins. He headed north, keeping to the centre to avoid falling objects just in case. Everything above him, except the sky, was rusty. A neon sign or air-conditioner or window hanging from its last screw might let go any moment.

The area was deserted. Without a fresh water source, surrounded by tumbledown buildings, everyone had left, leaving behind a panoply of dangling signs – relics of their civilisation.

Nude Dancers All Day – FREE DRINKS!
Jesus Saves!
XXXX-Movies
Darling Escort Service (satisfaction guaranteed)
Praise the Lord! (Cantonese Bible Studies 6B, ALL welcome)
Horny Housewife (escalator press 6E)
Believe in God – Get Eternal Life!

This was a final battle ground for God's soldiers and their depraved counterparts. Like antagonists in the last century's classic, *Star Wars*, they fought Armageddon with fluorescent tubes, competing for human souls.

* * *

Not a single soul left.

A dog or two watched guardedly from a distance. A lone cat lurked above. Occasional birds flitted past the strip of deserted sky trapped between skyscrapers. Devoid of urban trash, the birds had migrated to the hills or the seaside. Even the rats had disappeared. Huan had envisioned a world taken over by rats and cockroaches. He was wrong. While there appeared to be more cockroaches, rats had become less common. The sneaky rodents had become dependent on human communities. People hated them but were no good at catching or killing them. Rats were much smarter than man in things that matter, such as self preservation. By hiding in the dark damp corners of the human underworld, they were safe from most natural predators except fat house cats and occasional dogs.

Now that their unwitting protectors and food source had disappeared, all kinds of predators had returned with an appetite. The lazy fat cats had lost weight, pursuing them as if it was a matter of life and death rather than plain old sadistic fun.

* * *

Huan had been looking for a bike all afternoon. When he had no need for one, they were all over. In abandoned shops, balcony apartments, street corners. Now that he desperately needed one, there was none – none that worked anyway. *Where did they sell bikes in this part of town!* He spotted a telephone directory in a collapsed booth. *Ah, great, Yellow Pages. Remember?* These antiquated things still existed in tourist districts for decoration rather than function. But the phone book had been digested beyond legibility by something that found paper tasty.

Finally, a whole row of them. He could see a line of bikes through a crack in the corroded shutter, next to shelves of colourful accessories. The owner evidently did not want to abandon his merchandise. He had locked up the store after his last visit, probably planning to resume business one day soon. Optimist. Miser. Jerk. Must have been a miserable man.

He expected the rusty gate to crumble like potato chips with a few kicks. But no. In spite of the thick oxide, it held up stubbornly. He threw everything he could find at it, and pried with anything he could get a grip on. Still no.

He was tired, frustrated, hungry.

If Song were here, we would break this in no time.

But Song was not there.

He found an old wheelbarrow instead.

Half a day into his self-discovery adventure, he was only three kilometres from Song on the other side of the water. It felt like a whole lifetime away.

*   *   *

He wandered into Kowloon Park, met by the vigilant eyes of a few dogs. They gave the impression of a runt pack in half-hearted formation. They kept a respectful distance, trying to figure out where this intruder stood in their section of the food chain. Inter-species encounters in the post-modern primal world once again hinged upon who eats who. The way they stared would have freaked his son right out. Huan smiled.

Dogs are dogs. Having lived like dogs for centuries, they could still sense who was boss by instinct, an instinct that had been hard-coded into their blood. "If you appear confident and dominant, they'd leave you alone," he had told Song, who would not believe his father on this one. Huan wondered where Song's canine phobia came from.

He spread out his backpacks to dry on a bench, and prepared his bed on another, calmly whistling. They watched. One tested a growl tentatively, then quieted down when no one else joined in. He ate a preserved chicken thigh and tossed them the bone. They fought over it noisily.

"See what I mean? Treat them like dogs, and they'll behave accordingly. Come, Doggie, come!" he snapped his fingers. They raised their ears, and reacted to his friendly gesture with suspicion. They were too young to know humans intimately, and refused to take a chance on Huan.

Dogs are hardcore racists.

Once released from human domestication, big dogs hung out only with big dogs, preferably of a similar breed. Small ones got eaten.

Hong Kong had been pooch haven. Their squeaky yelps could be heard in every apartment block. Some poodles were taken out for walks in prams, to be let out at their favourite lampposts. The owners collected their turds in plastic bags, or wrapped them in newspaper like fish and chips, to avoid getting fined. Some would wipe their canine asses with sanitising tissues before returning them to the prams. When it was coolish outside, the dogs wore coats. When it rained, some had rubber boots on all four feet. Most had forgotten they were dogs, just like their owners had forgotten they were members of Homo sapiens.

Huan was right about dogs still being wary of people, but the bigger breeds reverted to their atavistic instincts more readily than the annoying and inferior members of their own species. It became a dog-eat-dog world the day after the humans.

He witnessed a terrier rushing straight up to a German Shepherd. Its judgement had evidently been fatally warped by generations of la-di-da breeding. *Yap Yap Yap! Stay off my pee you stupid dog! Yap!* The big guy was ominously silent. Then, snap! It happened so fast the next thing Huan saw was the terrier twitching and withering in its captor's mouth, silent for the first and last time.

The German Shepherd regarded Huan, as if out of courtesy. *Not yours? Mind if I eat it?* Sensing no objection, it carried the little one away for private consumption. It had calmed down, limp; probably it had fainted from the sight of its own blood.

Watching hungry dogs consume a human corpse was more troubling. His son was devastated although he agreed that canine burial is not a bad way to get rid of rotten neighbours.

Huan, Song Sung, and John were tracing the stench of a neighbour to an apartment, expecting to give someone an incendiary funeral. As soon as they entered the sizeable flat, they heard dogs gorging and wolfing at the far end. Song turned to run but John signalled him to stay. He grabbed a chopper from the kitchen, and wrapped a big towel around the other forearm. He sidled along the corridor, towards the feasting party. The Songs equipped themselves similarly and inched along behind him.

Here they were: three german-shepherds shoving their muzzles into the bowel of an ex-human. A cloud of flies buzzed impatiently above. The dogs looked up to regard John at the head of the party, but continued to eat, yanking out tissues and organs with powerful jaws.

"Move to one side, back against the wall to give them room." The old soldier ventriloquised the command. Song reacted with funny gurgling noises from his throat. When everyone was in position, John charged with a war cry, brandishing the chopper. They fled, viscid intestines flapping in their blood-soaked mouths, leaving a trail of dark blood.

The flies immediately resumed.

FIRST STOP

Song Huan summons up what seems to be his last calorie with a deep breath, and props his swollen feet up on the window sill to reduce the throbbing.

Under his chair, a mosquito coil incenses the air. The intoxicating scent of pyrethrum powder gives him a sense of power over his lifetime antagonist. He imagines dazed skeeters bumbling in the dark, dreamily crashing into walls, and dying – yes! – leaving behind tiny, despicable smudges of stolen blood.

But the burning incense is also another tick in his countdown to a depleting future. When they have run out, he might not find replenishment out here. If he is not yet dead, he will have to lie back and let them draw blood. They would be the final victors. Humans, in the long run, are no match for mosquitoes in the survival game. The thought disgusts him.

For many years, he was allergic to mosquitoes. They gave him giant bumps the size of fried eggs, sunny-side-up, and he would itch for weeks. They were warm to the touch, and throbbed indistinctly yet persistently. The urge to scratch had been irresistible and maddening; but the harder he scratched, the itchier they got. Any attempt to tamper with their course of torture was punished with sadistic vengeance.

Huan hates mosquitoes, loathes the phantom monsters. Look at them. Sneaky hair's-breadth legs; surreptitious, filmy wings; a filthy stylet finer than most human instruments, and a tummy for blood. How can there be room for anything else? But there is. They can detect the faintest signal of danger, and pull out just in time, taking off at impossibly obscure angles.

Spooky.

Once, when a teenager, he was driven to submerging himself in a bathtub of ice and water after a particularly buggy camping trip. Numb the body down; freeze the bites to death. It worked for a little while. After a painful acclimatisation, the first thing he felt was a flush. Then – *beep, beep, beep. Oh shit!* – one by one, the bites would return, thudding stealthily under the ice like Arctic submarines on manoeuvres, getting into position, ready to attack, to itch.

Fortunately, his allergy had calmed with age. Bug bites no longer irritated. One advantage of getting old – there are very few of them – was losing his itch. He had expected ageing to take away his teeth, appetite, sex-drive, ability to sleep well, agility, and so on. But itchiness? What a pleasant surprise. Nothing itches now. Bug bites don't even swell up. His epidermic nerve fibres must have wilted. His skin has deflated and shrivelled up like an old balloon's. Due to whatever biochemical excuse, his body has stopped reacting to insect bites. It feels numb instead.

Without the natural selection exercised by swatting human hands and insecticides, mosquitoes had become less alert and easier to hit, but much more populous. Nevertheless, he had three dozen coils in his runaway luggage. His number one foe must be checked, for as long as he can manage. It is not so much their exasperating bites that he fears now, but malaria and dengue fever. Although he has come out to die, he does not want it triggered by a skeeter. Anything but the damn skeeters. He cannot let them have the last bite. No way. Furthermore, his instincts are still intact and headstrong, driving him to live on, and on, for as long as possible.

Every day counts.

* * *

Yuen Long. Song Huan had planned this to be the first stopover, at the end of Day One of his new life. He would rest for a day or two, then cross the border into the mainland. From there on, let's see.

It had now taken him nearly a week to get here.

It was a rural town near the border with mainland China. A few tiny villages had for centuries miraculously resisted the encroaching city. They carried on farming in the midst of sprawling junkyards, makeshift recycling factories and clusters of randomly oriented, square and ugly townhouses. For generations, they snubbed progress, disregarded time.

Huan had expected to find a few surviving farmers here. But when he arrived in the late afternoon, limping from tiredness, aching joints, and bubbly blisters, all he could find were dogs, monkeys, herds of impassive cows, and the odd snakes. Not a single human in sight. Finally, it took extinction to break this tenacious community.

Wild hemp-vine was the new dominant species. They were not indigenous. The warming climate had made Hong Kong hospitable to them not long ago. Without the weeding hands of humans, they had gone rampant, strangling the native plants in their advance.

A brook ran through the fallow fields. It probably once served as a two-in-one irrigation channel and open sewer. Huan sat down on a flat rock to rest. He took his shoes off, and soaked his feet in the cool water. Jumping mud carp and Chinese perch squeezed by, but he was too exhausted to take out his net. He had planned to rely in the future on gathering and netting rather than farming. Tomorrow. The fish can wait. There're so many of them.

He looked up, and noticed a bungalow on a knoll a few hundred metres to the left. "Nice spot." Without pumping out the water, this low-lying country would frequently get inundated. A house on the small hill would be quite safe from the floods. "Doesn't matter, anyway. I'll move on in a few days." He was too tired to pay attention to his own half-stupefied soliloquy, not to say judge its sincerity.

"Well, let's check it out." He reached for his socks, and put them back on in slow motion.

*   *   *

Huan stares at his feet, supported by the wooden window frame, projecting outside. They are now thankfully numb rather than painful. He can hardly make out their swollen outline. No moon. No stars. Just a one-dimensional pitch darkness. The tip of the incense glows like a lone star, burning faintly from a depthless distance. He suddenly realises he can bask in darkness, just like in sunshine, but less hot and sticky.

Is he going to settle here for a day or two as planned? Or the rest of his life? Who knows? "I'll find out. Quit planning," he reminds himself. He desperately needs rest, but is too exhausted to sleep.

The hut overlooks the creek and clumps of abandoned vegetable fields. It is nearly free of hemp-vine up here. Perhaps the owner left only recently. Where did he go? There might be some goodies left under the soil. He will check it out tomorrow, before setting up the fish net. "Hey, what's that? Planning again!"

This is a sturdy bungalow, made of big chunks of granite held together by cement mortar. It looks hand-built, probably by some old man and his wife and half a dozen kids, in the last century. The wooden beams and door frame are rotting, but should outlast Huan. The roof is made of traditional clay tiles. The bed is assuringly dry, also wooden, primitively plain. He sprayed it with insecticide, hoping to get rid of any resident bugs.

Right outside is a tidy row of fruit trees. Might have been a mini orchard in the past. A few dead papayas had been taken over by adjacent mangoes and guavas. The mangoes probably taste awful, but might be fine cooked. The gentle slope leading down to the field is lined with lychee and old peach trees.

At nightfall, the frogs come alive, filling the air with deafening croaks. In his next life, which may not be far away, he would like to be a frog, since being a human is no longer an option. He will eat mosquitoes all night. But before then, they would have to become him. Steamed frog is one of his favourite dishes.

He wonders what had become of Sari...

He rocks back on the old wooden chair, wriggling his feet, trying to get some feeling back. A soft breeze passes freely through the empty frame. Two giant blisters hang from his big toes.

"Hey skeeters, suck that," he says to the unseen mosquitoes around him, visualising them taking mistaken bites at the blisters, and chuckles impishly.

His can feel the circulation in his feet again – they hurt.

His heart has been the sole source of an overbearing pain in the past week. One good thing about heartache is, that it masks all other pains. Nothing else matters when the heart is immersed in deep grief. Now that time has eased the emotional twinge, a myriad sorenesses are trickling back, bit by bit, like musicians straggling onto the stage before a concert starts, fiddling with their instruments, waiting for the maestro.

In this symphony of agony, his feet are doing a solo while the rest of him hums a variety of discomforts. His head hurts. That's nothing new; but a dying tooth and slightly infected jaw are highlighting his familiar headache with added complexity. Most of his joints creak.

Fine. Go ahead. Torture me. Time's on my side.

Pain, however loathsome and fierce, can only attenuate with time. The nerves will get used to it, or, even better, snap. The body will learn to ignore it. If the worst comes to the worst, he will die and leave pain behind without a host. *Ha! There you go.* Huan expects death to be an imminent prospect. A few months? A few years? Let's say ten very unlikely years – a blink of the eye.

He is seventy-two, only seventy-two, and not a hypochondriac. He does not think so anyway. He would still be a long way from death according to his original projection made years ago. Seventy-two was a relatively young age. Not too long ago, people in their seventies were working full-time to help postpone the collapse of the pension system, expecting salary reviews and promotions. Otherwise, they might starve.

Huan is largely healthy, except for mildly high blood pressure, and a multitude of muscular and arthritic pains that come and go. Nothing that he cannot get used to. Besides, when he was young, there was no awareness, not to say enjoyment, of a perfect body. It was taken for granted. What a waste. Now, in the odd days that he wakes up painless, he would feel fantastic, and spend the rest of the day enjoying a trouble-free body, appreciating every minute of it. Well, he thinks, that's another good thing about getting old, besides thumbing his nose at mosquito bites with neurological indifference. But in the primitive post-modern world, even minor accidents can be life-threatening...

He nods forward with a start, breaking into a cold sweat. He has nearly dozed off. He takes his feet down and sits up. A fall can mean hell. One can't be too careful at this age, under the circumstances.

Wait!

Something is missing in his dreary inventory of bodily pains. That zinging in his chest, neck and temple has, for the first time in a long while, nearly disappeared. No. Not nearly. It has been totally absent for perhaps a day or two. That would be ironic wouldn't it? It was mainly that exasperating zing that told him, in louder and louder thuds, it's time to leave.

Thud. Thud. Thud.

Time to go Huan.

Start packing.

But it's all quiet now. Now that he's on the dentist's chair, the tooth hurts no more. Maybe he is after all not dying of a burst artery anytime soon, as he had been expecting for months? Maybe it was just a figment of his imagination to start with? Maybe the long march from Tsim Sha Tsui fixed it? Maybe something had burst, temporarily relieving the pressure in his system until...?

Until whatever. Cannot plan now. Just let it be.

He is a meticulous planner. He puts everything on a blueprint, then follows it up step by step in a particular sequence, covering contingencies as much as possible. No surprises; surprises are for the incompetent. This one-way trip is different. He has planned it to be different. He has decided to let go, to follow the flow for once, while he can.

From here on, no more plans. Come what may. He has planned no more plans.

For the first time, Song Huan willingly lets surprises take over, leading him to the end. "Surprise me."

So far, as he has always suspected, the surprises have been unpleasant.

REMINISCENCES

Has it been five days? Six? Not more than seven, he is sure, almost sure.

It's not senility, Song Huan assures himself. It's the stress of walking zombie-like for days, pushing a wobbly wheelbarrow through rubble, giant blisters squishing inside his shoes. He did not have a clear destination in mind or the entire journey fully charted out in advance. He was trying to enjoy the empty feeling of aimlessly following the flow.

During the slow slog north, haphazard daydreams piled upon each other like fallen leaves. One day slipped into the other, mixing a jumbled past with a vacant future. The constant daze was broken occasionally by unpleasant surprises. A twinge or cramp, or the startled escape of hidden animals.

The past few days were the culmination of a journey that began two years ago, soon after he had updated his projection of life expectancy, and concluded that his time was up. Ma had a good laugh. "How can a serious and rational man like you do such a goofy thing?" he asked.

Perhaps Ma was right; but the goofy thing highlighted something sobering. What will his death mean to Sung? And what if he dies slowly, painfully slowly...

He had asked himself that question before, without answering. He was facing Death down at the time, sleeping beside it in the hospital, taking in its sickly breath, challenging it to take him along with Sari, or instead of Sari. "What would happen to Sung if I die?" The thought came, and went; came, and went. He just watched.

Death eventually retreated, taking Sari with it. The question vanished with her. He became numb, not feeling the nauseating worry. He had worried enough about his son living or dying since the minute they left the delivery room. As euphoria calmed, the portentous statistics returned to centre stage. Two out of two in five years. Both died. That's a hundred percent. Would Baby Song live to celebrate his first birthday?

Finally, he did. The statistics were wrong that time.

Humanity continued with its protracted demise, more or less the way Huan had projected. His forecast could not be wrong every time.

Two years ago, he revised his projection manually, updating the parameters. Just something to do. His new estimate showed a starkly reduced life expectancy of just under seventy-one. He was seventy at the time, therefore due to die soon according to his calculation. The question returned, stern and sober this time. "What will happen to Sung when I die? And if I die slowly."

But expectancy is merely a forecast isn't it? A forecast is a forecast. Reality is reality. They don't always agree. Didn't his own son sleep, eat, pooh and smile through the most confidently sinister forecasts?

Ma was right. Projecting his own life-span was goofy; the results meant nothing.

Then the rotten corpse came along, followed by the nightmares. He did not believe in omens but was good at taking a hint, even one from his own subconscious. He started to plan, and prepare Sung for the last time. Then he procrastinated, until recently, when his head started to zing. Not much time left. Let's start packing, old man.

Ironically, the zing that drove him packing is now gone. When did it stop? He hadn't noticed. Can't recall. Oh well, it doesn't matter anymore. What matters now is the end, not the beginning. The end has been mobilised, set in motion. It's no longer a threat that lurks, troubling everyone. It's now his own business, a private matter for Song Huan, the only thing left that has a future.

Looking back, the long-march of life has taken very little time. He can see fragments of the past with uncanny clarity. Just like yesterday, like they say. As he approaches the present, strangely, focus and memories become fuzzy. It is as if he's staring back in time without his reading glasses. The closer it gets, the blurrier it becomes.

When did it start being like this? It must be recent, for he has absolutely no idea.

* * *

One of his earliest memories was a monk sending phone messages under the table. It was his father's funeral.

His parents were diligent accountants with their own small practice in partnership with an old friend. "We sort beans according to size, then count them," was how Mum described her work. When Huan was about to turn six, his father was killed in a traffic accident. He was coming home unusually late one night, after a professional function. According to the police surveillance camera, he spent one minute and seven seconds waiting for the pedestrian signal to turn green, displaying a patience which the officer unthinkingly called *incredible*. There was not a single car on the road all that time.

Huan's father was law-abiding to the extreme. Waiting for the green light was a matter of principle. "If everyone makes their own judgement, it'd be chaotic. We all judge differently, and very poorly when in a hurry," he had told Huan when he was way too young to understand issues of principle.

When the red man turned green and striding, he exercised his right of way, not noticing the 5.2-litre V-10 engine under a red composite body spinning drunkenly around the corner at 120 kph. It must have made a hell of a roar that time of the night, but the traffic signal was indisputably in favour of the pedestrian. Perhaps his father was drunk too but the police said he showed no outward sign of intoxication in the video. He stood attentively, looking straight ahead all that time.

He died on the spot – a spot less than two hundred metres from home. Mother was informed four hours later.

That was Huan's first exposure to death.

He was not quite old enough yet to grasp its tragic nature. The only thing he remembered years later was the funeral. It was a Daoist ceremony. As the only son, he played a central role in sombre costume. It was like being a swordsman in a Cantonese opera; but he was aware enough to know nothing was supposed to be amusing that day.

Loud and clanky music dominated by a blaring deeda trumpet overwhelmed the mournful occasion; perhaps that was the intention. Mercenary monks, beating wooden fishes, gongs and drums, chanted in mesmerising unison. From a child's vantage point, he saw a dextrous monk sending phone messages under the table with his free hand. Huan was fascinated by telephones at the time.

The eclectic monks could also do Buddhist ceremonies, Christian memorials (for a surcharge), and Islamic Janazah (for a yet higher surcharge). It was all up to the clients. To customers without a preference, such as the Songs, they would recommend Daoist or Buddhist; rites they knew best. Since Buddha and Laozi had no taste for pomp and circumstance, the authenticity of their elaborate new-age show could never be challenged. They danced and swung a sword to break the Gate of Hell and scattered rice to bribe the equine and bovine guards.

Mum told him Dad had gone to a faraway land. He was not convinced even then, but nodded to show understanding. In the following year, Mum sold the family's shares to her and her late husband's partner, and joined a large accounting firm as junior director. "Life's more stable that way," she said, mainly to herself. He wondered what a more stable life would be like.

As it turned out, losing his father had very little impact on his daily life. Their maid Rose continued to take care of his needs. Mum continued to be mum when not working. In addition, she encompassed whatever paternal attributes Dad might or might not have had. His parents were similar – nearly identical – in each and every way. The redundancy only became obvious after one had been accidentally removed. The family became more efficient. His parents had been merged, eating and spending as one, in perfect harmony.

Huan grew up in this steady and harmonious environment.

* * *

Song Huan was pragmatic and useful by nature, full of *nous*, and brought up to be even more so. Instead of a mind, he proudly proclaimed that a processor had developed between his ears. It took seventy years and a dramatic change in circumstances to show him there might be something else hidden in the folds, which he had avoided exploring.

After secondary school, he studied engineering in Canada. He returned to Hong Kong in 2035 and joined a Finnish company as trainee. He was a good worker. Young and steady, enjoying challenging tasks, indifferent to tedious ones. He never asked irrelevant questions. He was aiming to be an engineer, a specialist, and happy to leave the rest to others. The company loved him.

Five years later, he was promoted to senior engineer. During a year-long secondment to the Shanghai office, he met Sari.

"God I forgot everything about women all these years!" he told himself.

Sure, sure. But what he told himself was not the whole truth.

He had not forgotten everything about women all these years, though romance had indeed been a marginal affair. He was more absorbed in building a career with nuts and bolts and electrodes. A few girls showed interest. He was a handsome dude with a sound education, good job and concrete career plan. But he found most Hong Kong girls – the ones attracted to him anyway – giggly. Giggles confused him. He did not know how to read them, not to say react with charm.

"Why do girls giggle?" he asked a buddy over a beer, sharing his confusion.

"Cos it's cute, I think," suggested his taciturn friend, a thoughtful young man with deeply furrowed brows that tightened as he gave the subject thought.

"I took Lucy out for Japanese last night. I told her I liked sushi more than sashimi when we looked at the menu, and she giggled."

"Hmm..." The furrow gaped like a toothless mouth.

"It was a comment, an empty remark, a bland statement to fill an odd moment. Not meant to be funny."

"It wasn't."

"That's right. It wasn't meant to be. So I told her, maybe too bluntly, that it wasn't meant to be funny."

"What'd she say?"

"She giggled at a higher pitch. This time, unstoppable!"

"Hmm..." The furrow withdrew so tightly it closed up. "Maybe she found you funny, not what you said."

"Know what? I think that's possible. They all do."

They were his first dates. Typically, after twenty minutes of awkward conversation, he would be calculating, assessing if she would make a good partner for life. Would she be sensible and understanding while he paved his career path brick by brick? Would she be supportive at times of crisis? There was supposedly a fertility crisis out there. Did she look fecund with those tiny hips? Would she be a loving mother? Grandmother? Would she be luscious in bed, for the next forty years? He would be half a century ahead before they finished aperitif. All the irrelevant thoughts he smothered at work would come out in social situations, and flare.

None of them came close to passing his objective evaluation. These girls were all too shallow, too deep, too loud, too timid, too serious, too easy, too fat, too thin, too smart, too dumb, too tall, too short, too this, or too that.

Too much hassle. Too much commitment. Not worth it.

Huan was a serious young man, an earnest techie. The kind of women attracted to him were from similar stock and in their early twenties, the kind he did not like. They were looking for a textbook husband to show off to old school friends, and to share a lifetime mortgage. Time was running out so let's get on with the check-list. Degree? Professional membership? What do you do at work? Do you have any dream of promotion? You've started saving for an apartment already? How commendable! "What? In Tung Chung?" One girl could not hide her distaste. She told him, jokingly of course, *ha ha*, she fancied bank managers because of preferential mortgage rates. Or expatriates who were provided with quarters in Island South or the Peak. Well, not Tung Chung anyway.

No wonder Hong Kong was a city of bachelors and old maids. Social researchers had studied the phenomenon. Some said the price of real estate was responsible. It had made young people desperate. Having one's own property had become *the* social selection force. Others said those who grew up in a virtual environment of video games were uncomfortable with real humans. Yet others said it had been like that since the invention of free love. In any event, dating had apparently become a lost art among urban professionals.

ONE NIGHT STAND

Memory has a mischievous mind of its own.

Important information sternly committed to memory is inexplicably lost when urgently needed. On the other hand, reckless moments that are best forgotten might stick for life, secretly embarrassing.

Song Huan analysed everything. He believed there was a reason for everything, but could not find one to explain his unremitting recollection of a one-night stand half a century ago. He could smell her sour skin and cigarette breath. Perhaps the experience was so unlike him that it had left a lasting impression. But when planning his runaway, other possibilities emerged. Strange possibilities, rather disturbing thoughts, especially for an old man.

Could the aberrant derailment from his disciplined life be a rare glimpse of his other side, a side that had been muffled all his life? Did that mean the way he had been for seventy years was just as equally unlike him? Maybe his spontaneous affair released something in him, and inadvertently prepared him for Sari? But that must be stretching things too far. Sari was a love from past lives, he was sure. How else could it click just like that for both? And Sari was beautiful. She, whatever her name was, was ugly. God, was she ever. But irrepressibly memorable.

* * *

He was heading home after a party at a colleague's. A beautiful place that would have cost a successful engineer half a century of salary before tax, food, transportation and shelter. It was his parents' house on Island South. There was a lavish barbecue table and two competing karaoke machines. He had planned to leave early but, after a few beers, ended up being one of the last to leave.

When his taxi passed through the old Suzie Wong district of Wan Chai, he made an impulsive stop at a late-night watering hole. He relished these occasional indulgences, watching weirdoes doing their normal things. Nothing too adventurous, just a taste of an alien atmosphere, and to savour the feeling of not being himself, brewed by a few drinks in the bloodstream. He would suspend his responsible normal self for a few hours, for as long as he knew he was not really overstepping any mark.

The subdued attention of other customers – people who ate breakfast in the evening – gave him secret satisfaction. He was a conspicuous geek in a smoky joint, like someone with a full frontal dragon tattoo in the Royal Golf and Country Club's change room. Everyone wanted to stare, but pretended not to.

Most of them smoked. No one in their right mind there would observe smoking or underage drinking regulations; and no government inspectors in their right mind would visit during these hours. One world closed at five; another one took over.

The regulars chatted insouciantly, competing to be more cool.

Hey, you know, I don't give a fucking shit.

Fuck, no! Me neither.

Ha, ha, ha. No shit, man!

Every now and then, they would throw a nonchalant sideways glance at Huan, betraying suppressed curiosity.

Who's that fucking geek there? What's he doing here?

A corpulent figure smelling like mosquito repellent approached.

Hello Darling! Her bubbly voice had a background crackle, like static.

Hi...

Bright red lips, heavily waxed, glinted psychedelically in the dim light. They parted lazily, all kissing muscles at ease. A slim cigarette dangled jazzily from the bottom lip by adhesion. She let out an unrestrained laugh, propelled from the diaphragm, or lower. She did not giggle. Phlegm bubbles burst in her throat when she laughed. About what, though? Did she just sit down and laugh? The hearty guffaw was no less puzzling than girlie giggles to Huan, just more forceful.

Her deep and thunderous voice rumbled over the background music as if it had a private niche in the frequency band. The pendulous fag threw off smoke, synchronised with her speech like pulses on an oscilloscope. Huan missed most of what she said; he was thinking about her laugh. Behind the vibration was a certain disregard, a contemptuous defiance of the next arriving moment which fate had lined up. Come on darling, just come along.

Huan felt small and anal. Anal? Now he felt insulted by himself, although he was for the moment not supposed to be himself. He was all of a sudden self-conscious of being uptight and pretentious among a bunch of low-lifers. This can't be true! But nothing seemed true right then.

"What're you laughing at?" He screamed through the music. "You find me ridiculous?"

She laughed so hard she had tears in her eyes, dissolving the lashes. He ordered drinks for both. His irritation had ebbed. In its place was adoration for the enormous presence and palpable confidence of this stranger. She filled the moment, completely. So free of... everything!

Another few drinks later, she had become oddly seductive.

There she went again – talking and laughing simultaneously as if she had parallel voice-boxes. "Aaah, ha, ha, ha! Don't worry. Most people are like that. Don't feel like that about yourself darling. Aaah, ha, ha! Oh, you're so sweet darling; what's your name?" Her laugh triggered a micro-landslide on her heavily powdered face.

"Hey it wasn't meant to be funny! What the fuck are you laughing about!" He was offended by her reaction to his confidences although he could not remember what he had just told her.

Another blast of penetrating and fearless laughter arrived at his face like pressure wave. Residual smoke escaped from her smouldering mouth, accompanied by a sour odour sweetened by volatile lipstick. It paused for a brief second, then blended into the anoxic ambience. Even her smoke rings were unfettered. They drifted off, just like that. Supernova. No waffling. No calculations or sentimental dithering.

"Another beer?"

"Of course. Two more!"

Huan's vision shifted between focal planes like a wobbly time machine. She looked like a mosquito coil as well as smelling like one, but strangely sexy in a bizarre way.

"Could I have one of your cigarettes please?"

"Please?! " She laughed her head off again. "Yes please!"

"Hey, what's so funny? Tell me, really. Darling." He leaned closer, and thought he saw powder sloughing off her face.

He screamed, "Avalanche!" and broke into a guffaw, an unrestrained roar. She joined in at full force.

She had made him laugh just like her, no speed bumps, from deep within, for no reason. Is this freedom? So dumb. But he was in the company of a happy and sweaty person – a real person who was afraid of nothing, expecting nothing. She fucked tomorrow precociously, rather than planning for it. Funny. He laughed, and couldn't stop.

He had an idea. He wanted to bury his face in her immense cleavage.

* * *

He woke up smelling like an empty beer barrel someone had vomited into.

Darling was snoring next to him, one arm over his head, covering his crown with her armpit. Her other arm rested on his thigh. They were facing each other. They might have passed out in the middle of an euphoric embrace. Her right breast, slippery with sweat, pressed against his face. Her weary nipple and bumpy areola appeared unreal from up close. It reminded him of ferrous atoms under an electronic microscope. Branching out from the areolate cluster was a network of purplish and faintly bulgy veins. Half of them disappeared down the mammalian gorge into which he had buried his face.

Her skin had a unique funk. Sour. Huan involuntarily gave it another intrigued sniff, not expecting the odour to stick in his memory for life.

Late morning light charged into the room through bare windows. Her sizeable breasts threw dark shadows over her chest. At the bottom end of her cleavage, a birthmark the size of a pancake dribbled towards the stomach. It looked like Velcro with bristles. Huan suppressed the urge to touch. As she laboured subconsciously to force air into tar-coated lungs, the pelt of Velcro heaved like oil spill, shifting rhythmically.

His head hurt badly. He felt sick.

Some details trickled back.

Oh dear. Oh fuck. Oh no.

He got up quietly, went to the toilet to empty his bladder, put on his clothes and tiptoed to the front door.

"Thanks darling. You were lovely," she said without opening her eyes, then pulled a pillow over her head.

"Thanks. See you," Huan mumbled with one hand on the handle, then got out at a canter. He had not brushed his teeth.

Mum had left a dozen messages on his phone. He was still living with her. Rents in the city were out of reach for a young engineer. He sent her a reply instead of calling. "Stayed at friend's last night. Forgot to call. Sorry. Don't worry," then turned it off again. He bought a cheap T-shirt, then went for a long shower and massage at a nearby spa, then a medical check-up.

He did not imagine a one-night stand could be so unsettling. It left a bad taste in the mouth, then compunction for having that bad taste. "I'm disgusted because she's fat and ugly. Not fair," he confessed to himself. He tried pretending that an internal moral code or issue of principle had been violated, hence the regret, but failed.

What's-her-name was not an alcoholic illusion. She was real, vivid, too goddamn real. She walked up and read him as if he had been dissected and laid open with surgical pins. Then she laughed. So humiliating. Ugh! More than humiliation. Something in him had changed, something had become fundamentally different, but he could not put his finger on it.

SONG

The one-night stand left Song Huan with an emotional clarity that seemed disoriented.

He did his damnedest to forget – just one of those drunken escapades at his age. These things happened. But the close-up image of her breast would pop up, staring him blank in the face whenever his mind drifted off, even during work meetings. He was infuriated by how much he thought of her. Giggling girls became more insufferable, now that he had seen a powerful alternative which was not really an alternative. He impetuously devoted himself to bachelorhood.

He did not confuse bachelorhood with celibacy. To balance yin and yang, he would pay occasional visits to girlie bars. Just a pragmatic compromise, he was aware, as long as it's done with clinical discipline, restraint, and sanitation. He used their service responsibly like the emergency in hospitals. To buddies with imminent marriage plans, he would defensively jest with borrowed wit. "Why keep a cow if all you want is a glass of milk every now and then?" Half meaning it; half sour grapes.

"I don't think I have passion. Don't think I want to experience it. Passion is for poets," he told his laconic buddy.

"You've got the genes of two accountants in you."

"What's that supposed to mean?"

"Hmm..."

The arrangement worked. He was content, if not exactly happy, devoted to work, buying affordably packaged comfort from womankind whenever he felt his yin and yang losing equilibrium. Everything was under control. Neat, tidy, predictable.

Until he met Sari in Shanghai.

Sari did not giggle. Finns never did. When she smiled or laughed, it would be for reasons that Huan could understand. Suddenly, he was tormented by passion. Song Huan the romance paraplegic got up and walked, as if commanded by Christ. More, he got up and flew. He seized every opportunity to go to Finland for training or a meeting. He started to write love letters, romantic e-mails, even a poem so overrun by passion it made no sense, and forgot to rhyme.

But Sari loved it.

* * *

Song Huan did not need love, and fell madly in love.

Then he did not want kids. The Fertility Crisis suited him just fine. Sari wanted a baby or two. *Or two!* Yes, a girl, followed by a boy. "Wouldn't that be perfect?" Huan did not bother to disagree. "Sure," he said, knowing the chance of pregnancy to be near zero. He believed in statistics. "In the long run, nobody escapes the dictatorial grip of statistics; not the average guy anyway," he had said. "People want to know what God's like, how he handles things? Forget the Bible. Study stats."

Statistics could be sardonic like God though. Against all odds, Sari was pregnant. A new life was being expected in a big way. To his surprise, pregnancy was not all about life. Sari became compulsively morbid, preoccupied with death. Death was not Huan's favourite topic but Sari's new obsession got him thinking, analysing. What comes after life? He attempted a few conjectures to satisfy his wife.

But they never discussed their most obvious death concern; the death of their baby.

In Hong Kong, the only two births in the previous three years ended in massive funerals. Sari did not raise this with Huan, who did not raise it with her. He pretended not to notice her researching this eerie phenomenon. Privately, he could not help expecting their baby to be stillborn, or to die soon after birth. He tried positive thinking but it felt like insulting his own intelligence. He mentally prepared himself for the likely outcome, and secretly rehearsed staying cool, composed and supportive when that happened – no! no! no! – if and when that happened.

Song turned out to be a healthy little thing. He was born alive, right into a delivery-room party with champagne and hope, plenty of hope, effusive hope, overflowing.

Song started his lifelong job to live on.

Day one, lived. Day two, lived. Day three...

Soon, he outlived the attention span of the journalists camping outside their home, awaiting patiently for Song Sung to die, competing to be the first to report it. – Exclusive! – Day by day, Song gained strength, adding a miraculous sense of life to Sari and Huan's existence. They kept him in their room until he turned two. In the beginning, they got up every half hour to check his breath with a small mirror – a trick the doctor casually suggested would show whether their son was still "alive and breathing", as if the two could happen independently.

"Okay?" one of them would whisper, heart pounding.

A smile from an exhausted face. A nod that jiggled wonton-size bags under the eyes.

After six weeks, night feeding stopped. Huan started to sleep for hours in one stretch. Sari had grown accustomed to not sleeping at all. Motherhood could indeed make a woman remarkably irregular.

Huan wished that Sung were ugly, nasty and colicky so that when he died, it would hurt less. Instead, he was wonderful and adorable, a perfect baby. "When he dies, our hearts will burst." He wanted to say this to his wife, but did not. Anxiety mounted as Song's first birthday approached. Every morning, Huan had to summon up his courage before opening his eyes to scan the room first for Sari (to make sure she was not sitting on the floor at one corner, sobbing noiselessly), then his son. Is he breathing? What's his colour? Not blue please...

He was given one year's paternity leave. It was extended to two with the support of the government. They were two tense and enjoyable years which passed slowly.

*   *   *

Miracle! Song Sung turned one! This or something similar was the headline of the day.

There was overt excitement, genuine jubilation, with an undertone of bathos that verged on disappointment. The suspense was over. Heck, nothing happened. Journalists did not make a living reporting "everything okay as usual." At long last, they admitted openly, though indirectly, that they had been waiting for Baby Song to die. Not that anyone really wished him harm. That would be very far from the truth. They all adored him. Had Song died, the world would have wept for days and weeks, and held candlelit-vigil anniversaries. But the subconscious anticipation of a social tragedy – a tragedy that belonged to society, not just the Songs – was equally compelling and irresistible. People shed tears for Romeo and Juliet. But if the lovers did not commit suicide, and walked off-stage to live happily ever after instead, the audience would be disappointed. Bathos. Boo.

Sari was euphoric, proud, and triumphant for the family. Yes! They had prevailed.

Huan was euphoric, relieved, and secretly ashamed. While Sari maintained a single-minded faith in Song's viability every second of the past year, he had cowardly crouched over the other side – dark and negative. Was he just being faithful to probability? Was he preserving himself, preparing for the worst? A bit of both? He did not wish to think further. Let it pass. It no longer mattered. For once, he did not analyse.

Logic told Huan his son's anniversary was an entirely arbitrary milestone; but was nonetheless relieved that the psychological threshold had been crossed. His son had become viable, endorsed by statistics. Huan had had enough of death worries by then. Death! What an unexpected acquaintance he had made during this lively period. It could now come out in the open.

He once regarded death as an abstract threat best left unspoken. Then he gave it some perfunctory thought to please Sari, and came up with nothing. Life and death remained utterly inexplicable. The only conclusion he drew was that once life has happened, death is inevitable.

Why fret over something inevitable? Accepting the inevitable calmed him. Realising there was no escape allowed him to plan and pace life more sensibly. Death gives life dimension, makes it complete, with a beginning and an end. Life – the flurry of activities in between – is a bit like a school exam. To do well, he must note how much time has been given to tackle how many problems, and pace himself accordingly.

So he looked at how much time had been given. He assumed he would live till ninety like the average male, and die the day before his birthday in 2102. What should he do in the interim? And in what sequence? He started to lay things out on a spreadsheet, adapting a template designed for construction programmes.

When he scrolled into the future, it dawned on him how different the world would become. On a spreadsheet, it became starkly obvious that Song would have to survive in a dramatically different world. There had been a mind-boggling denial of what the future held. Everyone still pretended it would be business as usual, forever.

For the sake of the next generation – Song specifically – Huan realised they must stop pretending. The world needed proper shutting down, decommissioning, before too late.

PLAGUE

Ring around the roses
A pocketful of posies
Ashes, ashes
We all fall down... .

Bugs in your tummy
Eating you up yummy
Pus here, pus there
We all get drowned... .

"I like the song Mama."
"I knew you would."
"What does it say Mama?"
"Just people dying Sweetie."
"Why do they die?"
"Germs eat them."
"But germs are so tiny, and we're so big!"
"They nibble until we're soft like jelly, then drink us drop by drop. And they are many!"
"Will they eat us?"
"Probably not."
"Are they full?"
"Maybe. Maybe we no longer taste good."
"Maybe we're dead!"
"We're not dead. No! No! We're not dead! No! Never! Don't ever, ever, ever, say stuff like that!"
"Sorry, Mama."
"It's okay Sweetie. Sorry I yelled at you, Sweetie. Come, give Mama a hug."

* * *

It happened. It had always happened. They said, on average, three times per century.

That was in the past. Since the twenty-first century, epidemics and pandemics had been striking once or twice every decade, depending on how it was defined, and whether the press was preoccupied with other calamities. Some plagues were alarming, but with so few deaths in the end it mortified those who sounded the alarm. Then, when all seemed well and everyone grew weary of neurotic warnings, a deadly one would hit mercilessly out of the blue.

It was like the viruses had a war plan.

"Now, you take H1N6 to create a panic in Brazil and Japan, confuse them with the unlikely geographic link; make it sensational, but take it easy on lives. Then you birds distract them with an outbreak of H5N1 in the wild. Make it visible okay? I want hundreds of thousands of carcasses piled up for the photo session, maybe somewhere in Alaska. Still, don't bother with the humans yet; tire them out, keeping their guard up continuously.

"You Pigs – *hey wake up!* – work on a nasty mutation in the meantime, better be good this time. Sneak in through Eastern Europe, Central America and Western China simultaneously. Make sure you go for the body count before they develop a vaccine. Questions?"

"Nope."

"Okay. Let's go bugs. Good luck!"

*   *   *

Some were deadly, but localised.

The Simian-flu pandemic of 2020 killed thirty million in nine months, mostly in Africa. The rest of the world watched dumbfounded, shivering and shrieking. They beefed up the quarantine mechanism. International relief efforts were confounded by the cost of vaccines. Some accused the manufacturers of rip-off margins. Others explained they were a business, not charity.

The *International Community* exchanged impassioned pleas and indignant accusations, urging each other to do something. Before a philosophical consensus on international justice was reached, the virus had retreated, disappeared, probably never to return again before putting on a new coat of genetic make-up.

Another patented drug for the archive. *See? See? We only have a small window of opportunity to recover research investments, not to say making a profit.*

Other plagues affected practically every country with a paltry death toll. The H5N8 of 2033, for example, killed only twenty thousand. Just a dozen or so per country after China contributed eight thousand. It came and went like a hurricane, posturing to wipe out humanity according to prime time news in over one hundred countries.

Then there were the economic consequences.

The deadly Simian-flu was relatively negligible in economic terms. Even the price of precious metals – a key concern for many – remained stable during that tragic year for Africa. Thanks to resolute management policies, strong governments and a hungry populace, most mines stayed open. Once over, people soon referred to it as endemic, inching it out of collective memory. It was just another internal turmoil of Africa's.

The H5N8 thirteen years later was a different story. It raged for five months, with casualties hardly worth mentioning. But air traffic was down by sixty-eight percent, retail down by twenty-two, restaurants and entertainment a staggering eighty percent down. Global GDP slipped fifteen percent, enough to send the world tumbling down another recession. It was devastating for the global economy, a pandemic for sure.

The ranking of plagues depended on priority and politics. Nonetheless, people generally agreed why epidemics had become more fierce and frequent. Climate change, high density livestock husbandry, population density, frequent international travelling, et cetera, et cetera. Same old reasons. These things would not change, and no one could change them.

Conspiracy theorists offered more exciting reasons. Laboratories all over the planet were working round the clock, playing with the genes of bacteria and viruses. They worked overtime to tinker with the deadly unknown under microscopes, cutting and splicing the DNA and RNA of microbial Frankensteins, wondering what might happen to the Company's stock price if this hemagglutinin is surgically mated with that neuraminidase.

One stupid mistake, one inadvertent lapse in safety procedure, one leak for whatever reason, theft.... Terrible thoughts.

* * *

To Song Huan, only one plague mattered. The one of 2066. On the league table, it was neither here nor there – mediocre. Deaths: about forty thousand. Sad, medium sad. Duration: twenty-two weeks. So, so. Affected countries: Nine.

Economic impact: fifty billion DEY (the International Currency Unit introduced in 2032, initially at one to three thousand US Dollars). Not insignificant, but affordable.

A few places were hit harder than others. Hong Kong was one of them, with a final body count of 11,753. Had it been 11,752, Huan wondered, would Sari have been spared by a one-in-eleven-thousand-seven-hundred-fifty-three chance?

Possibly. But it was 11,753, not 11,752.

Swine-flu, they said. How could that be? Pigs were practically extinct in Hong Kong outside frozen meat counters. Huan was neither a conspiracy theorist nor one who would question the professional findings of virologists. Nonetheless, he was puzzled.

So, the pigs killed Sari, or, rather, the mutant of a virus that killed pigs killed Sari. The Swine Flu first invaded Thailand, then mainland China, followed by Canada and a few European countries before making a U-turn to catch Hong Kong by surprise. Within twenty-one days of first occurrence, Hong Kong was at the top of the score board, with the highest number of deaths.

Sari did not make breakfast for her family that day, as was her habit. "Breakfast's the most important meal," she often said. "Nothing's more important than eating together first thing every morning." She felt lazy that day, with a sore throat. Father and son made toast, oatmeal, and soft-boiled eggs themselves. She had an orange, a third of one, then went back to bed. "Mum never goes back to bed after breakfast," Song noted. "Yes she does sometimes." Huan said, unsure. She had been home during most of the past week, it could not possibly be the Pig Flu, he figured.

By the evening, she was in hospital. Ten days later, she was dead.

Huan spent her last three days by her side, watching her slipping away, giving up. The only thing she could utter was, "Go, go, don't let Sung come." Sung did pay a brief visit, and Huan did not leave. Each visit was followed by a heavily drugged quarantine.

He knew the bugs might take him too; but the prospect felt like a relief at the time. The alternative of being left behind was more stressful.

For three days, he sat next to Sari, nodding off continuously. He had to wear a mask, looking like a pig himself. Sari sank deeper into delirium in spite of increasingly strong and experimental drugs. Huan held her hand during the final hours, stroking her hair, not knowing what else to do. The transition was unstoppable. Anyone could see that.

He waited for her to die, thinking nothing, hoping nothing, saying nothing. The room stank of disinfectants and drugs, mixed with urine and faeces. If odour can pass through the mask, why can't the bugs? he wondered. Maybe that was why the doctors and nurses had bigger masks. They came and went, changing the drips, trying new drugs, changing diapers, measuring temperature, imperceptibly shaking their heads.

Only the medics' activities marked the passage of time. Otherwise, life had come to a standstill.

Suddenly, she opened her eyes, as if remembering something that she had meant to tell Huan. Then blink! everything was extinguished.

Ten interminable days consolidated into half a blink, a one-way blink that did not light up again.

Huan sat there, holding her hand, gazing glassily at her pale and peaceful face. He tried to grasp this farewell moment. When exactly did it happen? He closed his eyes to conjure snapshots of their lives together. Maybe Sari could take them with her, wherever she was going. But he was clamped by a total blankness. Not a single moment of their years together would come to mind.

Everything was lost.

Sari, the only person, the only thing he had ever loved with unreserved passion, was dead.

The hospital staff would normally have pulled him away but they themselves were dazed by death and fatigue. They had become very understanding, readily willing to ignore rules and protocols, but not sentimental. They were numbed by bereavement.

"She's gone, Mr Song," a nurse said. Huan did not hear.

"She's gone, Mr Song. Take care of yourself." Was it the same nurse?

Finally, he let go of her icy hand, and drew a deep breath through the mask. Has it been half an hour? Two? More?

"Would you like the week-long quarantine? Or the twenty-four-hour discharge, Mr Song?"

"The quick one, please."

"You know the additional medication, side effects and charges, I suppose?"

Huan nodded. Sari's face appeared soft, but her lips had parted slightly, making her look dead now.

"Just take a rest in the quarantine quarter. My colleagues will guide you through the discharge as well as ash handling and delivery," the nurse said, yanking at tubes, expertly unplugging Sari from the system. Now that Sari was a cadaver, she could do it more efficiently, like taking down laundry from the line. Song Huan cringed.

Cremation would be handled directly by the hospital. The ashes would be sent to the family later for funeral.

The nurse had run out of commiserative words. Thirty-two medical workers had died. The living ones had permanently quarantined themselves in the hospitals, staying away from their families. They simply could not afford emotional support for the relatives of equally unfortunate patients.

Everyone was following their destiny like a zombie.

Huan removed his mask and kissed Sari on the forehead. He intended to kiss her on the lips like he always did, but could not. Not because he was afraid of the bugs. They did not seem to like him anyway. But he felt he could not kiss a dead person in the mouth no matter how much he loved her. A few hours ago, he could. Even one minute before she died, he could; but no longer. It all changed from one minute to the next, he realised, but did not bother to analyse why.

SEVEN

BIRTHDAY PARTY

Whenever it rains, the sky opens right up. Drizzles are rare these days.

Rhea does not mind a downpour. It is the best fix for a muggy day. Paradoxically, a big storm gets things properly wet, and flushes out the lugubrious moisture.

She closes the piano lid. It lies there like a coffin, black and shiny, with a few copper nails. "That's it," she says, giving it a gentle tap, then gets up.

She takes out a brand new diary, and starts writing. After a few words, she pauses to marvel at the handwriting. Hand written words are so quaint.

Entry One: 13 June 2090: Big rain.

This is my first diary. I rarely wrote in the old days. Nobody did. Everyone used keyboards. It feels weird to see my hand twirling out words, like a toddler watching his own first steps.

Don't think Song will come in this torrent. Thunder is pealing next to me, not the sky. I can barely start counting after a blinding flash. The lightning rods have mostly rusted away, but this is a low-rise surrounded by tall trees and apartments. I hope I'm well protected if nature actually works this way.

I just played the piano for the last time. Tchaikovsky's Number One. I thought it might go well with the storm, but it did not. I know I have lost whatever I had for music. Maybe I never had it. I feel strangely relieved, like having signed the papers for an overdue divorce. Could this be just another symptom of pregnancy? How many symptoms am I suppose to have?

I've played the piano all my life without a purpose. They all said I was a natural, probably because of Gong Gong. But whether I was truly gifted or not, I never bothered to find out. I had no reason to.

The job of music was to kill time. Looking back, it seems we hated time, as if we had too much of it. We were always looking for expensive ways to "kill" it. Shopping; travelling; Geneva; ballet; pottery; movies; parties; internet; piano.... Everything was to *kill* time. Yet we were afraid of dying.

Time is now precious. I've been wishing to do something different, something more meaningful; that would leave a trail, a signpost for the future. For my baby.

A journal like this is perhaps a start.

Okay...

We had a birthday dinner, the day before yesterday, just us two. At first I expected Ma and John too. It was after all John who reminded us of Song's birthday. We all depend on his calendar for festivals and anniversaries. But the birthday boy preferred a small party, as if it was possible to have a big one. It was his birthday, so.

He made beggar chicken. The best. The aroma must have reached Guji's on the other side of the ravine. After having ignored each other all these years, I wonder if I should renew attempt to make contact. Maybe I can bribe her into being friendly with a chicken. It'd be so nice to have a neighbourhood girlfriend.

I made Salade Niçoise à la Stone-Age topped with chicken breast. He arrived in good mood and it got better after a bottle of Gong Gong's Chateau d'Yquem 2062. He was chatty and animated, talking about reviving his father's windmill project, so that we can have some electricity one day. That was the second time he has mentioned it lately. I wonder if he was serious.

We talked about Ma and Sashti. We often do. There's no one else to gossip about. We are forever puzzled why these soul mates who love each other live miles apart. Love is strange... like ours I suppose.

He kept asking if I was okay, which vexed me a little. I know I look tired these days. Of course I do. I wanted to use the opportunity to tell him but didn't. He would think me crazy, I know. I should wait till my tummy is 100% obvious. Then I'll just say, "Yes, I'm tired. Very tired," when he asks again.

Then we made love. It was beautiful, but felt a bit strange towards the end. I think we tried too hard. I enjoyed him more when we simply held each other afterwards, me pressing my ear against his chest, listening to his heart.

His mood swung from one extreme to the other in the morning. He woke up cheerful, then turned gloomy without reason, as if possessed. I pumped his blood-sugar up with three eggs and a stack of potato pancakes but it didn't work. He was beyond first-aid.

Good thing men don't menstruate. They would be more impossible if they did.

* * *

"What are you doing Mama?"

"Grinding the chopper Sweetie."

"Why?"

"To defend ourselves."

"What's 'defend'?"

"To stop people making us into what we don't want to be."

"Who's doing that?"

"Them. They came back."

"They scare me, Mama."

"That's right. They scared you and Tommy away twice. Enough is enough."

"Don't worry, Mama. We'll always come back."

"Always?"

"Ya."

"Promise?"

"Pinky promise! How do you defend us with that, Mama?"

"If they come again, I'll chop them up! up! up!"

"Can I chop too?"

"No, not for kids."

"Please! Mama! Just once."

"No. Only I can chop."

"Why are they so bad?"

"Because they don't know what they're doing, but think they do."

WHAT IS LOVE

From now on, Rhea nods determinedly to herself, she will write everything down, everyday. After the first few entries, she's become haphazard with her diary, and soon lost track of the date. She should ask John to make her a calendar, too. He would be delighted, she knows.

She must leave her footprints in time, make herself visible to the future. Music comes and goes, leaving no trace. Writing is different. Perhaps it kills time too, but preserves it at the same time. Her journal is a time-morgue. Moments frozen on paper can be retrieved later, savoured in reminiscence. What's done is done. But what's written on the spur of a moment can be thoughtfully reviewed later. Life on paper is given a second chance, to become sensible, like history books. We always write for the future, for their consumption. The future needs to know where it came from.

She rereads what she has written so far. Just a few pages, but enough to offer a glimpse of her own mind as if someone else's. It seems at once narcissistic and voyeuristic, also reflective and fulfilling. Her life preserved in literary formaldehyde.

She leaves the diary on top of the piano, hoping that he might get curious...

Entry Nine: 27 June 2090: Nice day.

I've been given a five-year calendar by John. What a wonderful man. I must remember to check everyday off – EVERYDAY – from now on.

I estimate that I'm due end of December. Sagittarius?

We had a good (lively anyway) chat about love today. Love is not something we normally talk about. Musicians talk music.

Sportsmen talk sports. Fishermen talk fish. But lovers shouldn't talk love unless it's other people's. It's too risky to examine the mystery. Does that mean we're no longer lovers? I hope not.

I was the one who brought up the subject, but I did not intend to turn it into a philosophical debate, dissecting love like a mental disorder.

I asked, a bit out of the blue I admit, whether he loved me. Of course baby, he said. (If I heard others calling their spouse, *baby*, I'd puke. Pet names may not be love, but are only tolerable because of it. I can't wait till he calls me Mum.) Anyway, I asked if he knew what love is. He replied "No," curt and categorical. I said, annoyed, "So you love me without knowing what it is?"

"That's right," he said.

He did not notice my irritation, although he did have a passable explanation. He said love is to be felt, not known. It's unknowable, like happiness, or a bad mood, or premenstrual syndromes, ha ha. Say you're happy one day because of the weather, a good meal, a nice chat. But repeating the same things later may not reproduce that wonderful feeling. Why? When you're happy, you just are, even though you don't know what happiness is, or what causes it. No?

Very intellectual. Downright unromantic. Utterly fallacious. He spends too much time with Ma. No doubt.

I interrogated him further. What about love as a selfless state of the mind? An unconditional feeling for the persons you love? What about love-inspired sacrifices?

He said he wasn't so sure about love being unconditional. If it is – he actually said this – then what's the big deal? It occurs by mere chance, and is sustained arbitrarily. If my love for him is *unconditional*, he exclaimed, touching his own heart unnecessarily, then he should be allowed to take it for granted, and abuse it if he wishes. It won't matter. Unconditional love should be there no matter what, unchanging regardless, like gravity, he said. "How could something that blind be precious? How could mindless devotion inspire poetry?"

He compared love to gravity. I felt like crying.

"Only if love *is* unconditional, which I don't think it is..." he attempted to clarify with more fuddle duddle, grinning sheepishly. I told him I did not wish to talk about it anymore. He said, "*Hey hey hey.* I didn't start it, you did."

So what.

*   *   *

"What's love, Ma?" asks Song.

"What?"

"You heard me, Guru Ma. What is love?"

"I'm a Daoist for Chrissake. Do you know how long I've worked on purging love, hate, expectation, disappointment, happiness and sadness and so on, from this illusory existence? You're contaminating my spirit with your question, Grasshopper."

"Let me put it differently then. Do you love Sashti?"

"*What*?!"

"Can you at least say pardon?"

"Of course I do," says Ma. "Why?"

"What is love, then?"

"I don't know, although sometimes I think I do, but not often."

"I got into trouble with Rhea for saying something like that."

"So you should."

*   *   *

Sashti taught yoga part-time at the gym where Ma had just become a member, joining Tai-chi and yoga classes that he could easily have taught. He was newly back to Hong Kong, and thought he might find like-minded people there. But most members just wanted to lose weight. Some were also seeking part-time enlightenment on a special monthly package of HK$680, including a free drink at the Om Bar. The yogis whispered, the body-builders guffawed. All quite friendly and jolly, but mentally unlike Ma.

Sashti had the kind of body curves that gave yoga a good name. Ma saw her in the hallway, and followed her to *Yoga for Beginners* in a trance.

"Very good." She towered over his upside-down face. "Beginner?"

He had doubled up into a perfect utanasana, head between knees, showing off. He felt the heat of her knees on his face, and swallowed against gravity. Embarrassed, he dropped his gaze to look up at her, but was blocked by his own bum.

He had found his like-minded person.

Sashti was born in Hong Kong to Indian parents. The family moved to London when she was thirteen. She had returned alone to do her post-doctorate in biochemistry at the University of Hong Kong, and be away from her parents.

She was a brilliant chemist. Her research on the degradation characteristics of polymers was supported by a generous grant, and she taught yoga in the evening for a few extra bucks. Most important of all, she was cynical. "Biochemical research is fully controlled by vested interests, supervised by committees who think a Periodic Table is something you fold away after each meal."

"What's your specialty?"

"Cut and paste. *Managing a One Experiment Many Papers* show." She took a sip of gin and tonic. "Just one way of making a living I guess, like theft and prostitution."

That was in 2056. They were in love three hours later, and kind of married a year later.

They shared many things: hobbies, writers, music, outlook, as well as, in Sashti's words, attitude problems. A couple destined to live happily ever after. Well, they did, still do really, but separately for the past ten years. Just before Ma started work on the hanging garden, Sashti told him she wanted to move to Repulse Bay. "When?" he asked. "I'll come check it out with you." The rest was operational. They never discussed why, as if the reasons were too obvious for discussion.

"They've always been soul-mates, but not lovers in the conventional sense," Song once speculated to Rhea.

"What makes you say that?"

"They never torment each other. Don't even argue."

"I suppose you're right."

Ma and Sashti had too much harmony. Two independent soul-mates with no kids might as well live apart after twenty years. Since neither small-talked, they eventually ran out of things to say, and drifted out of each other's sight. Living apart actually gave them the distance to see each other again.

* * *

"Do you think you two might still be living together if you had kids?" Rhea asked Sashti. They were at her beach-side villa in Repulse Bay, not far from Rhea's old family castle, making salad. The guys were preparing beggar's chicken and a giant cod in the garden.

"Why? To maintain a family setting for middle-aged offspring?" Sashti smiled teasingly. "Neither of us wanted kids actually, though it turned out not to be an option. You know, ironically, I was named after the Hindu goddess of fertility."

"Really? Is that what Sashti means? Bless me then!"

"You want kids?" She sounded surprised, then changed her tone. "I guess most women do. I'm just weird. There's a broken spring in my biology." She stopped slicing the tomato and turned to Rhea. "Not too late?"

"Don't think so." Rhea answered as if she had been waiting for the question. "Never."

Sashti raised her thin curvy eyebrows incredulously, then smiled warmly.

Entry Ten: 30 June 2090: Windy.

Very unmotivated. He's fixing the front window, broken by a branch last night, using a pane from next door. Don't feel like writing. No one's curious about my secret thoughts anyway. I thought about the old man he saw two weeks ago. It's not so much about him, although I do pity the poor fellow. It's the chance of something similar happening to us. Song can leave here one day and not return, and I might never find out why.

It also made me think of Guji. Haven't caught a fleeting glimpse of her for a long time. I wonder if she's still alive, or if she's moved again. Does anyone ever check on her? What does she do all day? Perhaps I'll be like her one day? No, I won't. I'll have a son. I think he's a boy. Maybe we should go pay her a proper visit one day soon?

Can't stop thinking about love. Must have been the chat the other day, or pregnancy again? I am unusually sentimental. Is this to prepare myself for love, big and unqualified, like gravity?

Going to Ma's for dinner tonight. Don't really feel like socialising but I guess I will. The walk would do us good, me and the little one.

Entry Eleven: 2 July 2090: Breezy and pleasant evening.

Ma gave a surprising discourse on love last night; it's such an unlikely topic for him. Timely though. It was inspiring and annoying as usual, but I found the premise of love being an extension of self particularly relevant in my situation. He would be flattered if he knows I'm recording his *lecture* before I forget it.

* * *

The four of us were having an after-dinner drink in his garden (I had soya milk). Ma had been at Sashti's for a couple of days, and just returned in the afternoon. John started it. The big guy is evidently just as curious about this odd couple as we are. It was the usual question. "Why aren't you guys living together, at least in the same area? You're too old to run a marathon every time you want to see your wife, for Chrissake."

"We need space." Ma smiled cheekily.

"Like," I said, "twenty-five kilometres?"

"It's nothing when there's love, my young lady." He could be infuriatingly patronising. But somehow I wasn't infuriated because it was Ma, and because he called me *young lady* with unmistakable sincerity.

"So Ma Shi Fu knows what love is! Great. Can you enlighten us then?" I had him trapped. I threw Song a glance, remembering our chat a few days ago.

Ma thought for a moment, then said, "We (excluding himself, I assume) talk too much and think too little about love, making it unnecessarily perplexing. Left alone, love would be one of the most natural attributes of a social animal like humankind.

"The over-glorified man-woman love, for example, is fundamentally *eros* – a basic animal instinct that doesn't need sweetening with poetry. It happens naturally, often by chance – " he looked at Song and me "– like you guys." We gave a synchronised shrug. He grinned. "Men and women are attracted to each other instinctively, like cats in heat. But unlike cats, civilised humans are uncomfortable with their nature. We need a reason for everything we do. Love is one such rationalisation. It idealises an innate desire that shouldn't require moral or intellectual justification, changing its true face as a result."

He paused to regard his audience.

I gave him a mmm-hmm look.

He continued, "In that sense, romantic love is a condition initiated by the genitals, then spread to the heart." He swept his hands up from his tummy to the chest, discreetly missing the starting point.

Song and John laughed, boosting his spirits.

"Hey," he added. "Don't forget! For millions of years, men and women met mostly by wild chance. They bumped into each other and?" He looked at the boys, inviting an answer.

"Sniffed at each other's butt!" John shouted like a school-boy. Song giggled, slapping his own thigh. The boys were having a good time discussing love. I suppose that was a positive step forward in evolution.

Ma complimented – or insulted – John by saying he would make a good *Homo erectus*. I remarked that they both would. Song protested with a neglected face, "What about me?"

Ma resumed. "As we became more *civilised* –" he said it with unmistakable contempt "– sex became controlled through marriage arranged by family elders for expedient reasons, or later on, registered by civil servants and stored in a Government database. Not long ago, things became even more spurious when love came to be regarded as a moral prerequisite for sex, as if our animal nature could be redesigned at will. It's like saying we won't eat unless there's healthy food on the table, or we won't even feel hungry unless the vitamin content on our dinner-plate is perfectly balanced."

"I don't feel hungry unless there's good food on the table," John said.

Ma noticed my questioning eyes instead, and clarified that he wasn't agreeing or disagreeing with what he'd described. He was merely stating what he had observed to be the way of modern civilisation. "Before the last couple of centuries, the majority of humans did not pretend to be in love before they screwed. Duty and family interests were the most common foreplay preceding legitimate intercourse. The awkward association of impalpable love and a carnal relationship is historically speaking a recent fad. That's all I'm saying."

"If *eros* is primitive love, so romantically animal, are there higher levels? If yes, what are they? What about love for children? And you still haven't defined love, Professor!" I said, a bit sarcastic. I knew Ma wouldn't mind.

"Wow! I'll need another drink to get into all that, my young lady." Song jumped up to pour him one.

"Thank you, Grasshopper." He took a mouthful as if he could quench thirst with cognac, and swallowed hard with a gratified grimace. "Yes, one love, many levels, all fundamentally the same. In my humble opinion, what we vaguely call love is an extension of self, or projection of one's existence – an expected trait of all social animals."

"Oh no... Philosophy." John muttered loudly, tapping his forehead.

Ma bobbed to him and said, "Zoology." Then turned back to me. "First and foremost of this projection is *eros*, as I've just mentioned. It biologically extends one's genes – through sex, of course. But other attributes can be projected as well. Parents, for example, are infamous for subconsciously wanting to pass ambitions and anxieties on to their kids. Some try to recapture lost opportunities in life through their children, hoping that they will undo the regrets of the previous generation. If these projections are love," he raised his fingers to bracket himself in quotation marks, "then yes: sympathy, encouragement, nurturing, desire, sacrifice, possessiveness, pressure, support and so on can all be interpreted as love. *Eros*, by comparison, is relatively pure, simple, honest, and pleasurable."

"Sounds like your favourite Shi Fu." Song sniggered.

Ma smiled. "Parental love is probably the next easiest to understand, after *eros*, because it serves to protect our gene carriers – the children. Other glorified *love-forms* are more questionable. Zealous nationalists, racists, and religious fanatics, for example, sacrificed their own lives and murdered others to serve a notional purpose, or whatever principles they were stuck with for the time being. Was that love? I'm not sure, but those who benefited from their sacrifice would say yes. Don't forget, most people who effusively eulogised martyrs were themselves very much alive and in power, probably due to the encouraged death of their *brave young men and women*.

"In short, basic love is instinctual, like hunger or thirst. It's innate, entirely natural to social animals, whether insect or human. No need to make a big glittering deal out of it. *Civilised* love, on the other hand, is artificial, often entwined with delusions. That's why it's impossible to define."

"What about a wider love for humanity – like Jesus's – or environmentalists' love for beasts and bugs or the natural environment in general?" asked John.

"They are just a tiny step up from the patriots or devout martyrs aren't they? The idea of Jesus of Nazareth promoting *universal love* was a post-Ascension fantasy anyway. Jesus' original messages of peace and forgiveness were directed at his own brutal and unforgiving world, with a racial focus on his tribesmen the Chosen Ones only. You can't blame him. He didn't know much about the rest of his Dad's secondary creatures, did he?

"And those who sincerely respected the environment as a whole were indeed projecting our existence onto a wider plane. Preserving the environment was good for long-term survival. Very sensible, yes, but nothing outlandishly noble about it." He paused, then added, "I haven't met many environmentalists who truly loved the environment, though."

"So, love beyond *eros* isn't necessarily a positive development of the human spirit in your view." I tried to stop him from wandering too far.

"Not to me. Like most things, love could be *good* only when given and taken in sensible and balanced measures. Otherwise, it could turn destructive. While so-called *love* from an enlightened person can be liberating and enriching, blind passion from a fool is annoying at best, murderous at worst. Fervid love chokes us when happening, and pains us with regrets when dead. It's an incredible cause of suffering.

"Truly great love is actually not something that catches the fancy of pallid sugary poets. Ultimate love has no preference; it appears impartial and impassive –"

"Like gravity!" Song nearly jumped.

"Gravity?" Ma was puzzled by Song's sudden burst of enthusiasm. "I suppose that's one way of putting it; a big background force that holds things together. When all is one and one is all, there's neither distinction nor favouritism. This is love at the highest level, attainable through enlightenment, not instinct or faculty, therefore, *Aiya*, not really the thing for us average humans."

John applauded. "Well said Monk Ma. Everything you've said is probably not true, and I now have less idea what love is than an hour ago, but you've made it sound great."

"Thank you." He bowed.

I actually found most of what he said made sense, but something was missing. Men don't seem able to feel the full power of love the way we women do, even on an instinctual level. It's a genetic defect, congenital deficiency. They either follow their erectus instincts and are unbearably basic, or think too much about it. Brain and penis are both wrong organs to seek love. Unfortunately, feminine feelings are no match for rationality in a debate of words, especially with Ma.

Instead of challenging his premise, I asked the question which interested me most. "What about our love for children. You haven't said anything about that yet."

"No? Thought I did. Didn't I say parental love is the easiest to understand? Okay, children carry our genes and project it into the future. They serve to keep basic love alive in a relationship, thereby prolonging it. Not that I have any personal experience, but I believe our instinctive love for kids is much stronger and more durable than that for spouses. Our mates are just interim *vehicles*. (How can I not love the way he turns beautiful things into existentialist gizmos?) *Eros* is tenuous and vulnerable, attenuated by time. Kids galvanise a couple's emotional and social bond, and give it a future dimension." Then he added an important afterthought. "Most people probably don't know the true force of instinctive love until they become parents."

"I agree, fully agree. And that includes you." I pointed an emphatic finger at him.

"Of course. That includes all of us childless people here."

I smiled. Just you wait and see, I thought.

I turned to Song. He had been staring at me without my knowing it, smiling like a kid. He had no idea what was in my mind, but enjoyed the discussion and company. Me too. I needed to talk about it.

I love him I love him. I can't explain why, nor need to. I just do, with all my instincts, and much more.

* * *

"Do you love me, Mama?"

"Of course, Sweetie."

"Tommy too?"

"Of course, Tommy too."

"What's love, Mama?"

"Love is everything."

"Good and bad?"

"Only good, Sweetie. Love's always good. Love's the best. There's nothing like love."

"How do you love us, Mama?"

"I care about you all the time; I worry about you every minute of the day, every second of the night; I want to be with you always; I won't let anyone hurt you, or get near you, or take you away from me. I'll kill anyone who tries to take you away from me. I'll do anything for you two. I'll never, never, leave you and Tommy. Forever and ever."

"Forever and ever?"

"Yes Sweetie. Every minute of forever and ever."

"Until we die?"

"Don't say bad things Sweetie! Spit and wipe your mouth!"

"What if we disappear and never come back?"

"You won't! You're saying bad things again!"

"No! Mama. Just pretend, please!"

"Pretend what?"

"Pretend we've disappeared."

"I'll just die."

"Yeah! I love you too, Mama."

ANNUNCIATION

Entry Fifteen: 5 July 2009: Disastrous.

I finally told him after breakfast.

I couldn't hold it in any longer. It came out just like that, as if involuntarily. "Haven't you the slightest idea that I'm pregnant?"

He gaped at me as if someone had just dragged him out of bed at three in the morning. I waited, smiling. He then said in a serious voice, "You're kidding." We sank into a moment of awkward silence. An explosive mixture of sadness, disappointment and humiliation flushed through me. I wanted to slap him. I exaggerated my smile instead.

I had been right. He thought I had gone nuts, and, more infuriatingly, suffering from menopausal delusions. He and his menopause and andropause. I had much better reasons to question his sanity than he had to question mine.

He then asked, "Did you test with a kit?" I said, "Of course. But darling, you know, unlike spam, these kits are hard to find. The market for them vanished decades ago." The one and only I found at Manning's, stuck behind a shelf in a store room, expired eighteen years ago. It had dried up completely. Whatever chemical there was inside had turned into a faint stain. Didn't even smell anymore.

Besides a hint of sarcasm, I was still trying hard to be charming, patient, and understanding. I expected him to doubt me. But...! His reaction upset me nonetheless. I took a deep breath, and explained how I knew I was pregnant the best I could. But he seemed as thick as cowhide lantern, impossible to enlighten. He didn't appear to know the basic biology of pregnancy. Not surprising. He had never seen a real baby in his entire life. Babies and pregnancy had never been a topic of concern to him or his father's survival game. Survival to boys is a man's game. To appease his intellectual vanity, I even tried to explain from a philosophical angle, blah, blah, blah.

In the end, he said, "OK, if you insist. How are you going to give birth?"

If I insist!

"How?" I remained calm even at this point. "Like all women before me."

"What if it's stuck?"

"What do you mean stuck?"

"Stuck, you know. Stuck."

"Cut me up if you have to."

"Alive?"

"If that's what it would take to save the baby."

He suddenly seemed truly angry. He said I was crazy, and accused me of grossing him out with violence.

I told him to fuck off, and he did.

I hate him. He hurts me so much when I need him most. I never thought I could hate him but I do. I never want to see him again unless he apologises. No! Not even then.

Let him watch. For million of years, women gave birth without their men. We're back to the Stone Age now. We're savages. I'll do it without him. I'll have the baby delivered myself. Come to think of it, it'd be easier without his dumb distractions.

Maybe I'll move to Sashti's. She'll understand right away. She would be able to help. Maybe I'll even go tell Guji. She's a woman after all. I'm sure the news of a baby would bring her out of her lonesome curse.

I'm crying again as I write. Good. I'd cry all I need to, then do some breathing exercise to calm down. I shouldn't let myself get upset. I can feel my heart racing right now. That's not good.

Getting rid of him is a good thing. One more cry, then a new beginning.

TIGER

Out in Yuen Long, solitude has no recourse.

When there were jails, even a prisoner in solitary confinement had the hope or knowledge that his punitive solitude might end one day. The outside world was only a brick wall away. He could hear the guards chatting, doing their job. They depended on his incarceration for a living. They had to serve and feed him regularly. They had to be nearby, attentive, in order to monitor, torture, toy with him. They were there for him, because of him. The prisoner was keeping his guards confined just the same, on possibly more intolerable terms because it was a job; they had the choice to leave, but could not.

A lighthouse keeper's job was lonely. He was far away from people, but would occasionally visit town for provisions or breaks. At night, he could see the faint glow of a familiar place in the sky. He could visualise people living their congested lives over there, in a land he knew. Ships sailed past. Sailors and passengers were sweating, labouring, resting, eating, looking his way, curious if there was a keeper on duty, and what he might be doing at that moment.

A shipwreck victim marooned on the cartoonists' single-palm island might appear stuck in a situation similar to Huan's; yet there is one big difference. The forlorn survivor would spend his days looking out to sea, craning his neck longer, hoping for rescue. One day, perhaps even later today, his loneliness would end. There would be welcome-home champagne, and a lifetime right to tell his story over and over again.

Unlike them, Huan's solitary confinement is voluntary, absolute, endless, till death.

* * *

Solitude has given him a more prominent role in his own life. He daydreams freely, ranging over boundless territories. He talks to himself without worrying about being overheard, or what others might think. He laughs at his own jokes. Ironically, he is in much better shape than he's been for a while. Is it the agreeable diet of freshwater fish, frogs (and one vole so far), wild fruits and vegetables? Or the healthful effect of relaxing into his death position?

His stopover is looking permanent. A few days' rest has turned into three months – ninety five days actually, with a potential error of two. On two occasions, he was not sure if he had missed marking the time chart in the morning, so he did it in the evening anyway, knowing that he might have duplicated. He has since made it a habit to mark the day first thing every morning, before emptying his brittle old bladder. He realises how silly and pointless it is, but can't help it. He will start a new sheet in a few days. One hundred days per sheet.

A hundred days – believe it or not.

In spite of his high spirits, he does not seem to have the energy to cross the border, as he originally planned. It looks like Yuen Long is where he will die.

He wakes before sunrise. A good long sleep is rare at his age. When it occasionally happens, he feels sluggish and limp rather than well rested. Young people wake up from a good sleep rejuvenated. He wakes up from deep slumber feeling like a disturbed corpse.

After breakfast, he takes a walk through the field to the village. The round trip takes an hour. Sometimes he continues all the way to the ghostly town centre, which is twice the distance, to scrounge for stuff. Must keep those legs fit. Might need them to find a good roof to jump off in case he needs to. He does not intend to commit suicide; not at all. But the natural course of things can become unbearable. He might need to self-administer euthanasia for humane reasons.

When death arrives, he hopes it will be in his sleep. He has experimented focusing his mind on terrible things before sleeping, hoping to induce a nightmare. Dying of a heart attack in a bad dream would be a nice clean way out. Death is the final thing Song Huan still tries to manage in this life.

There are chores after the morning walk. Pruning fruit trees, gathering vegetables, collecting firewood, making jam, getting water, fixing leaks around the house, doing laundry. Sometimes – not often – he eats a small lunch. Then he naps. In the late afternoon, he might fish, bathe in the stream, or set up snares for pigeons and voles.

After dinner, his mind would drift.

Most days, he sits back to listen to the frogs and insects, and to reminisce. He indulges in the happiest years, replaying them over and over. He is in Shanghai or Finland, or at home with Sari and Song, chatting, cooking, doing dishes, reading sitting next to them, walking up the Peak, sharing a stupid joke. Nothing exhilarating. Just plain and simple contentment, the felicity of not wishing for anything else.

Sometimes, to his surprise, he would be at work, figuring things out, feeling accomplished or frustrated. Occasionally, bits and pieces of younger days would surface. He would see his mother, someone he has not thought of for many years. Maybe it is time to refresh his memory, in preparation for the reunion.

Other days he stays in the present, planning chores. Sometimes he rehearses contingencies in his head: a broken hip, a debilitating attack of flu, dengue fever, even a tiger attack. He plans what he can do to better the chance of surviving with minimum pain.

Every now and then, he daydreams about the final moment. If he knew he had one minute left, how should he spend it? Most likely, he would not be able to do anything physically. But if he does not panic, if his mind remains sound, what should he occupy it with for the next sixty seconds, while he's still a human on Earth? What impression would he like to take with him when crossing the big divide?

On a starry night or moonlit evening, he might stray off the planet. He would sit at the cockpit of the expanding universe, rushing towards a starless infinity, penetrating an endless space. Stars explode into sight – one, two, ten, a hundred, millions, billions. They pop up out of nowhere and multiply endlessly at a dazzling rate, like a firework that keeps flaring, layer after layer. These are neighbouring universes, also expanding, rushing for infinity; a celestial stampede. Huan tries to catch up with the front runner, but cannot. He does not know which way to look.

Without the encumbering body, he can travel faster than light, breaking all physical limitations. *Just imagine.* But still he cannot reach the end. Infinity is out of bounds even for the imagination, too far even for ghosts.

He comes home to the Milky Way. Sari has been waiting. "Hei muru, what took you so long!" She takes his hand for a tour of the heavens. Sometimes she looks twenty-five – her age when they met. Sometimes she looks forty-eight – her age when she died. He is always an old man in his seventies, looking even older than in real life, exhausted from the cosmic flight. She is like his daughter, even granddaughter. He tries but cannot visualise himself younger, or Sari older.

* * *

Song Huan cannot make himself young again in his dreams, but can still be adventurous.

He has crossed the border, walking towards the hinterland of Guangdong province. For centuries, this was one of the most fertile lands of China, supplying fragrant rice and organic vegetables to millions. Not too long ago, lush green fields were smothered by dusty grey factories, turning into miles and miles of square concrete blocks – a grey Wall of China. Tonnes and tonnes of stuff were churned out from it day and night. Stuff the world wanted but did not need. The eighth pair of sneakers for Johnny, Daddy's 36th polka-dotted tie, Jane's third i-Pod, water bottles with blinking caps. It was a junk yard in reverse, taking in useful resources, cranking out junk.

The world depended on affordable throw-away items to keep its economy expanding, to keep inflation down and the Christmas spirit up. Millions of workers' pay-cheques depended on people throwing stuff out. Now that the rice fields were producing golf balls and running shoes, the people needed money to import rice. This was the inside of a global economic engine. It looked and smelled like the inside of an engine.

Some factories are green again. Trees have reclaimed the world's last industrial heartland, turning assembly lines of i-Dreams and Virtual Sneakers into Angkor Wat.

Huan expected to see more people this side of the border, but has not seen a soul. He is leaving the city centre. The grey wall is changing hue, shedding dust. The setting sun imposes a coat of orange over the emerald jungle he is about to enter. The freshness of moss and sweetness of wild fruits fill his nose. Apple, guava, lychee, papaya, mandarin, water melon, banana as well as exotic species he does not recognise. Finally, he is in the place he had in mind when he left home long, long ago.

There is a waterfall nearby. The sound of it invigorates him. Perching at the top watching water plunging off is an ancient pine – a Hospitality Pine – just like in old paintings. It has witnessed the incessant flow for millennia. It has watched the world beyond change from green to grey, grey to brown, then back to green.

Huan is exhausted, but happy and peaceful. He lies down next to the bank, listening to the water, feeling the mist landing on his face, gently refreshing him.

Before long, he is fast asleep.

Something is sniffing his head. He keeps his eyes closed and body still. He breathes as evenly as he can, but his heart pumps fear all over. His temples thud.

How stupid of me to fall asleep in strange territory.

All of a sudden, it licks the crown of his head.

A big tongue. Strong, steady slurps.

A tiger? Oh shit. This is near where the Shenzhen zoo was.

Don't move. Stay calm. Let it lick. Maybe it will find his wizened head flaky and distasteful, and go away after a little sampling.

More likely, it will eat his face afterwards.

What does he want to think of now, now that there's only a minute or two left?

He cannot think of anything.

Instead, he dozes off again.

* * *

He drifts in and out of sleep. Every time he comes out of it, he blearily senses the tiger nearby. Its breath, carnivorous and raw, reeking of undigested blood, is upon his face.

Finally, he feels awake. It is still dark. He must have slept the whole night. It's about 4.30, his biological alarm says. The tiger is still around, he knows. But why hasn't it eaten him?

Early birds are singing. Where is he?

He opens his eyes a crack. Everything looks blurry but familiar. Isn't this the hut in Yuen Long? So it was just a dream? But the unmistakable stench of a beast is in the air, right here. He can faintly hear its breath. Shenzhen might have been a dream, but the tiger is not.

Huan stays motionless, and waits for light.

An hour feels like eternity when one waits in bed. Every cell in his body aches to twitch. At long last, the first glow of dawn seeps through the windows, gradually increasing in intensity. God is slowly turning up the dimmer. The warbling of birds reaches a crescendo.

He opens his eyes gently, reminding himself not to panic if a tiger's face is against his. Only the ceiling. Gingerly, he turns his head to the side, and sees it sitting two metres from the bed.

The chow chow notices him waking, and stands up, alert, spotty tongue hanging slightly out. Its tail is lifted, wagging hesitantly from side to side, pausing after each swipe.

"Hey doggie," Huan says in a coarse morning voice. "You scared me. I thought you were a tiger."

In reply, its tail swipes three times. One, pause, two, three. Tentative and noncommittal, but clearly not hostile.

Huan slowly sticks one hand out, gesturing it to come closer. "Come on, good boy. Hungry?"

It comes closer, and lets Huan pat its thick and scruffy coat, sticky like cotton-candy. "Good boy. Or are you a girl? Don't have a pack to join?"

The dog seems relaxed now. It comes right against the bed, wagging vigorously, inviting him to continue patting.

"Had enough of freedom? Wanna be a pet again?" The dog seems to agree. "Wow, you need a bath!"

"What should I call you?" He pushes himself up like a rusty robot. His bones creak in unison. "*Tiger*, of course! Yeah! Good! Come Tiger, let's make breakfast!"

LONELY AWAKENING

Melody lay in bed with the worst migraine she had ever had. She wanted to find a wet towel to cover her head, but could not summon the energy to get up. She slipped her T-shirt off and placed it over her eyes instead. Light was everywhere, stabbing, gnawing.

She breathed with mouth wide open, moaning long and deep. The pain was excruciating. Some single-minded madness was slashing up her inside savagely. Here! Here! Here! Here! Her brain twitched and convulsed, unaware of anything but pain – a sharp searing pain that darted from front to back, then to the front again, then the crown, poking for a weak spot to crack open. It aimed to kill.

Big teardrops rolled down her cheeks. They were cold.

* * *

She woke up, emerging from a dark abyss of lost time, and was surprised. I'm still alive? She noticed the damp T-shirt next to her. Her mouth was dry, her tongue stuck to the roof. Her lips were chapped and flaky. She wondered how long it had been.

So quiet. The music had stopped.

The kids!
Sweetie?
Tommy?
Sweetie!!!

* * *

"Sweetie!
"Tommy!
"Oh no...
"No... no... no...."

243

*   *   *

She sits on the parapet wall where Sweetie and Tommy first appeared; music was playing then. She's not sad. Sadness had been promptly taken over by rage, an intense rage that scorched every organ. Kidney, stomach, liver, heart.

Then the rage died out, burnt no more.

The night is dark. A weak yellow light flickers in the distance. She stares at it, zooming in mentally with a vampiric flutter. Rhea, the other woman, the other lonely woman, is sitting there, watching the reflection of a candle in the window. Then the vision dissolves, replaced by darkness, the darkness that engulfs her.

The night is dead quiet.

She wonders why God is doing this to her, robbing her of a self-containing love and happiness that bother nobody. What has she done wrong? What pleasure can He possibly get from teasing her until she breaks?

"What!" She screams, looking up towards Heaven.

The moon glows behind a veil of clouds, hiding.

"Cowards! You're all cowards!"

She wants to smoke, but has no cigarettes.

She starts to sing instead, her voice deep and brittle tonight.

From the far side of the ravine
blows a gentle wind.
Sweeping over the silver moon
Sailing across the purple sea
It's come a long long way
to be in your dream.

Sleep O baby sleep
Only when you dream, I can come in
Only when you dream, everything's real
When the sun comes up
We'll disappear
Like the wind, gone, gone
Blowing beyond
Never to be seen.

She freezes, listening intently to her own voice resonating in her head, hoping it might rekindle the music, followed by Sweetie and Tommy. "Come on Mozart." But there is only silence. It's deafening. She shudders.

She looks down at the darkness underneath, so dense and bottomless, and plunges in.

In her flight through the warm moist air, Melody hears the sibilance of wind passing through her once silky long hair, and the gentle flapping of her favourite purple dress.

James Tam

O SOLE MIO

Song trudges down Old Peak Path without his the staff he takes when walking. He has left it at Rhea's when leaving in a hurry.

"If I slip and kill myself, it'd be all her fault." The thought of Rhea bearing the guilt for the rest of her life gives him a tinge of satisfaction. When passing the bend where he encountered the old man, he wonders what has become of him, and is tempted to check. Then he walks on. Better just let him be.

He has been replaying the fight with Rhea in his head over and over again, discovering more and more regrets. He could have been more patient and sensitive. Perhaps he was a bit petulant and unnecessarily retaliatory. He should simply have said less. Why was he so unforgiving, even mean and harsh, to someone he loves so dearly? Was it menopause clashing with andropause? He wonders how many women had mistaken menopause for pregnancy. Not many, he concludes. Most women died before the menopause until recent centuries; then they stopped getting pregnant.

Come to think of it, the same folly would have been comical rather than vexing earlier on in their relationship. He would have taken the news with humour instead of exasperation. Is this how love matures?

Rhea may be being ridiculous but her delusion is excusable, and her reasoning sound. Why couldn't he just play along, and let her discover the difference between pregnancy and menopause in due course? Why was he so gung-ho about proving her wrong right away? Why couldn't he shut up and wait? Was he subconsciously threatened by the idea of a baby, even as a remote possibility?

He plods on.

When he reaches Robinson Road, he continues downhill. He does not feel like going home yet.

* * *

Where did it go wrong?

They were chatting after breakfast. Song leafed through the calendar from John, asking why she wanted one.

"Because I'm pregnant." She looked at him, a big smile on her face.

"*Mmm Hmm.*" He sensed that it was not just a weird joke, but did not know how to react.

"I am." She repeated, still looking at him with the same exaggerated charm and happy face. "Maybe approaching the end of my first trimester."

"You're sure?" Song sat bolt upright, giving the impression that he was only starting to pay attention. He said the first thing that came to mind, "Have you checked with one of those kits from the pharmacy?"

"Of course, but darling, these things expired long ago." She sounded sarcastic. "By the way, I'm a woman. I can tell I'm pregnant without consulting chemical indicators."

"You sure it's not the menopause?"

"What?" She seemed shocked and offended by his reasonable speculation.

He tried to clarify. "I mean, it could be the menopause, you know. Don't they have similar symptoms, like no more periods?"

"Song, I don't believe you!"

A silly argument had started, deteriorating quickly. The news was more than a surprise to Song; he found it ludicrous, outrageous. His first reaction was indignation. Rhea is forty-eight. Even in the bygone fertile world, women rarely became pregnant with their first baby at this age. Furthermore, even if it were true, he told Rhea, why would they want to bring a new life to a dead end? To grow up all by itself? To be the only person on Earth, wandering aimlessly all day engaged in soliloquy?

She turned a furious red, but quickly calmed down to a bit of philosophy. She cautioned against speculating too much about the future. "Doesn't Ma call us *Post-Modern Savages*?" she said. "He's got a point there. We're now savages. We need to rely on instincts – not hypothesis and wordy intellectualism. Remember

247

your *Homo erectus*? They wouldn't have become *Homo sapiens* if our primeval ancestors had wondered whether it was a good thing to have kids, because a million dreadful fates awaited them. If they had thought about it, they would have realised that the chance of us large monkeys with stubby toes surviving in the brutal world was pitifully slim. "What's the point?" they would have asked.

"But NO!" she nearly hollered. "Our ancestors were real men and women. They just went ahead and did it. Their duty was to reproduce, as much as they could, and leave the future to the future.

"Who do you think we are?" she stood up and asked, like a lawyer in court. "Some kind of god, responsible for planning the future of mankind? Had you lived in the tenth century, and been blessed with the knowledge that Song Sung now has, would you have decided against having kids because mankind might die out a thousand years later? Would you?"

Song said he might have, if he had had that vision.

"Well," Rhea said, discharging a lungful of exasperation. "Song, humans have known for quite a while that, one day, we'll all be dried up by the expanding sun. So why live today, since all lives will be incinerated? Because it's our instinct to carry on, to keep the species going!

"Fine, for a while there were far too many of us; but we're now leftovers of a dying race on its last breath. There's no time for contemplation. We can't afford it. Turn on your instincts. Imagine yourself the very first man, serial number 001. You don't even know you'll grow old and die sometime in your twenties. You have no idea. Just live, a minute at a time, one day at a time, and make babies at every opportunity."

Maybe she *is* pregnant, Song thought. How else could she become so impossibly eloquent and aggressive all at once? There's got to be some hormone with a monstrous molecular structure behind all this.

"Dream! " Rhea resumed.

"Pardon?" Song was dreaming about hormones, wondering how they might look.

"I said dream," Rhea repeated, this time softly. "Dreams make us a different animal. Dreams make us special. They are above rationality and irrationality. Dreams allow us to ignore statistics and achieve the unlikely, even the so-thought impossible. Dreams help us to challenge destiny, redefine fate."

"Wow!" Song smiled slyly, trying to tone down his amazement. "Nightmares are dreams too."

Rhea paused and looked away.

"Rhea," Song said to her back. They had dropped their pet names for this present conversation. "But there's something called judgement. Assuming that you are pregnant – Okay, correction, since you are pregnant – we're going to be parents. As parents, we love our kid, and want it to be happy. But to the best of my judgement, it will have a pretty miserable life. What do you say to that, Mum?"

"Were you listening?" retorted Rhea. "In the post-modern world, it's not felicitous niceties like happiness, job satisfaction, a wonderful marriage and a good pension that we care for. It's survival. Survival of self. Survival of the species. Nothing else!

"You once said you don't know what happiness is. How do you plan happiness for your kid if you don't know what it is, huh? You're still thinking too much, or refusing to switch from thinking to acting. You're totally out of context, and out of time for that matter. Come back to here and now! Forget history! Forget the future! Quit analysing! Quit weighing one impossible outcome against another! Look at us Song, the way we are – now!"

Rhea then realised she might have sounded too personal and critical. She softened her voice to plea. "Come on Baby, I know what's happening. I'm not crazy. Trust me. You must. We have a baby coming. Let's focus on that."

He was thinking. A technical concern entered his mind. "Okay, if you insist. How are you going to give birth?"

"How? Like all the women before me."

Song inexplicably found that answer unreasonable. "What if it's stuck?" he asked.

"Cut me up if you have to."

"Alive?"

"If that's what it'll take."

Song could not believe his ears. The idea stabbed him like an electric shock. It saddened him for a split second, then provoked him with a sense of violence he had never experienced before.

Blood rushed to his head. "You're gross." – He sounded icy cold. – "And insane."

She burst into tears, and told him to fuck off.

He turned to leave, forgetting the favourite staff he took with him when walking.

* * *

Song slouches on John's bollard at Queen's Pier. His anger has ebbed away. Remorse has taken over. She was right, whether she's pregnant or not. He does spend too much time thinking and talking inconsequentially rather than acting.

Why wouldn't he be like this, though? He has never had to do anything about most things!

His father told him it's a tough world, so, be tough son. But in what way? He's strong, He could run two marathons a day if he had to. But physical strength and stamina have turned out to be much less critical than Huan had anticipated. With knowledge, durable leftovers, food, shelter, and clothing are reasonably easy to come by. The wind and rain are no more threatening than before. The animals are only just beginning to learn to be wild again. In fact, as John once noted, there are not even any bad guys to worry about any more. With nothing to gain or lose, villains have become extinct.

Song's life is much easier than his father had imagined. An excessive past had left him with a surplus of nearly everything; and a terminal future has relieved him of the anxious preparation. Compared with past generations, he is practically worry-free. His duty to himself and others is to live for today. He does not even need meditation.

He was often told how wonderfully different and lovable he was for a Generation-Zeder. Even at the age of forty-two, he remains somewhat unworldly. How can he not? He has never faced any pressure to grow up, whether into a tough caveman, an ambitious middle-class urbanite, or anyone else in particular. He has never had any real responsibility. He does not know the burden of a mortgage, a career, family, children. Up until now, all that has been required of him is to live – eat, drink, bullshit, sleep. Do a few chores. Make love if available. Tough life, huh?

His biggest test supposedly awaits him in the future. To be alone when everyone else has died; if everyone else indeed dies ahead of him. Then he must wait courageously for his turn, and die mankind's last hero. No one has ever expected more from him. No one has ever expected anything from him.

Except Rhea.

When she moved out of Shek O, she expected to move in with him. His mild panic perplexed them both. When he suggested a separate house in the same neighbourhood to give each other more space, she moved to the Peak instead. She was disappointed, but did not show it. "Fine. Good idea. I think I'd pick a house on the Peak instead." The issue of cohabitation had not been mentioned since.

This morning she did it again, much more shockingly this time, expecting him to become a father.

He has been praised and sympathised with for having the admirable courage to live a life without future. *Poor Song*. It suddenly dawns on him that living without the burden of history or anxiety for the future is freedom – *real* freedom! No wonder the world was full of rapturous eschatologists.

Continuity and expectation bring nothing but headache. People looked at history, and got aggravated by events that had long become irrelevant. They then wasted today stockpiling for an unknowable tomorrow, then waited anxiously for it to materialise.

Song has been free of this fettering cycle since birth, until just now. Rhea's news of pregnancy, illusory or otherwise, was an affront. For the first time, he was forced to face today and plan for tomorrow. She forced him to face a totally different life, an alien life which brings back burdens and responsibilities. It was an assault on the free rein he has always enjoyed.

What about Rhea? She's a Generation-Zeder too, though at the front end of it, and spoiled by a super-wealthy upbringing.

She's a woman. That why!

Gender makes a big difference under the circumstances. Basic biology like menstruation keeps women in touch with their raw bloody instincts. Rhea has evolved unaware, way ahead of Song, becoming fitter for survival, for long-term survival of the species – the overwhelming goal of all living things.

With pregnancy – or the illusion of it – her instincts have resurfaced, covering all the stains of civilisation. She has completed her transformation. She is a full-fledged post-modern savage now. Her life is no longer distracted by interpretation. No nonsense. For the future's sake, she doesn't care whether there is a future or not.

But may be there is!

Looking back, his own birth was statistically impossible; it happened. His surviving the first year was unlikely; it also happened. Meeting Rhea was a one in a million chance event; and it happened as if by design. According to Ma, the appearance of humanity itself was infinitely unlikely, but it happened, didn't it?

So, what is impossible?

Nothing seems impossible if he stops analysing. What has he got to lose anyway? Maybe they are destined to rekindle the human race, restarting it from scratch? Rhea's only forty-eight, much younger than many child-bearing geriatrics in the Bible.

But... Rhea is no mythical figure. She's forty-eight after all, living in a world with neither medical assistance nor guardian angels. What is her chance of surviving a first pregnancy?

What if...

He is captivated by the frantic aquatic community around the sunken barge. Hundreds of fish mill about, searching for food, searching for mates, playing out their roles in nature. Unthinking. Searching.

That's it. No more what ifs...

All of a sudden, he hears a baby crying. It rings in his head the same way he used to hear his mother calling him to dinner, years after she had died. Was it a real cry? He holds his breath to listen. Water splashes against the pier. Could have been a sea-gull.

Just like the fish... No more what ifs...

Rhea is right. I have not been a good caveman. Not even a bad one. Not even a fish.

His mind drifts to Rhea's breasts. They did seem fuller recently. Is that because of pregnancy? Or just her getting fat? Or menopause. *Who cares!* Time will tell. No more what ifs. No more menopause.

In the last couple of hours, since the *idea* of a baby entered his head, his perception of life has made quantum leaps in all directions. "Wow, powerful stuff." He takes a deep breath. "I have great responsibilities ahead, perhaps." Better be strong! He might be a Father Abraham figure to a congested world two thousand years from now.

He turns towards the Old Peak Path. Many silly questions line up for his attention. Should Rhea move to Robinson Road to live with me? That should have happened years ago. Yes, with or without a baby. I'll propose to her.

But Baby Song the Second would grow up all alone...

No it won't. He recalls Rhea's words when they first met. There'll be someone else. And they'll meet, somehow, just like us. What if they finally meet against all odds, and discover each other to be of the same sex? What's this *what if* again!

Perhaps they should move to Kowloon, and be connected to the mainland?

What about a name? "Now this is more than silly," he mutters with a silly smile. He goes through a few options anyway. Xing can suit a boy or girl in Chinese. It can mean star, or *spark*. A spark of hope; a pilot light for the next civilisation? What about a Finnish name instead. Jari? Satu?

But what if it's just the menopause? That means we're not going to have a baby after all. He can't help feeling slightly disappointed. Nah. She's right. She must know. And no more *what ifs*, remember?

As he climbs the path, he feels a rejuvenating lightness, and starts to sing his favourite song.

Che bella cosa e' na jurnata 'e sole,
n'aria serena doppo na tempesta!
Pe' ll'aria fresca pare già na festa
Che bella cosa e' na jurnata 'e sole!
...

O sole mio...

POST-PUBLICATION REVIEW

It's Hong Kong – but not as we know it. The year is 2090 and Song Sung, 42, is the youngest person alive. James Tam's debut novel, *Man's Last Song*, is a complex-yet-compelling exploration into the balance of mankind – for individuals, as well as for humanity as a whole. This superbly written dystopian novel is appealing on many levels: for its dramatic use of Hong Kong, for the intriguing characters, for the questions raised and, more importantly, for those which are left unanswered. A highly recommended read.

—Laura Besley, first published in *Time Out Hong Kong* (Issue 133).

WRITE TO US!

We are interested to read **your** response to
James Tam's *Man's Last Song*.
Please write to our email address, proverse@netvigator.com,
giving us a few sentences
which you are willing for us to publish,
giving your comments on this book.
If what you write is chosen to be included
in our E-Newsletter or website,
we will select another title published by Proverse Hong Kong
and send you a complimentary copy.
Please include your name, email address and mailing address
when you write to us, and state whether or not we may cut or
edit your comments for publication.
We will use your initials to attribute your comments.

ABOUT PROVERSE HONG KONG

Proverse Hong Kong is based in Hong Kong with long-term and expanding regional and international connections.

Proverse has published novels, novellas, fictionalized autobiography, non-fiction (including autobiography, biography, history, memoirs, sport, travel narratives), single-author poetry collections, children's, teens / young adult and academic books. Other interests include diaries, and academic works in the humanities, social sciences, cultural studies, linguistics and education. Some Proverse books have accompanying audio texts. Some are translated into Chinese.

Proverse welcomes authors who have a story to tell, wisdom, perceptions or information to convey, a person they want to memorialize, a neglect they want to remedy, a record they want to correct, a strong interest that they want to share, skills they want to teach, and who consciously seek to make a contribution to society in an informative, interesting and well-written way. Proverse works with texts by non-native-speaker writers of English as well as by native English-speaking writers.

The name, "Proverse", combines the words "prose" and "verse" and is pronounced accordingly.

THE PROVERSE PRIZE

The Proverse Prize, an annual international competition for an unpublished book-length work of fiction, non-fiction, or poetry, was established in January 2008. It is open to all who are at least eighteen on the date they sign the entry form. Unusually for a competition of this nature, there is no restriction based on nationality, residence or citizenship.

The objectives of the Proverse Prize are: to encourage excellence and / or excellence and usefulness in publishable written work in the English Language, which can, in varying degrees, "delight and instruct". Entries are invited from anywhere in the world. Semi-finalists to date include writers born or resident in Andorra, Australia, Canada, Germany, Hong Kong, New Zealand, Nigeria, Singapore, South Africa, Taiwan, The Bahamas, the Peoples' Republic of China, the United Arab Emirates, the United Kingdom, the USA.

FOUNDERS: Verner Bickley and Gillian Bickley. To celebrate their lifelong love of words in all their forms as readers, writers, editors, academics, performers, and publishers.
HONORARY LEGAL ADVISOR: Mr Raymond T. L. Tse.
HONORARY ACCOUNTANT: Mr Neville Chow.
HONORARY JUDGES: Anonymous.
HONORARY ADVISORS: Bahamian poet Marion Bethel; UK translator, Margaret Clarke; UK linguist & lexicographer David Crystal; Canadian poet and academic, Jonathan Hart; Swedish linguist Björn Jernudd; Hong Kong University Librarian, Peter Sidorko; Singapore poet Edwin Thumboo; Czech novelist & poet Olga Walló.
HONORARY UK AGENT AND DISTRIBUTOR: Christine Penney
HONORARY ADMINISTRATORS: Proverse Hong Kong.

PROVERSE PRIZE WINNERS WHOSE BOOKS HAVE ALREADY BEEN PUBLISHED BY PROVERSE HONG KONG

Laura Solomon, Rebecca Jane Tomasis, Gillian Jones, David Diskin, Peter Gregoire, Sophronia Liu, Birgit Linder, James McCarthy (Scotland, UK).

PROVERSE PRIZE WINNERS WHOSE BOOKS WILL BE PUBLISHED BY PROVERSE HONG KONG IN NOVEMBER 2014

Celia Claase; Philip Chatting.

Summary Terms and Conditions
(for indication only & subject to revision)

The information below is for guidance only. Please refer to the year-specific Proverse Prize Entry Form & Terms & Conditions, which are uploaded in April each year onto the Proverse Hong Kong website: <www.proversepublishing.com>.

The free Proverse E-Newsletter includes ongoing information about the Proverse Prize. To be put on the E-Newsletter mailing-list, email: info@proversepublishing.com with your request.

The Prize
1) Publication by Proverse Hong Kong, with
2) Cash prize of HKD10,000 (HKD7.80 = approx. US$1.00)

Supplementary publication grants may be made to selected other entrants for publication by Proverse Hong Kong.

Depending on the quality of the work in any year, the prize may be shared by at most two entrants or withheld, as recommended by the judges.

In 2015, the entry fee was: HKD220.00 OR GBP32.00.

Writers are eligible, who are at least eighteen on the date they sign The Proverse Prize entry documents. There is no nationality or residence restriction.

Each submitted work must be an unpublished publishable single-author work of non-fiction, fiction or poetry, the original work of the entrant, and submitted in the English language. School textbooks and plays are ineligible.

Translated work: If the work entered is a translation from a language other than English, both the original work and the translation should be previously unpublished. The submitted work will not be judged as a translation but as an original work.

Extent of the Manuscript: within the range of what is usual for the genre of the work submitted. However, it is advisable that novellas be in the range 35,000 to 50,000 words); other fiction (e.g. novels, short-story collections) and non-fiction (e.g. autobiographies, biographies, diaries, letters, memoirs, essay collections, etc.) should be in the range, 80,000 to 110,000 words. Poetry collections should be in the range, 5,000 to 30,000 words. Other word-counts and mixed-genre submissions are not ruled out.

Writers may choose, if they wish, to obtain the services of an Editor in presenting their work, and should acknowledge this help and the nature and extent of this help in the Entry Form.

KEY DATES FOR THE PROVERSE PRIZE IN ANY YEAR
(subject to confirmation and/or change)

Receipt of Entry Fees / Entry Documents	14 April to 31 May of the year of entry
Receipt of entered manuscripts	1 May to 30 June of the year of entry
Announcement of semi-finalists	July-September of the year of entry
Announcement of finalists	October-December of the year of entry
Announcement of winner/ max two winners (sharing the cash prize)	December of the year of entry to April of the year that follows the year of entry
Cash Award made	At the same time as publication of the work(s) adjudged the winner / joint-winners of the Proverse Prize
Publication of winning work(s)	In or after November of the year that follows the year of entry

NOVELS, SHORT STORY COLLECTIONS
AND OTHER FICTION
Published by Proverse Hong Kong

If you have enjoyed **Man's Last Song** by James Tam**,** you may also like to read the following (all titles in English unless otherwise stated):

A Misted Mirror, by Gillian Jones. 2011.
A Painted Moment, by Jennifer Ching. 2010.
An Imitation of Life, by Laura Solomon. 2013.
Article 109, by Peter Gregoire. 2012.
Bao Bao's Odyssey: from Mao's Shanghai to Capitalist Hong Kong, by Paul Ting. 2012.
Black Tortoise Winter, by Jan Pearson. Scheduled 2015 / 2016.
Bright Lights and White Nights, by Andrew Carter. 2015.
cemetery miss you, by Jason S Polley. 2011.
Cop Show Heaven, by Lawrence Gray. 2015.
Death has a Thousand Doors, by Patricia Grey. 2011.
Hilary and David, by Laura Solomon. 2011.
Instant Messages, by Laura Solomon. 2010.
Mila the Magician, by Zhang Jian. 2013. (English / Chinese bilingual)
Mishpacha – Family, by Rebecca Tomasis. 2010.
Odds and Sods, by Lawrence Gray. 2013.
Paranoia (the Walk and Talk with Angela), by Caleb Kavon. 2012.
Red Bird Summer, by Jan Pearson. 2014.
Revenge from Beyond, by Dennis Wong. 2011.
The Day They Came, by Gérard Louis Breissan. 2012.
The Devil You know, by Peter Gregoire. 2014.
The Monkey in Me: Confusion, Love and Hope under a Chinese Sky, by Caleb Kavon. 2009.
The Monkey in Me, by Caleb Kavon. Translated by Chapman Chen. 2010. E-book. 2010. (Chinese)
The Perilous Passage of Princess Petunia Peasant, by Victor Edward Apps. 2014.
The Reluctant Terrorist: in Search of the Jizo, by Caleb Kavon. 2011.

The Shingle Bar Sea Monster and Other Stories, by Laura Solomon. 2012.

The Snow Bridge and Other Stories, by Philip Chatting. Scheduled 2015.

Tiger Autumn, by Jan Pearson. 2015.

The Village in the Mountains, by David Diskin. 2012.

Tightrope! A Bohemian Tale, by Olga Walló. Translated from Czech by Johanna Pokorny, Veronika Revická & others. 2010.

Tightrope! A Bohemian Tale, by Olga Walló. Translated by Chapman Chen. 2011. (Chinese)

University Days, by Laura Solomon. 2014.

Vera Magpie, by Laura Solomon. 2013.

OTHER GENRES

We also publish in other genres, including autobiography, biography, children's illustrated books, educational books, Hong Kong educational and legal history, memoirs, poetry, teenage / young adult books, and travel. Other genres may be added.

James Tam

FIND OUT MORE ABOUT OUR AUTHORS
AND BOOKS

Visit our website
http://www.proversepublishing.com

Visit our distributor's website
<www.chineseupress.com>

Follow us on Twitter
Follow news and conversation: <twitter.com/Proversebooks>
OR
Copy and paste the following to your browser window and
follow the instructions: https://twitter.com/#!/ProverseBooks

Request our E-Newsletter
Send your request to info@proversepublishing.com.

Availability
Most titles are available in Hong Kong and world-wide
from our Hong Kong based Distributor,
The Chinese University Press of Hong Kong,
The Chinese University of Hong Kong, Shatin, NT,
Hong Kong SAR, China. Email: cup-bus@cuhk.edu.hk

All titles are available from Proverse Hong Kong
and the Proverse Hong Kong UK-based Distributor.

We have stock-holding retailers in Hong Kong,
Singapore (Select Books), Canada (Elizabeth Campbell Books),
Principality of Andorra (Llibreria La Puça, La Llibreria).

Orders can be made from bookshops in the UK and elsewhere.

Ebooks
Most of our titles are available also as Ebooks.